THE TRAITORS

Tom Becker studied history at Jesus College, Oxford. He won the Waterstone's Children's Book Prize for his first novel, *Darkside*, at the age of 25. He lives in London.

Other titles by Tom Becker:

THE DARKSIDE SERIES

Darkside
Lifeblood
Nighttrap
Timecurse
Blackjack

THE TRAITORS

TOM BECKER

SCHOLASTIC

First published by Scholastic Children's Books
An imprint of Scholastic Ltd
Euston House, 24 Eversholt Street
London, NW1 1DB, UK
Registered office: Westfield Road, Southam
Warwickshire, CV47 0RA
SCHOLASTIC and associated logos are trademarks and/
or registered trademarks of Scholastic Inc.

ISBN 978 1 4071 0952 7

A CIP catalogue record for this book
is available from the British Library.

Printed and bound by CPI Group (UK) Ltd, Croydon, CR0 4YY
Papers used by Scholastic Children's Books are made
from wood grown in sustainable forests.

1 3 5 7 9 10 8 6 4 2

www.scholastic.co.uk/zone

*For Damon Jackman and Magda Nakassis, the
most dastardly pair of scoundrels I know*

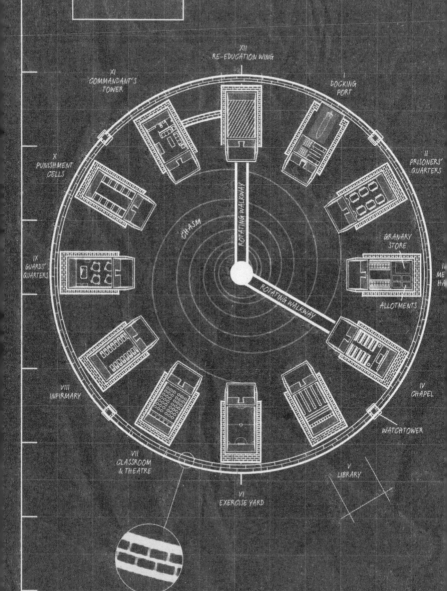

THE DIAL

XII
RE-EDUCATION WING

XI
COMMANDANT'S
TOWER

I
DOCKING
PORT

X
PUNISHMENT
CELLS

II
PRISONERS'
QUARTERS

CHASM

ROTATING WALKWAY

GRANARY
STORE

IX
GUARDS'
QUARTERS

ROTATING WALKWAY

III
MESS
HALL

ALLOTMENTS

VIII
INFIRMARY

IV
CHAPEL

WATCHTOWER

VII
CLASSROOM
& THEATRE

V
LIBRARY

VI
EXERCISE YARD

"Escape . . . escape . . . escape . . . by God!
Never mind hunger pains, discomfort, or
any other agony. Let escape become your
passion, your one and only obsession until
you finally reach home"

(Wing Commander Douglas Bader in
Boldness Be My Friend, by Richard Pape)

THE DIAL	SERIAL NO. 0115978
DATE: April 5th	PROJECT: Re-education of traitors
PLAN: D	
VERSION: 2	WATCHTOWER

PROLOGUE

The sirens wailed into life at dusk, as darkness descended over the prison like a denial. In the prisoners' quarters, a dense jungle of bunk beds and washbasins, the inmates returned their playing cards to the deck and trudged outside. Over in the mess hall, there was a loud clatter as the prisoners on cleaning duty dropped their dirty pots and pans and hurriedly dried their hands. The alarm even reached down beneath the chapel floor, where two boys were painstakingly tunnelling through the ground – nudging each other, they wiped the grime from their faces and began scrabbling back towards the surface. In a matter of minutes, all the inmates had gathered in the exercise yard, shivering in the cold as they waited for the evening headcount to begin.

All the inmates bar one.

In a tower above the guards' barracks, the Traitor walked up a flight of stone steps; soft, deliberate footfalls untroubled by guilt. There was a crackle of loudspeakers, and then a high-pitched voice rang out above the siren: *Attention! One minute until roll call! Any prisoners who fail to present themselves will be subject to one week in the punishment cells!*

The inmates responded with a rowdy chorus of boos and jeers. The Traitor smiled.

The stairwell was steep, and coiled like a serpent. The Traitor had spent hours hiding in a disused cellar beneath the guards' quarters, and it felt good to be moving again. It had taken an age for the siren to announce the roll call, and then for the scrape of chair legs and the thunderous tread of jackboots above the Traitor's head to mark the guards' exit from the barracks. Waiting until the coast was clear, the Traitor had crept out of the cellar and moved soundlessly through the empty building. Steam rose from half-drained cups of coffee; books were jammed open on chair arms. A snooker table had been abandoned mid-game, leaving balls strewn across the scuffed green baize.

At the tower's summit, the staircase came to an abrupt end at a door. The Traitor knocked twice, and entered a study dominated by a burnished desk and a phalanx of pockmarked metal filing cabinets. A couple of dusty books lay supine on a shelf on the far wall. The air was filled with smoke, the atmosphere heavy with the burden of countless cigarettes.

Mr Pitt stood stiffly by the window, his back as straight as a baton. The Traitor was aware how scared the other inmates were of this man – how Mr Pitt strode, bloody-knuckled, through their dreams. The Traitor wasn't scared of him, though. The Traitor wasn't scared of anything.

"You wanted to see me?"

Mr Pitt didn't turn around. "Who am I?" he asked finally.

The Traitor paused, taken aback by the question. "You're Mr Pitt, sir. The Assistant Chief Warder."

Mr Pitt nodded. "I thought that once, too." He removed a monocle from his eye and gave it a thorough wipe in a white handkerchief, still staring out of the window. The distant bark of the guards carried up to the study as they herded the prisoners into formation in the exercise yard. "But, as the years have gone by, as the centuries have amassed out here in no-time, I have realized that my official rank is meaningless. I am not the Assistant Chief Warder. I am not a prison officer of any stripe or description. I am a zookeeper. Overseeing a menagerie of *rats*." He spat out the word as though it had curdled in his mouth, before continuing calmly: "Now, in all civilized cultures, rats are considered a pestilent menace to decent human society, and are exterminated – snared in traps, or torn apart by dogs. But not on the Dial. Here you are free to live, to run around, to fill your little faces with food. My one comfort is that you do not breed."

Sensing that now was not the time to interrupt, the Traitor stayed silent as Mr Pitt turned away from the window, stalked over to one of the filing cabinets and selected a bulging brown file from the top drawer. He flicked through the pages, a look of disgust on his face.

"I've been looking over your case," he said, "and you are without doubt one of slipperiest specimens I've had the misfortune to come across. You'd sell out your own mother for a handful of loose change. Ordinarily, I'd take great delight in making you suffer here for a few centuries, but you have been fortunate enough to catch me at a time when I have lost patience with this entire process." Mr Pitt snapped the folder shut. "In short: I am willing to offer you a deal."

The Traitor tried not to look surprised. "What kind of deal?"

"I've know how the rats pass their time here," Mr Pitt replied. "Sniffing around nooks and crannies looking for a way out, burrowing little tunnels underground. Praying that one day they'll be able to get back through the warp-hole to their homes. I know that the Tally-Ho are planning something big – I want you to tell me how, and when, they're looking to make a run for it. Is that information you could obtain for me?"

The Traitor nodded slowly. "There's usually someone who'll talk – as long as you know the right way to ask them. But it's risky. Ever since Luca betrayed them, the Tally-Ho have been on the lookout for anyone who might be a rat. If they catch me, I'll be in big trouble."

"If they catch you, the Tally-Ho will be the least of your problems," Mr Pitt retorted. "You make a deal with me, you better hold up your end of the bargain."

"I'll do everything I can, sir, believe me. And if I succeed. . .?"

Mr Pitt opened a carved wooden box on his desk and

pulled out a hand-rolled cigarette. Striking up a match, he lit the cigarette in his mouth, then held the wavering match near the Traitor's folder.

"Records can be made to vanish," he said. "Prisoners can disappear. Unless, of course, you're happy to spend the next five hundred years here?"

Mr Pitt extinguished the match with a sharp flick of his wrist, and jabbed the blackened stub at the Traitor.

"You understand that *no one* can know about this? If anyone gets so much of a sniff of this conversation, it will be very bad news for you. A single loose word, and I will have a long time to make you regret it. Do I make myself clear?"

"Absolutely," replied the Traitor, with the faintest trace of a smile. "You can trust me."

CHAPTER ONE

There was no escape for him in dreams.

For three nights Adam Wilson had been stalking sleep like a hunter through the undergrowth. He lay in ambush, eyes clamped shut, trying to tempt it closer with a selection of boring thoughts: his dad's fishing stories; the rules of cricket; all the words he could think of beginning with the letter Q. But no matter how much Adam shifted underneath the covers, or how carefully he rearranged his pillows, he couldn't get comfortable. He got up and crept through his dark, silent house to pour himself a glass of water in the kitchen, only to steal across the landing an hour later to use the toilet. He turned on the light and read chapters from his favourite book until his tired eyes could no longer grip on to the page. Still the clock on his wall ticked relentlessly onwards: 1.15; 2.45; 4.30...

With a sigh, Adam reached over to his bedside table and turned on his radio. The station was playing slow love songs, presumably to relax all the other listeners who were lying awake out there. In between the music, the DJ whispered heartbroken confessions as though they were lullabies.

As the songs merged into a soft purr, Adam finally felt the tension in his limbs begin to ease. He was drifting into unconsciousness when the speakers gave out a sudden violent crackle. Loud static drowned out the music, as though someone had sharply twisted the tuning dial. Two pips sounded above the static, and then a voice announced:

"Greetings, traitor."

Adam's eyes snapped open. He glanced at the radio, which had settled back into a dull fizz. It felt like it had been talking to him. He shook his head wearily. The lack of sleep was making him imagine things.

The radio spat into life again. "This is the Dial calling."

He wasn't imagining things.

Even though the announcer's voice was faint, it didn't endear itself to the listener. It had a childish, nasal tone that gave the impression that the speaker was curling his lip as he talked.

"Repeat: this is the Dial calling, traitor. We know who you are, Adam Wilson. We know what you've done."

At the sound of his name, Adam's heart began pounding. It wasn't possible. This had to be some sort of bad dream. How could they know his name? How could they know what he'd done?

Adam scrambled out of bed and stretched his arm down the back of his bedside table, yanking the radio's plug from the socket. As the "on" light died, the nasal voice sent him a parting shot.

"We're coming for you, traitor. . ."

CHAPTER TWO

That morning, a letter was waiting for him on the breakfast table.

Adam didn't see it as he sat down and blearily reached for the cereal packet. It was only as he was drenching his cornflakes with milk that he noticed the small rectangle propped up against the sugar bowl, his name and address printed neatly on the front. There was no stamp or postmark. Adam couldn't remember the last time he had received a hand-delivered letter. For some reason, the sudden appearance of one now – after what had happened the night before – troubled him.

His mum bustled into the kitchen and kissed the top of his head, laughing at his instinctive flinch.

"Morning, sleepyhead," she said cheerfully. "See you've found your letter. What's it about? Your dad and I couldn't think who on earth it could be from."

Adam didn't reply. He picked up the brown manila envelope with the tips of his fingers, as if fearful that it might explode.

"Well, aren't you going to open it?" his mum asked, a curious note in her voice.

Adam carefully returned the envelope to its post by the sugar bowl and picked up his spoon.

"Not right now," he said finally.

Adam joined the reluctant flow of schoolchildren tramping up the main road, the letter stuffed in the bottom of his bag alongside his textbooks and games kit. He was feeling strangely exposed, as though every wink and nudge, every laugh was aimed at him. Outside his school gates, factions of girls huddled together trading gossip and secrets, while slouching regiments of boys exchanged rapid-fire insults with one another. Usually Adam would hang around with them until the bell rang; today he hurried inside.

Friday morning meant assembly for Adam's year – he took a seat at the back of the hall with resignation, well aware what was coming. Sure enough, after a lengthy speech about fulfilling potential, the headmistress's face became serious.

"Now, as most of you will be aware, following Tuesday's unfortunate events, the chemistry lab will be off-limits for at least another week, as we try to repair the damage. The pupil responsible for the destruction, Danny Lyons, has been excluded. There is no place for such behaviour in this school."

Adam could feel eyes looking in his direction. There were a few suppressed sniggers. A couple of rows in front of him, Danny's girlfriend, Carey, shifted uncomfortably in her seat, her cheeks reddening. She glanced back over her shoulder towards Adam; he looked quickly down at the floor.

There was only one topic of conversation as the pupils filed out of the hall.

"They kicked Danny out? Bit harsh, that."

"You reckon? I heard he totally lost it – nearly decked Old Robbo when he tried to stop him smashing up the lab."

"What was wrong with him?"

"Who knows? It was only a matter of time with Danny. He's a complete nutter. Remember when he beat up that kid outside the bus station?"

"Hey!" A hand grabbed Adam's arm. "You're Danny's mate, aren't you? Have they put him away yet?"

Adam shook off the hand and ploughed through the crowd, resisting the urge to make a run for it through the school gates. He kept his head down all morning, ignoring the empty seat next to him as he muddled his way through a maze of French verbs, quadratic equations and insect parts. At lunch time, he played football for the first time in years, earning screams of frustration from his teammates as he misplaced passes and mishit shots. On his way back to lessons, he heard Carey call out his name in the busy corridor; Adam hurried into his classroom without looking back.

The last lesson was PE. After a sodden game of rugby, Adam padded out of the showers into a battlefield of muddy socks, battered kitbags and wet towels. The air in the changing room was a combustible brew of sweat and deodorant. Most of the boys were hurriedly changing to escape school for the day, but Adam dried off and dressed slowly. By the time he was finished, the last bell had long since rung, and the only sound in the empty changing room was a drip echoing off the shower walls. As he crammed his kit back into his school bag, Adam saw the letter still waiting patiently for him. He pulled it out and sat down on the wooden bench.

His hands trembling slightly, Adam peeled open the envelope. There was a single crisp sheet of paper inside, stamped with a red crest of a snake entwined around a dagger, the serpent's forked tongue darting into the air. The lettering was slightly clunky and haphazard, as though it had been composed on an old typewriter rather than a computer. It read:

Dear Adam Wilson,

Agents from the Dial are on their way to collect you. Make your farewells now, as you will not be seeing anyone you care about for a long time. Such are the consequences of treachery.

If you feel you are being unjustly
treated, show someone this
letter - a family member, perhaps,
or a figure of authority. Tell
them that you are innocent,
and that you deserve their
assistance.

But you won't tell anyone, will
you? You're too guilty and
ashamed. We know it and we're
coming for you.

Regards,

Mr Cooper
(CHIEF WARDER, THE DIAL)

Adam scanned the letter again, convinced that he had
misread it. He noticed with a chill that it mentioned "the
Dial" – just like the radio message had the previous night.
It was clearly a threat. Maybe the best thing to do was to follow the letter's suggestion and show it to his mum and dad.
They'd find out who this Mr Cooper was and stop him. If
they had to, Adam knew, they would take the letter to the
police. They'd do everything they could to sort things out.

But instead of showing his parents the letter, Adam ripped it up into tiny pieces and, on his way home, scattered them over the patch of scrubby wasteland behind his house, like the ashes of some little-lamented family pet.

CHAPTER THREE

Adam kept the radio switched off that night. In the silence, his bedroom felt as though it was under siege: creaks on the stairs threatened the nearing tread of intruders, while the tap of tree branches on the window sounded like animals' claws. Sometime after midnight, Adam could have sworn that he heard someone outside shout his name. He raced over to the window and tore open the curtains, but there was no one standing in the street below. Eventually, overwhelmed by exhaustion, Adam slumped into a dreamless sleep.

He slept in late the next morning, grateful that it was the weekend. Eventually he crawled out of bed and into the bathroom, where he glumly inspected the bags beneath his eyes in the mirror. After a shower, Adam surprised his parents by volunteering to go into town with them. Usually he avoided shopping trips like the plague, but the truth was that he was too jumpy to sit in the house alone. His mum gave him a thoughtful look but didn't say anything.

The town centre was quiet. Adam lived in a seaside resort that was sliding into disrepair, haunted by the absence of crowds on the promenade and the echoes of decades-old laughter. With summer long since faded away, the tourist shops were boarded up, and the machines in the amusement arcades bleeped and fizzed with lonely desperation. The cries of the seagulls sounded like taunts as they wheeled through the air above their heads.

For once, Adam was pleased to have his parents for company. While absent-mindedly accepting a flyer from a man standing on the corner of the high street, he even agreed to his mum's suggestion that they go clothes shopping. He tried on a few shirts, and didn't argue when she chose to buy the one he least liked. As his mum chatted to the sales assistant and paid for the shirt, Adam retrieved the crumpled flyer from his pocket. It was a plain piece of card with a short message written in a familiar typeface:

You can run, but you can't hide.

Adam dashed to the doorway and scanned the high street. There was a steady stream of people going in and out of the shops, but the man handing out the flyers had vanished. A group of teenage girls were gathered around a bench, talking excitedly with one another as they ate fast food. Seeing the look of alarm on Adam's face, one of the girls burst out laughing.

"Adam?"

He whirled round, only to see his mum standing behind him.

"You look like you've seen a ghost!" she exclaimed. "You've been like a cat on a hot tin roof all morning. What's the matter?"

For a second Adam was tempted to tell her. Then he shoved the card back into his pocket and shook his head. "Nothing," he muttered. "Thought I saw a mate, that's all."

As he trailed after his parents back to the car, Adam made up his mind: he had to end this. Which meant that there was only one place to go. He waited until after lunch before slipping out of the house, pulling up the hood on his tracksuit top when it began to spit with rain. Adam followed a familiar route through residential streets, cutting through the back of the old people's home and on to a patch of waste ground, where a tall, broad-shouldered boy with cropped hair was sitting on top of a skateboard ramp, staring moodily out into space.

For years the skate park had provided a retreat for all the kids in the area, until a young boy had fallen off a ramp and smashed his head on the ground. As he lay in hospital in a coma, the council had declared the skate park unsafe and closed it. Now the ramps were pitted and scarred, covered in graffiti and broken glass, and thick weeds flourished in the cracks of the concrete. But as everyone else had drifted away, Adam and his best friend had secretly adopted the place as their own, marking out their overgrown territory like New World explorers.

Now, at the sight of Adam threading his way through the undergrowth, the other boy stood up angrily.

"What the hell are you doing here?" he spat. "I told you to stay away from me."

"I know, Danny," Adam replied. "Had to talk to you."

"I've got nothing to say to you."

"Yeah? Then why are you following me around?"

Danny frowned. "What are you talking about?"

Adam clambered up to the top of the ramp until he was standing face to face with Danny. There was a grim set to the boy's jaw, and his fists were clenched. Everyone in the town was wary of Danny's temper, but Adam had been his best friend for over a decade, and at that moment he didn't care.

"You know exactly what I'm talking about," he said. "I know you were in town this morning, and outside my house last night."

"You're crazy!" Danny replied, breaking out into bitter laughter. "I've only just got up. And I was at my dad's last night. You think I've not got anything better to do than stalk you?"

"What about the letter, then?" Adam persisted. "And that trick with the radio? It had to be you – no one else knows. . ."

He trailed off.

"No one knows what?" Danny asked, pushing his face into Adam's. "Why I smashed up the lab? Why I got kicked out of school? Why I was so angry?"

Adam took a step backwards. "Have you spoken to Carey?" he asked quietly.

Danny's face darkened. "I don't need to talk to her. We're finished. You two can have each other."

"I know what you saw looked bad, Danny, but it wasn't her fault," Adam protested. "She was upset and I was just trying to make her feel better. It was a stupid mistake. It didn't mean anything. Honest!"

"Yeah?" Danny kicked a stone off the ramp and into the tangle of weeds. "Well, it did to me."

"You can't stay angry with me for ever. We've been best mates for years!"

"I know. But it was my best mate I caught kissing my girlfriend. Be grateful the lab got it instead of you."

Adam rubbed his face wearily. "But it doesn't make any sense," he murmured. "If you're not doing any of this stuff, who is?"

"Don't know." Danny shrugged. "Don't care. It's your problem."

As his friend turned away, Adam reached out and grabbed his wrist. Danny spun round, his eyes blazing with menace. Slowly, very deliberately, he prised Adam's fingers from his arm.

"You're really pushing it, you know that?" he said softly. "If anyone else had done to me what you did, I would have beaten the hell out of them. And now you come round here accusing me of all this crazy stuff?" He pushed Adam firmly backwards. "Get out of here before I lose it."

With a shake of his head, Adam climbed down the ramp and walked out of the skate park without looking back. He drifted aimlessly towards the seafront, where fierce gusts of wind were blowing sand in off the beach, forming dirty brown eddies on the esplanade. Wet ropes slapped desultorily against the flagpoles. Slipping through the barriers, Adam dropped down on to the sand and began trudging along the shore. Whenever he was depressed or confused, he always gravitated towards the beach. To him, the roaring of the waves felt as comforting as an arm around the shoulder.

The town fell away into the distance, before disappearing behind the row of dunes rearing up steeply on Adam's left-hand side. Dark clouds fomented in the sky, above a flat horizon of sea broken only by the outline of an offshore oil rig and a ghostly army of wind turbines. A seagull perched at the water's edge gave Adam a baleful glare.

Lost in thought, Adam trudged along the beach for hours, until the joggers and the dog-walkers had long since turned back and he was completely alone. By the time he had turned round and headed back for home, the coastal dunes were shrouded in gloom. The rain was coming down more heavily now, dappling the sand with fat drops.

Suddenly, the hairs on the back of Adam's neck prickled in warning, and he was assailed by the feeling that someone was watching him. Adam scanned the dunes for movement, the wind whipping his blond hair into his eyes.

"Danny?" he called out uncertainly. "That you?"

The heathery tufts on top of the hillocks swayed silently in response. Adam picked up his pace, silently cursing himself for having walked so far. He hadn't taken more than ten paces when a voice called out above the wind:

"Adam!"

There was a loud, fuzzy quality to the voice that suggested it was coming through a megaphone. He stopped in his tracks and looked around again, but the dunes refused to reveal their secrets.

"Adam Wilson!" the cry came again.

A voice in Adam's head was screaming at him to run away as fast as he could. He ignored it. Whatever danger he was in, he was sick of all these games. All he wanted to do was see whoever was tormenting him.

"What?" he yelled.

There was a long pause, and then the voice gleefully replied:

"Nowhere to hide now, traitor. You're ours."

CHAPTER FOUR

Adam didn't wait for the voice's owner to reveal himself. His trainers churned up the sand as he sprinted off down the beach. Feeling dangerously visible on the deserted shoreline, he scrambled up into the dunes, plotting a tortuous course through the shallow valleys and waist-high beachgrass. This had to be some kind of sick joke, Adam told himself frantically as he ran. There was no way this could be happening for real.

A guttural bark brought Adam to a halt; diving behind the nearest dune, he peered over the top. His heart sank at the sight of a line of men fanning out across the dunes between him and the main road, the beams from their torches sweeping methodically over the hillocks.

"Anyone see him?" one of them called out.

"I lost the little bleeder in the dunes," another replied, a large German shepherd straining at the leash in his hand. "But he's here somewhere. Rex'll sniff him out."

Fear trickled like cold water down Adam's spine. Danny had been telling the truth – this was nothing to do with him. It was much, much worse than that. Who were these men? And what did they want with him? Panicking, Adam fumbled for the mobile phone in his pocket, only to discover that there was no signal: he was too far from town. Adam cursed and crept away from the dunes, trying to stay as low as possible. With the main road blocked off, his only hope of making it back to safety lay along the beach. Adam scrambled down on to the shore and was jogging towards the distant lights of town when a movement out over the sea caught his eye. He stopped in his tracks, a look of horror on his face.

The rain clouds had parted, revealing a black behemoth of a craft flying towards him. It was a long, cigar-shaped balloon fashioned from leathery canvas, powered by two giant propellers affixed to its rear.

"Help!" Adam shouted desperately, at the top of his lungs. "For God's sake someone help me!"

There was a loud clank, and a searchlight burst into life on the airship's prow, the froths of the waves glinting in the glare of its powerful beam. Adam stumbled away, racing full-pelt along the beach until his lungs were near bursting, too scared to look back at whatever might be following him.

There was a loud bark to Adam's right; a low shape bounded out on an interception course from the dunes. Automatically Adam zigzagged away from the dog towards the sea. He made it knee-deep into the shallows before the German shepherd barrelled into him, knocking the pair of them underwater. Freezing cold seawater rushed into Adam's mouth and nose as he sank below the surface. He struggled up for air, only for a wave to break over him before he could take a breath, knocking him back underwater.

The dog pressed down on him, barking triumphantly. Adam's head was growing woozy, and his limbs were weakening. Suddenly a strong hand reached down, grabbed him by the hood and dragged him out of the water. Adam collapsed in a sodden heap on to the sand, coughing violently. He was aware of a group of men dressed in dark clothing standing over him. The German shepherd had followed them out of the shallows and was waiting obediently by their feet, its eyes warily fixed upon Adam.

"This one's a bit of a sorry state," a man's voice said.

"Serves him right," another replied, panting. "I hate it when they run. Come on, let's get him out of here before someone sees us."

As Adam was hauled to his feet, he saw the airship swoop in over the beach like some giant mythological bat, its searchlight sweeping over the sands. Summoning his remaining strength, Adam lashed out with his foot, and was rewarded with a shout of pain and an oath.

"He's still kicking!" someone warned.

A scrum of hands descended upon him, each grabbing for a limb. As he was hoisted into the air, Adam twisted his neck and clamped his teeth down on the hand near his left shoulder.

"Aah!" a voice howled. "The little sod bit me!"

"Right," came the grim reply. "Enough messing around. Hold him steady."

Adam blinked as someone shone a bright shaft of light into his eyes. The last thing he saw was a man's arm coming sharply down, and then something heavy cracked into his temple, and he spiralled into unconsciousness.

CHAPTER FIVE

Adam sat bolt upright, spluttering and coughing. In the abrupt shock of waking, it took him several seconds to register the water streaming down his face and soaking his tracksuit top. Wiping his eyes, he saw a small red-headed boy standing over him. The boy was holding an upturned bucket over Adam's head, and there was a mocking grin on his face. He was dressed in matching dark-blue trousers, cap and jacket, with a yellow armband tied tightly around his sleeve.

"Wakey, wakey," he squeaked. "Mr Pitt wants to see you."

Adam's head was pounding, and there was a sick feeling in the pit of his stomach. He was sitting on the floor of a tiny windowless room, in the narrow gap between a cot and a washbasin. A single light bulb hung down from the ceiling, dyeing the other boy's features a grimy orange. There was a low rumbling noise in the background, and the cold floor beneath Adam's palms was trembling.

"Where ... where am I?" he asked, bewildered. "Who are you?"

"Save your questions for Mr Pitt," the boy retorted. "He'll throttle me if we keep him waiting. Come on."

The boy helped Adam up and ushered him out of the room. In the dingy corridor outside, the rumbling noise was loud enough to make Adam's head throb. He paused to get his bearings, only for the boy to push him sharply, sending him stumbling forward. As they walked past a series of identical wooden doors, Adam thought he heard a low whimper emanate from behind one of them. He wondered whether other people were trapped here too, or whether this was his own, entirely private, nightmare.

Fixing his eyes upon a circular window set into the wall, Adam broke away from the other boy and pressed his face against the glass. His cry for help died in his throat. He stared in shocked silence at a world of pitch-black night. Vague, wispy shapes slid past the window like forgotten memories. With a jolt, Adam realized they were clouds.

"We're flying!" he said, a note of wonder in his voice.

The boy clapped sarcastically.

"What gave it away?"

Adam was too busy trying to digest this new information to acknowledge the boy's derisory tone.

"So we're on a plane?" he asked.

"Zeppelin," the boy corrected. He snorted at Adam's look of incomprehension. "Airship? You know – big balloon thingy?"

"I know what an airship is," Adam said defensively.

"Good for you. Then I'm sure I don't need to tell

you that we're in the gondola. It's the cabin beneath the balloon, where all the crew and the ..." a smirk spread across the boy's face "... *passengers* stay during the flight. It's nearly two hundred metres in length from prow to stern."

Seeing Adam's underwhelmed expression, the little red-head stopped and grabbed him by the arm.

"This isn't any old airship, you know," he said. "This is the *Quisling* – pride of the Dial." The boy glanced up and down the deserted corridor before continuing in a whisper: "They reckon in the olden days the Commandant himself used to fly it."

The boy's eyes widened at the thought. Adam's brain was deluged by questions, but he didn't want to give his infuriating captor the satisfaction of answering any of them. Though he was a head shorter than Adam, and at least a couple of years younger, there was a casual superiority about the redhead's manner that made him seem a lot older. It was easy to act that way, Adam supposed, when you had all the answers. Inspecting the smaller boy out of the corner of his eye, Adam wondered whether it was time to teach him a lesson.

As if reading his mind, the boy jabbed him sharply in the back.

"Don't even think about it. I've worked on this ship for ten years now, and I've taken care of bigger and meaner kids than you."

Despite everything, Adam smiled. Did this boy think

he was an idiot? Ten years ago, he would still have been in nappies!

When they reached the door at the end of the corridor, the redhead stopped and carefully adjusted his cap in the window.

"It'll be all right, you know," he told Adam, in the friendly, knowing tones of an elder brother. "Even I was worried when they first came for me. But if you keep your head down and don't cause any trouble, things become much easier." He tapped his armband. "I'm a trustee now. I get taken on all the *Quisling*'s flights. You follow my advice, maybe one day you'll be allowed up here too."

"Um ... OK. Thanks," said Adam, utterly bemused. As he went to grasp the door handle, the boy stayed his hand.

"One more thing – a piece of advice from an old hand."

"What?"

"For God's sake, don't make him angry."

Before Adam could ask who he was talking about, the boy knocked on the door. From inside the room, a clipped voice called out, "Come!" The boy opened the door and peered inside.

"Mr Pitt?" he asked nervously. "I've got one of the new arrivals for you here."

"Very well, Carstairs. Send him in."

"Yessir."

With a farewell poke in the ribs, the boy shoved Adam through the door and closed it softly behind him.

To his surprise, Adam found himself in a plush lounge area, his feet sinking into a deep maroon carpet. Slanting, rain-splattered windows ran the length of two of the walls, providing a panoramic view of the shifting landscapes of the night sky. In the middle of the room, a circular bar stood unattended, bearing rows of spirit bottles that glinted in the light. Beyond the bar, a door was marked with the sign "Control Room – No Unauthorized Access".

Mr Pitt sat alone at a table in the corner, leafing through a stack of brown files, shrouded in a haze of cigarette smoke. He was a tall, angular man with slicked-down black hair and brisk, economical movements. A pencil-thin moustache sat in haughty residence on his upper lip, and a monocle was wedged over his left eye. There was a silver ashtray by his elbow, filled with a pyramid of cigarette stubs. As he flicked through his files, Mr Pitt scribbled notes in the margins, the light catching on a pair of chunky gold sovereign rings adorning his fingers.

Unused to the fug of smoke, Adam coughed. Mr Pitt didn't look up.

"Come on over then, lad," he said finally, not unpleasantly.

Adam stepped hesitantly towards the table.

"Name?"

"What?"

Mr Pitt looked up sharply. Behind the monocle, his left eye was filmy and unfocused. His right eye narrowed.

"Perhaps I should make myself clear," he said slowly.

"My name is Hector Pitt. You will refer to me as 'Mr Pitt', or 'sir'. Failure to do so will not be tolerated. I'm a fair man, but one has to draw the line somewhere. Have I made myself clear?"

"Yes . . . I mean, yes, sir."

"Ah! A fast learner." Mr Pitt smiled, revealing a row of stained yellow teeth. "Now, let us try again. Name?"

"Adam Wilson, sir."

Mr Pitt rifled through the stack of files, eventually pulling out one near the bottom. He began to scan its contents.

"Sir?" Adam ventured, halting Mr Pitt in the action of lighting another cigarette. He plunged on, as politely as possible. "Could you please tell me what I'm doing here? It's just that, one minute I was walking home, and then these men jumped me, and now I'm. . ." Adam faltered. "Well, I don't know where I am, or who you are, or what I'm doing here. Sir."

Mr Pitt paused, and then surprised Adam by breaking out into a raspy chuckle.

"Of course, Wilson." He struck up a match and lit his cigarette, before taking a deep drag. "No doubt you are finding this a most disorienting time. Let me try to explain things for you. Now then, you will be aware of your acquaintance Danny Lyons?"

Adam nodded dumbly.

"Good. And you'll also be aware that five days ago you betrayed him?"

"I didn't *betray* him!" Adam began. "You don't understand, sir. . ."

Mr Pitt held up a hand.

"It's all here in black and white," he said, looking down at his file. "Last Monday evening Lyons caught you kissing his girlfriend . . . at a skate park, it says here, not that the location is material to this matter. Understandably upset by the actions of his supposed best friend, the next day Lyons takes his frustration out on a chemistry laboratory at your school. He is summarily expelled." Mr Pitt snapped the file shut. "You, on the other hand, appear to get off scot free. . ."

"It wasn't like that!" Adam protested. "Danny and Carey had had a fight that night – I was just trying to cheer her up! I shouldn't have tried to kiss her, it was a big mistake, but it only lasted a second!"

"It's too late for excuses, Wilson. The powers that be – my employers – have already placed you on trial, on a charge of Low Treachery. Needless to say, you were found guilty. A unanimous verdict."

"What trial?" Adam exclaimed. "No one told me anything about a trial! My parents would have got me a lawyer!"

"Lawyer, *sir*," corrected Mr Pitt sharply. "Let's not fall out. Whether you knew about the trial or not is immaterial, Wilson. You know you betrayed Lyons, and *we* know you betrayed Lyons. No amount of legal tomfoolery could have helped you wriggle out of it."

He stared unblinking at Adam, daring him to protest again. The guilty silence was interrupted by the door to the Control Room sliding open. A young man poked his head into the lounge. In the cockpit behind him, Adam could see a team of crewmen busily working the zeppelin's controls.

The man gave Mr Pitt a crisp salute. "Sorry to interrupt you, sir, but I thought you should know – we've passed through the warphole and have returned to no-time, but the weather's pretty hairy out here. Might be a bumpy journey back."

Above the growl of the airship's engines, Adam could hear the wind flinging handfuls of raindrops against the windows. The floor wobbled slightly as the *Quisling* sought to navigate a path through the growing storm.

"I've been through worse than this," Mr Pitt said, after a dismissive glance outside. "Let me know when the Dial's in sight."

The crewman nodded and slid the door shut again. Adam's head was bursting with so many questions that it was hard to know where to begin.

"Excuse me, sir, but what is the Dial?"

Mr Pitt nodded. "Fair question, Wilson. The Dial is the prison where you'll serve out your sentence."

"Prison?" Adam gasped. "For how long?"

Mr Pitt consulted the file.

"Let me see ... ah, here we are: two hundred and seventy-four years."

"Two hundred and seventy-four years?" Adam echoed incredulously. "Are you nuts?"

He barely saw Mr Pitt move. There was a flash of light, and Adam's temple exploded with pain once again. He reeled away from the table, his head spinning. Mr Pitt rose up out of his chair, calmly wiping the blood from his sovereign rings with a handkerchief. After tucking the handkerchief back into his pocket, he shoved Adam to the floor and aimed two sharp kicks to his body. Adam would have shouted out, but the air had been buffeted from his lungs, and he found himself mouthing silent words of agony.

"You will call me SIR!" Mr Pitt screamed, drenching Adam in saliva and the stench of cigarettes. "Every day, for two hundred and seventy-four years, you will call me SIR! A good, solid stretch for a particularly vile young man who will learn the meaning of manners, if I have to tattoo it on his skin in bruises!"

As Mr Pitt clenched his fist and prepared to bring the rings down on Adam again, there was a loud bang, and the *Quisling* lurched sickeningly to one side.

CHAPTER SIX

The sudden tilt caught Mr Pitt unawares; with a startled yell, he went sprawling across the lounge. Bottles tumbled down from the bar on to the floor, smashing into pieces. The lights blinked on and off, as though surprised.

As the *Quisling* lurched back on to an even keel, Adam curled up into a ball, tears streaming from his eyes. His lungs were fighting for breath, and his forehead was sticky with blood. Mr Pitt had struggled to his feet and was now screaming in the direction of the Control Room. The young crewman reappeared in the doorway, his face ashen.

"This wind's too strong, sir!" he shouted. "One of the starboard engines has backfired, and I don't know how much longer the others can hold out for. I'm not sure we'll make the Dial!"

"Of course we'll make the Dial, you idiot!" roared Mr Pitt. "Get out of my way!"

He stepped over Adam's prone body and strode into the Control Room, barking out a series of commands. The *Quisling* banked sharply again, forcing Adam to roll out of the way as a chair toppled over next to him. He hauled himself upright, still clutching his stomach. As he looked for somewhere safe to hide, his eye was drawn back to the Control Room door, which remained invitingly ajar. Despite the pain, he couldn't resist it. Adam stole over to the door and looked inside.

On a calm, sunlit afternoon the Control Room of the *Quisling* must have afforded a panoramic view of a journey through the skies. But now the prow windows were black and drenched in sheets of rain, and the gondola was shaking like a leaf in the gale-force winds. Navigators wrestled with the steering controls, frantically consulting a complex panel of dials and gauges. As they shouted at one another, it seemed to Adam that they weren't speaking in English but a numerical language of coordinates and bearings. Mr Pitt paced up and down the raised bridge at the back of the cabin, exhorting the ship to go faster and faster. Engrossed as they were by their efforts, none of the men noticed Adam watching them.

The *Quisling* stuttered again, and a navigator looked up nervously from one of his instruments. Even from the back of the room, Adam could see the needle sinking towards the bottom of the gauge.

"We've lost a port engine now too, sir!"

"Dammit!" Mr Pitt crashed his fist down upon the metal railing at the edge of the bridge. "Keep her steady now!"

As the airship hurtled down through the cloud cover, Adam could make out a barren expanse of wasteland stretching out beneath them. It seemed to go on for ever, miles and miles of stony ground untouched by vegetation or wildlife. Then the *Quisling* banked again, and the flat horizon was brutally shattered by a soaring crag that rose like a clenched fist hundreds of metres into the air. Agelessly forbidding, composed of jagged rocks of black granite, the bluff looked as though it could support the weight of planets on its shoulders with disdainful ease. At the crag's summit, a cluster of buildings huddled behind a high, circular perimeter wall. Adam shivered. It was a sight bleak enough to chill his heart.

"The Dial's in sight, sir!" the navigator called out.

As they tried to plot a course towards a building on the north-eastern edge of the complex, it felt like the wounded *Quisling* was now entirely at the mercy of the elements. The airship barely crested the Dial's outer perimeter wall before sinking with alarming speed to a concrete-paved airstrip beyond.

"Thirty seconds until landing!" one of the crew called out.

"Set her down carefully!" said Mr Pitt, through clenched teeth. "Too hard and the fuel tanks will go up, and we'll all be burned to a crisp."

He remained standing as the navigators hastily strapped themselves into their seats, his sole concession to the approaching landing a one-handed grip upon the railing in front of him. As Mr Pitt braced himself, he caught sight of Adam out of the corner of his eye.

"What the hell are you doing in here?" he screamed. "Get out!"

Adam bolted out of the doorway and ran back into the lounge, scrambling beneath a table that was bolted to the floor. There was a final, pained splutter, and he heard a panicky voice shout: "All the engines are out!" They were in free fall now; brick walls raced past the windows as they plummeted towards the ground. Adam threw his arms over his head and whispered a quick prayer.

The *Quisling* hit the ground with a thunderous crash, scraping along the concrete with a high-pitched squeal of metal. The lights went out in the lounge, leaving Adam blindly covering his head as fittings rained down on the table above him. Just as he wondered, through gritted teeth, how much further the airship could slide across the ground, it came to a sudden halt. With a groan the gondola teetered to one side, threatening to topple over completely, before rocking back and coming to a precarious rest on the landing strip.

Adam emerged from beneath the battered table, panting heavily and picking fragments of plaster out of his hair. The lounge – which only minutes earlier had been a study in airborne elegance – now looked like a bomb site. Adam picked out a path through the broken furniture and headed over to the smashed port windows. Careful to avoid the shards of glass protruding from the sill, he hauled himself through one of the windows and dropped the short distance to the concrete below.

The landing strip was shrouded in darkness, hemmed in by high prison walls dotted with blacked-out windows. The only source of light was an orange beam emanating from a tower over to Adam's right. Craning his neck, Adam followed the beam as it traced an arc through the sky, broadening into a large whirling vortex of air tinged with sparks. When the beam of light abruptly winked off, the vortex collapsed, shrinking to a tiny orange dot before disappearing completely, leaving the sky a flat pond of midnight.

There was a loud clunk and a whirring, and then a battery of searchlights blazed into life around the landing strip, forcing Adam to shield his eyes. Suddenly the air was alive with shouts and whining sirens. "*Attention! Attention!*" a voice called out, over a crackling loudspeaker. "*The vortex has been closed. Power has been returned to the Dial. All emergency crews to the Docking Port immediately!*"

In the piercing glare, Adam saw two airmen awkwardly disembarking from the *Quisling* through a hatch in the Control Room floor; one propped up on the other, his right leg dragging uselessly behind him. Mr Pitt was already halfway across the landing strip, briskly brushing the dust from his jacket as he strode towards a gabled building. Men were running past him in the opposite direction, fire hoses looped over their shoulders and folded stretchers in their hands.

There was movement towards the rear of the

gondola, and a door banged open. A small column of children stumbled off the airship, shock etched on tear-streaked faces. As they were herded across the landing area by the guards, Adam caught a glimpse of red hair, and saw Carstairs urging a crying girl away from the *Quisling*.

"Oi!"

Adam turned round to see a burly man yelling at him.

"What are you doing over there? The fuel tanks could blow at any time! Go with the others!"

Adam's muscles tensed, urging him to make a run for it. But run where? He was surrounded by sheer walls, and there was nowhere to hide on the flat expanse of the strip. The only way out appeared to be through the gabled building at the edge of the concrete. Adam hesitantly joined the procession of prisoners, rough adult hands shoving him on his way. He passed through a high arched doorway and entered a crowded room alive with the sounds of distress and bewilderment. A hard-faced woman in uniform stood on top of an upturned box and clapped her hands together for attention.

"Listen up!" she called out. "New inmates will present themselves to the guards in the Registration Area next door, where you will receive a regulation prison uniform. You will shower and hand in your current clothes, which we will return to you on your departure from the Dial. You have twenty minutes before transportation to the inmates' quarters takes place – not a second more. Unless you want to find yourself standing outside in your underwear, I'd advise you not to dally."

The new prisoners filed through to the Registration Area, forming snaking queues in the hall as they waited to give their names to the guards sitting behind a row of tables. After shuffling forward for a few minutes, Adam was wordlessly ticked off in a register, and he was handed a blue uniform. He was then directed beyond the tables and through into the boys' showers, where others stood shivering under the icy jets of water. No one spoke. The air was heavy with shock. Adam washed himself mechanically, cleaning the dried blood from his forehead, and slipped on the blue uniform, the coarse fabric instantly making his skin itch.

Gathering his old clothes up into a bundle, Adam walked through into the next room, where more inmates with yellow armbands – trustees, Carstairs had called them – were standing behind the counter of what looked like a giant cloakroom, the back wall covered in a honeycomb of lockers. Adam went up to the nearest trustee, a tall girl his age, her face obscured by long lengths of mousey brown hair, and handed her his clothes. She reached up and placed them in one of the lockers before turning the key and handing it to Adam.

"Take care of it," she said quietly. "There aren't any spares."

Adam looked down at the key in his hand. "Will my stuff be safe in there?"

The girl nodded. "Not that it matters."

"What do you mean?"

"Unless you're really lucky, by the time you've finished your sentence, all your clothes will have rotted away anyway."

Adam was still trying to digest that fact when Mr Pitt loomed up behind the girl. She flinched as the guard leaned over her, beckoning Adam forward with a long, bony finger.

"Listen here, Wilson," he whispered, hissing into Adam's ear like a cobra. "Don't think I've forgotten about you. I can see I'm going to have to keep my eye on you. You even think about getting up to any monkey business, and I'll be on to you faster than you can say 'infirmary ward'. Understand?"

Adam nodded.

"Good. Now hop it."

As Mr Pitt turned on his heel, the girl trustee gave Adam a cryptic look. Behind her long curtain of hair she had a pretty face, albeit one shadowed with sadness. Feeling Adam's gaze upon her, the girl quickly called the next inmate forward. A guard pushed Adam on before he could say anything more.

Outside, in the freezing air, he stopped and stared at the scene before him. The Dial was a brooding complex of buildings – Adam counted twelve in total – arranged in a circle around a yawning black chasm. Adam shivered as he looked down into the bottomless abyss. Although a perimeter wall, reinforced at regular intervals by high watchtowers, ran around the back of the buildings, the only way to cross from one part of the Dial to another appeared to be over the chasm along a walkway, which separated into two independent parts at a circular stone platform in the centre of the abyss.

The new inmates were milling around a small patch of land in front of the gabled building, penned in behind a tightly meshed wire fence. There was a gate in the heart of the fence, above which a sign read: "Wing I: Docking Port".

Reappearing at the head of the crowd, the hard-faced female guard opened a metal box attached to the gate and played with a mechanism inside. There was a loud grating sound, and to Adam's amazement the two sections of the walkway pivoted around the stone platform, one branch stopping by the Docking Port's gate as another moved round to the large building to their immediate left. The female guard opened the gate, allowing the children to shuffle tentatively up on to the walkway, peering down over the chasm as they went. They passed over the circular platform and followed the second branch of the walkway to the new building, passing beneath a sign that read "Wing II: Prisoners' Quarters" as they stepped back down on to solid ground.

A male guard was waiting for them in the doorway to the quarters, passing a powerful torch beam over the prisoners' faces as they approached.

"Boys will follow me up to floors one and two," the man called out, gesturing at the building behind him. "Girls will continue upstairs with Miss Roderick."

The guard marched inside the building, up a flight of stairs and down a narrow corridor, reeling off names from a clipboard as he passed certain rooms: "Davies, you're in 7a – Roberts and Wilkinson, next door." Bewildered by the labyrinth of corridors and backstairs, Adam quickly lost count of the number of rooms they passed. Eventually the guard barked, "In there, Wilson!" and pointed at a doorway.

Adam hurried inside the room, which turned out to be a long dormitory filled with rows of bunk beds. Boys were huddling beneath their blankets in the darkness. Everyone appeared to be asleep. The odour of farts and smelly feet was overpowering. There was only one empty bed for him: a bottom bunk in the far corner of the room. Adam threaded his way soundlessly over to it and lay down.

As the sound of the guards' tramping feet continued down the corridor, someone stirred in the bunk above Adam's, and the outline of a head dropped down to look at him.

"Hey!" a voice hissed. "What's the news from outside?"

Adam said nothing.

"Come on!" the voice persisted. "What's going on?"

"Give it a rest, Mouthwash," another boy called out drowsily. "You can bother him in the morning."

"But Doughnut—"

"Shut it, or you can forget about me getting those comics for you."

Muttering to himself, the first boy pulled his head back up and rolled over in his bunk, drawing an indignant creak from the springs. As silence enveloped the dormitory, Adam gathered his blanket around him. His aching limbs were still trembling, and he had to bite his lip to stop himself from bursting into tears. He lay awake for hours, accompanied only by the snores and sniffs from the bunks around him, before finally falling into a dark, dreamless sleep.

CHAPTER SEVEN

A loud thud startled Adam into wakefulness; when his eyes flicked open, he was confronted with the sight of two pale knees close to his face. His bunkmate – a short boy with spiky blond hair – had leapt down from his bed, and was now scraping a lump of grey chewing gum from the side of the post.

"Rise and shine!" he said, popping the gum into his mouth. "The goons don't approve of lie-ins."

The dormitory was stirring into life, boys drowsily rubbing their eyes and swinging their legs out of bed, shivering at the pinch of the cold air on their skin. Adam closed his eyes and slumped back on to the pillow. At the back of his mind, he had been praying that he would wake up in his bedroom, surrounded by his music posters and his computer games, with the sounds of his parents bustling around drifting up from the kitchen. Things had happened so quickly the night before that there hadn't been time to take everything in. It was only now, lying there in his bed, as the other boys splashed water on their faces and brushed their teeth, that the truth hit Adam: this was real. He was a prisoner, behind bars for two hundred and seventy-four years. Nearly three centuries would have to pass before he could return home and see his family or his friends again. It was more than a lifetime – it was an eternity. Adam turned over in his bunk, determined that no one see the tears welling in his eyes.

"Looks like the newbie's taking it tough," he heard his bunkmate murmur.

"Bet he's crying his eyes out," a harsh voice sneered. "The girl."

"Leave it out, Caiman," another boy shot back. "I was here when you first arrived, remember? You were too busy wetting the bed to cry."

"Please don't make me sleep on the top bunk!" someone else added, impersonating a fearful girl's voice. "I'm scared of heights!"

Howls of laughter swept through the dormitory, drowning out Caiman's angry protests. Order was only restored by the sudden appeal of the sirens across the Dial.

"*Attention! Attention!*" a high-pitched voice rang out. "*Roll call will take place in ten minutes in the exercise yard.*"

Amidst much swearing and hopping around, the boys put on their boots and tumbled out of the dormitory. Adam looked up to see a heavyset, dark-skinned boy giving him a sympathetic glance from the doorway.

"Better get up," the boy said quietly. "You'll only get into trouble otherwise."

Adam laughed bitterly. "Things can get worse than this?"

The boy paused, then nodded slowly. "Yes, they can. But only if you're stupid. You'll get the hang of it before long. Everyone does."

With that, he waddled away after the others, leaving Adam alone.

Though he was tempted to roll over and go back to sleep, squirrel himself away from this dark world of zeppelins and roll calls and prison guards, the boy's words stayed with Adam. As the sirens continued to wail he dragged himself out of bed, pulled on his boots and ran downstairs.

The walkway gate from Wing II had been opened by the time he got outside, and prisoners were trudging over the chasm towards a flat gravel yard on the other side of the Dial. It was incredibly cold, the weak winter sunshine failing to dispel the biting chill in the air. As he joined the back of the queue, shivering in his thin uniform, Adam noticed ruefully that almost everyone around him had extra layers of clothing: overcoats and hats and scarves, thick pairs of gloves.

When the last inmate had stepped down on to the gravel yard, the gates were closed and the prisoners arranged in ranks. The guards strode up and down the rows, screaming for silence as they counted heads. At the front of the yard, two men stood apart, overseeing the proceedings. One was a paunchy, middle-aged man in a leather overcoat and a black peaked cap, a flicker of benign amusement playing across his face. The other was Mr Pitt, his filmy left eye roving hungrily behind his monocle as he surveyed the prisoners before him.

One of the guards hurried over to the larger man and saluted. "All present, Mr Cooper, sir."

A jolt of recognition hit Adam. Mr Cooper had signed the letter Adam had opened in the changing rooms at school – this was the Chief Warder of the prison! He looked somehow friendlier than Adam might have imagined, especially compared to Mr Pitt's furious demeanour. Mr Cooper smiled as he stepped forward, clearing his throat before addressing the crowd.

"It's a cold morning, so I shall be as brief as possible. First, matron has informed me that someone is stealing bedsheets from the infirmary. I can't begin to imagine who would be responsible for such a wanton and petty crime, but until the perpetrator returns the items in question no games of Bucketball will be permitted anywhere on the Dial."

A disgruntled murmur ran through the crowd.

"Silence!" shouted Mr Pitt. "Not a word while the Chief Warder speaks!"

The murmur vanished as quickly as it started.

"Thank you, Hector," Mr Cooper said mildly. "Now then," he continued, "you will no doubt be aware that there was a new intake of prisoners last night. En route to the Dial, the *Quisling* suffered severe mechanical failure and was forced to make a crash landing. It is only thanks to the skill of Mr Pitt and his crew that a terrible tragedy was averted. We do not yet know how badly the *Quisling* has been damaged, but it looks like it could be out of service for several months at least. This will have a grave impact on our food supplies, and I am forced to announce that from today lunch time rations will be halved. This will be a trial for all of us – but I will not allow the decrease in rations to be used as some kind of excuse for bad behaviour and unrest. Act up, and you will learn the hard way – as countless other prisoners have before you – that there are limits to our patience."

A hard edge had crept into Mr Cooper's voice, and suddenly he didn't look quite as friendly as he had before. The Chief Warder let his final threat hang in the air before dismissing the inmates.

Without any instruction or direction on how they were to spend their morning, the prisoners were free to drift away in groups across the Dial. Adam returned to his bunk in the prisoners' quarters, where he spent hours in a dazed huddle beneath the sheets, vainly trying to come to terms with what was happening to him. At one o'clock the sirens blazed into life again, and the inmates were ordered to Wing III – the mess hall – for lunch. As he waited to cross the chasm, Adam couldn't help but marvel as the walkway swung round the Dial, picking up prisoners from all the different wings and depositing them in turn outside Wing III.

A two-storey building filled with tables and a canteen

that ran the length of the ground floor, the mess hall bubbled with conversation – the atmosphere heavily spiced with gossip, rude jokes and sudden squawks of laughter. Feeling at once very visible and very alone, Adam picked up a tray and moved along the canteen, accepting a bowl full of unidentified slop and a mug of weak tea on the way. The rest of the boys from his dormitory had congregated together at a table at the far end of the hall. Wordlessly Adam went over to join them, taking a seat next to the dark-skinned boy who was known, he gathered, as Doughnut.

Looking down at his food, Adam poked the murky slop suspiciously with his spoon. He nudged Doughnut. "What is this stuff?" he asked.

"Stew," the boy replied laconically.

"What kind of stew?"

"Meat stew."

Adam wasn't convinced. He slowly lifted the spoon to his mouth and took a taste. Instantly he spat out his mouthful across the table.

"Everything all right?" Doughnut asked mildly.

"H-hot!" Adam spluttered, flapping his hand in front of his mouth. The boys around him chuckled knowingly.

"Trust me, it's best that way," said Doughnut. "The hotter the food, the less you care how it tastes."

"Well, well, well," a voice chuckled behind them. "What a surprise. I was just saying to Jonkers: now, where might our good friend Doughnut be? Never thought we'd find him here, eating."

As two large shadows loomed over his meal, Adam was aware of the boys around him hurriedly finishing their meals and leaving the table. Only Doughnut seemed unconcerned.

"It is lunch time, Scarecrow," he replied calmly.

Scarecrow scowled. "It's always lunch time for you." He leaned in closely. "Where's those gloves you promised us? It's nearly winter, and my hands are getting cold."

Doughnut didn't respond.

"I'm talking to you, fat boy!"

Doughnut calmly carried on eating his meal. Frustrated, Jonkers snatched Doughnut's lunch tray and hurled it to the floor, while Scarecrow grabbed the chubby boy by the lapels and hauled him to his feet.

"Where's our gloves?" he repeated.

Doughnut spread out his hands helplessly. "Look, there's been a hitch with the clothing supply. I promise you, as soon I get a new delivery you'll get your gloves."

Scarecrow glanced at his companion. "Did you hear that, Jonkers? Tonnage here is giving us the brush-off."

Jonkers shook his head slowly. "Can't have that, Scarecrow. Can't have people like him taking liberties with us. Better teach him a lesson."

Adam put down his spoon and slowly stood up. "Leave him alone," he said quietly.

For the past day it had felt as though Adam had reeled from one blow to another: from the face-off with Danny to the ambush on the beach to Mr Pitt's sovereign rings raining down upon him. And now Scarecrow and Jonkers were picking on the only person who'd been nice to him in the entire prison. But these two, Adam could deal with.

All three boys looked up, united in their surprise.

"Who the hell are you?" asked Scarecrow.

"It doesn't matter. Put him down."

Jonkers laughed incredulously. "Or what, tough guy?"

"Or nothing. Just back off."

Adam didn't like fighting. But he hadn't spent ten years around Danny without learning to take care of himself. Even now, he felt strangely calm. As Jonkers lunged at him, Adam picked up his bowl of stew and threw the scalding liquid in the boy's face. Jonkers cried out in pain, clutching at his eyes. Before Scarecrow could respond, Adam spun around and clattered him over the head with his lunch tray, knocking him to the ground. He clenched his fists, braced for more, but suddenly a whistle was echoing around the mess hall, and a red-faced guard ran over towards them.

"What the hell's going on here?" he demanded.

Before Adam could speak Doughnut stepped in and said, with a beatific smile: "Nothing to worry about, Mr Harker. My friend spilled his stew, that's all."

Mr Harker looked suspiciously at the sprawled figure of Scarecrow. "So what's he doing on his backside?"

"Must have slipped on the stew," Doughnut replied evenly.

Mr Harker turned round to face Jonkers. "Is he telling the truth?"

Jonkers was still wiping chunks of carrot from his face, his features twisted with fury, and for a second Adam thought he was going to drop them all in it. Then Jonkers nodded slowly.

"Yeah – it was just an accident, sir. No harm done."

As the guard examined their faces, Adam could tell he didn't believe a word of it. By his side, Doughnut remained a picture of affability, hauling Scarecrow to his feet and patting him on the back.

"All right then," Mr Harker said eventually. "But for God's sake clean this mess up before Mr Pitt sees it, or we'll all be for it. And no more messing about, you hear me?"

The boys nodded vigorously. As Scarecrow and Jonkers sloped away, murder in their eyes, Doughnut went to the canteen and fetched a cloth. Under the watchful eye of Mr Harker, Adam helped him mop up the mess.

"Thanks for stepping in there," Doughnut said softly. "I owe you one."

"Don't worry about it," Adam replied. "It was nothing."

"I wouldn't be so sure about that. Scarecrow and Jonkers don't tend to forget that sort of thing."

Adam made a dismissive noise. "They're all talk. I'm not scared of them." He glanced across at the guard. "I can't believe he swallowed your story, though."

"Mr Harker? He's all right, as goons go. He knows which side his bread is buttered."

"Eh?"

Doughnut chuckled. "I forgot what it's like when you first get here. You've got a lot to learn, my friend."

"Tell me about it," Adam said glumly.

"All right, then," said Doughnut, getting to his feet. "Let me show you around."

CHAPTER EIGHT

It took them an age to leave the mess hall. At every table they passed, people leapt up to stop Doughnut: watchful boys who pressed notes into his hand with meaningful nods; girls with ingratiating, feline smiles who slipped their arms around his back while they whispered in his ear. Doughnut received the pleas and entreaties like a benevolent monarch, clasping hands and promising to do what he could.

Having disentangled himself from one particularly persistent blonde girl, Doughnut finally led Adam out into the fresh air.

"Bloody hell!" Adam exclaimed, shaking his head. "Is there anyone here you *don't* know?"

Doughnut shrugged. "No one who counts. Most people come and find me eventually." Noting Adam's quizzical expression, he explained: "I'm a fixer. I get things for people. Things they can't get here."

"Yeah? Like what?"

"Mostly it's food and clothes, that kind of stuff. People are always on at me to get them TVs and computers and stupid stuff like that, but even if I could smuggle them in here, the Dial ain't exactly the height of modern technology. So I tend to get the lads comics and magazines. Girls are much harder to deal with. I mean, do I look like I know anything about eyebrow pencils?"

Adam smiled. "Not really, no."

"Doesn't stop them hassling me about it, though, believe me."

Doughnut waddled over to the mess hall gate and opened a box attached to the wire fence. There was an intricate mechanized diagram of the Dial inside, with two movable hands representing the walkway. Doughnut set the hands to a new position on the diagram, then closed the lid. He blew out his cheeks, tapping his foot.

"I hate waiting for this thing," he muttered. "God knows how many years I've spent doing it."

Feeling a light tap on his head, Adam looked up. The sky was ominous with black clouds. By the time the walkway had rumbled round in front of the mess hall, the air was alive with rain, and Adam and Doughnut hurried across the chasm with their jackets pulled up over their heads. A gaunt, dilapidated building rose up in front of them, brickwork smeared with grime, tiles missing from the sagging roof and water cascading down from the rickety guttering.

Dashing off the walkway and through the gate marked "Wing V: Library", Adam heaved open the thick wooden door and ran inside. He stopped and caught his breath, waiting for his eyes to adjust to the gloom. Rows of leatherbound volumes stared down at him from the bookshelves, bathed in orange lamplight as soft as a whisper. On either side of the library, two wrought-iron spiral staircases led up to a tier of balconies lining the walls, where more books were stored behind glass cases. Silence nestled amongst the undisturbed shelves and the empty reading desks.

Adam glanced over at Doughnut, who was glumly rearranging his sodden hair. "What are we doing here?" he whispered.

"Going to meet a friend of mine." Doughnut peered through the half-light. "You hear that?"

Straining his ears, Adam could just make out a faint squeaking sound coming from somewhere deep in the library. "Your friend's a mouse?"

"Very funny. Come on."

As they followed the squeak through the labyrinth of bookshelves, Adam's nostrils were overpowered by a musty smell of neglect. The drumming rain was seeping through the ceiling, landing with a splash into metal pails dotted at intervals across the floor.

Rounding a corner, Adam came face to face with the source of the squeaking. A young boy was pushing a wooden trolley of books along the aisle, occasionally filing away a volume on the shelves. With every revolution, one of the trolley wheels let out an anguished squeak.

"Bookworm!" Doughnut called out, his voice echoing round the library.

The young boy winced. "Keep it down, will you? I can't tell everyone else to shush if you're screaming the place down."

Doughnut spread out his hands in protest. "We're the only people in here!"

"Even so," Bookworm replied solemnly. "You've got to maintain your standards." He pulled down a book from the shelves and placed it on the trolley. "Would you like a cup of cocoa?"

Doughnut grinned. "I was hoping you'd ask that." He turned to Adam. "Bookworm's famous for his cocoa."

The portly fixer took control of the trolley as they followed the shuffling Bookworm back towards the reception area. There was something about the little boy – the way he talked, the way he carried himself – that made Adam feel strangely ill-at-ease, no matter how friendly Doughnut was towards him.

They sat down around one of the reading desks, nursing mugs of black liquid that Bookworm produced from a Thermos. Adam had been looking forward to cocoa, but he was disappointed to find it bitter and thick with coarse granules. Nevertheless, he smiled politely as he sipped it. Doughnut slurped away with relish, coating his upper lip with dark liquid.

"Adam here just arrived yesterday," he told Bookworm.

The librarian looked over towards him. "Guess you're feeling pretty strange right now."

"Strange?" echoed Adam incredulously. "I think I'm going mad."

"You wouldn't be the first," Bookworm said. "The Dial is a lot to get your head around, and not everyone can cope.

Some of the kids get so upset they lose their mind. They end up in the infirmary, drugged up to the eyeballs. Not a place you want to end up in."

"No kidding," replied Adam.

"How long's your sentence?"

"Two hundred and seventy-four years."

Bookworm shrugged. "That's pretty standard."

"Standard? What's a long sentence here?"

Doughnut burst out laughing and clapped Bookworm on the back. "You're asking the right guy. This here's one of the oldest nine-year-olds you're ever likely to see. How many years you been here now, Bookworm?"

The little boy scratched his head. "About six hundred and fifty, give or take a few."

An incredulous laugh died in Adam's throat as he saw Bookworm's serious expression. It couldn't be true, there was no way it could be true . . . and yet it did explain why the librarian's manner unsettled him. There was a crushing melancholy to Bookworm's demeanour at odds with his unlined face, a weight of experience that seemed to press down on the shoulders of his young frame.

"This place. . ." muttered Adam in disbelief. "I don't understand . . . I mean, how?"

Bookworm took another sip of cocoa, then disappeared into the bookshelves. He returned a couple of minutes later, blowing the dust off a slender dark-blue volume that he showed to Adam. The title of the book had been marked out on the cover in gold lettering: *The Inmate's Handbook*.

"Maybe this will help," Bookworm said. "It was written for new inmates." He cleared his throat, then began to read aloud, in a thin, faltering voice:

Welcome to the Dial. I imagine you have a lot of questions. Where am I? What is this place? Why am I here? The last one is easy enough: you are here because you betrayed someone. Don't bother trying to deny it. The sooner you accept it the better. Questions about the prison itself are rather harder to answer, but hopefully this brief introduction will serve as a useful starting point.

The Dial is located in no-time, a place far beyond the outer reaches of the known universe. Although the seasons turn as normal, the Dial's planet must revolve around a different sun, for a year here lasts as long as a blink of an eye back on Earth. The prison can only be reached through a warphole in the sky, which is activated by the machinery located in the Commandant's Quarters. If anything or anyone else exists in no-time beyond the prison walls, then it has remained hidden. As far as we know, this world is entirely barren. There is only the Dial.

The prison can hold a thousand prisoners at any one time, and the plentiful supply of traitors from Earth ensures that a bunk is never empty for long. The total number of inmates to have passed through the Docking Port is anyone's guess. Many thousands? Certainly.

Millions? Probably. Given that the Dial exists beyond time, it is possible that everyone has been sent here at one time or another. After all, nobody's perfect. . .

"But wait!" I hear you say, "if there have been all these prisoners, how come I've never heard of the Dial before?" Allow me to explain. At the end of their sentence, inmates are taken to the Re-education Wing, where their minds are wiped of all memories of the prison, save for a flicker on the edge of their consciousness. They are left only with an awareness of the steep price of betrayal, an awareness that prevents them from even thinking about committing the same crime again. Then the inmates are allowed to resume their life on Earth, not looking a day older than when they left, and where barely a second will have passed since their arrest. After that, it is hoped that they will live their lives with a sense of honour and loyalty instilled by countless decades of imprisonment.

Bookworm closed the book and placed it down carefully upon the reading desk.

"Cheery read," Adam said, rubbing his face with his hands. "Who wrote it?"

"I did," Bookworm replied quietly. "A couple of centuries ago. Probably only five people apart from me have ever read it. People here would rather listen to rumours and fairy tales than anything I've got to say."

"I still can't believe you've been here for all this time," Adam breathed.

"You haven't heard the best of it yet," said Doughnut. "All of us prisoners were born within a few years of each other. Back on earth, it's probably only been a week between when Bookworm was taken and when the *Quisling* came for you. Only for him, that week's lasted over 600 years."

"But that's. . ."

"Impossible?" The librarian laughed. "That word doesn't very mean much here."

As Bookworm took another sip of cocoa, Adam gave him a curious look.

"What did you do?"

"Mmm?" said Bookworm.

"I mean – why are you here? Who did you betray?"

Doughnut held up a warning hand. "Dial manners, Adam. Don't ask anyone that. If they want to tell you, that's up to them. No one ever does, though."

"It doesn't matter what any of us did," Bookworm said quietly. "We're all guilty."

"So that's it?" Adam said bitterly. "I'm stuck in this place for two hundred years?"

"Not necessarily," said Doughnut. "If you don't fancy doing your time quietly, you could always try and do something about it."

"Like what?"

Doughnut's eyes twinkled. "Escape, of course."

CHAPTER NINE

Doughnut's words floated up into the rafters, where they were lost in the darkness. As the silence in the library assumed a meaningful tone, the fixer grinned, finishing off his cocoa with a flourish.

"Escape?" said Adam. "How?"

"Well, that's the question," replied Doughnut. "There've been all sorts of crazy schemes over the years. There was that time when Sanchez knotted loads of sheets together and tried to climb down from a window in the mess hall, or when Beanpole tried to get on the *Quisling* dressed as a guard. My personal favourite was when Price and Banjo tried to get over the wall on that ladder of theirs."

"You're kidding me!" said Adam. "Did they make it?"

"Make it?" Bookworm emitted a reedy laugh. "They were lucky they didn't break their necks!"

"Getting out of here is pretty tough," admitted Doughnut. "This place is a fortress, and the guards are watching you twenty-four-seven. Even if you do make it out of the Dial, what then? Sit around in no-time for the next few thousand years? You'd be better off in here."

"What about the warphole?" Adam asked. "Can't you get back that way?"

"That's the *only* way you can get back. Problem is, you've got to open it first, and that means strolling over to the Commandant's tower and turning the machine on. And that's the most secure wing in the prison."

Adam remembered standing on the landing strip looking up at the whirling mass in the sky, and the beam of light shooting out towards it from a tower on the Dial.

"I don't get it," he confessed. "Who's this Commandant?

"You saw Mr Cooper today in the exercise yard, yeah?" said Doughnut. "Well, he's the Chief Warder – in charge of all the day-to-day stuff – but it's the Commandant who's the main man. He was here at the very beginning. As far as we can tell, the Dial is all his work."

"What's he like?"

The fixer scratched his head. "That's the thing – no one really knows. The only time you ever meet the Commandant is in the Re-education Wing, just before you get taken back to Earth. Apart from that, he doesn't leave his tower. But he's the one opening the warphole, all right."

"And no one's been able to break in and turn it on themselves?" Adam asked, a note of excitement in his voice. "That's impossible?"

Doughnut gave him a sly look. "Well, maybe not *impossible. . .*"

"Don't encourage him!" Bookworm said sharply. The

small librarian wagged a finger at Adam. "Escaping is a fool's game. I've seen enough idiots try over the years, and no one's ever made it."

"That's not true, though, is it?" said Doughnut.

Bookworm pulled a face of disgust. "And you think Adam should use *him* as an example?"

"Wait!" said Adam. "Who are you talking about? Has someone actually escaped from the Dial?"

If Bookworm replied, it was lost in the deafening keen of a siren. Doughnut brushed his hands together and got to his feet with a sigh.

"Where are you going?" Adam asked.

"Same place as you. Lessons."

Adam's face fell. "Lessons?"

"And you thought this place couldn't get any worse," Doughnut laughed, patting Adam on the shoulder. "Let's get it over with. See you later, Bookworm."

They headed back outside, where the walkway was rumbling through the slanting rain, picking up bedraggled prisoners and depositing them in front of a large building on Wing VII. The classrooms occupied the lower floor, Doughnut informed Adam. Above them was a large theatre space, reserved for special occasions and off-limits for most of the year.

"Don't worry," the fixer assured him, as they trooped off the walkway and inside the building. "This isn't proper school or anything. We don't have to do it every day. Most of the time the goons leave us alone – they reckon sitting around bored for a few hundred years is worse punishment than breaking rocks or scrubbing floors or anything like that. But, every so often, they like to remind us why we're here."

Classes were arranged by grouping different dormitories together, creating a mixture of boys and girls in each room. Relieved not to be separated from his new friend, Adam followed Doughnut to a classroom and took a seat at the back of the orderly regiment of wooden desks. The windows were barred and there were no computers, and a dusty blackboard instead of a whiteboard, but still the atmosphere felt just like every other classroom Adam had been in: a mixture of boredom and a restless desire for mischief; stifled yawns and giggles; whispered secrets and daydreams of freedom. He took a seat beside Doughnut, directly behind two of the fixer's friends: the hyperactive Mouthwash from their dormitory, who talked as fast he chewed on his ever-present gum; and a serious-looking girl with dark hair and glasses, whose nickname, Adam learned, was Paintpot.

"Quiet!"

Miss Roderick strode to the front of the class, her face like a thundercloud as she handed each inmate a lined exercise book and a thick, leather-bound volume with the title *Betrayals: Vol. 653* embossed on the cover in large black letters.

"We'll start copying out from page one hundred and forty-five today," Miss Roderick declared. "And in silence!"

When he opened *Betrayals*, Adam saw that the pages were filled with handwritten testimonies, written in shaky hands, the ink smeared with tears. They were all the same in tone – trembling descriptions of how people had been let down by those closest to them. As he leafed through the book, Adam realized that there had to be hundreds of testimonies inside. And this was volume 653...

He made a start on his copying, and was halfway down the page when Doughnut nudged him.

"Check this out," he whispered.

The fixer flicked to the very front of the book, where the ink was faded and the pages were stained with mildew. Straining to decipher the tangled handwriting, Adam read:

> "...and even though I was really ashamed I told my best friend, Lydia, making her swear that she wouldn't tell a soul. But then the next morning I came into school and all the other children were laughing at me and I realized that they all knew, every single one of them. I ran out through the school gates and never went back again."

"Sad stuff," said Adam.

"You might not feel quite so sympathetic when you see who wrote it."

Adam inspected the signature beneath the testimony: Hortensia Roderick. He glanced up at the guard, then back at Doughnut.

"This is *hers*?"

Doughnut softly tapped the Betrayals. "All the guards are in these books somewhere. See, loads of kids get let down and betrayed. But the guards are the ones who never get over it. So they come back here, as adults, to take it out on us. Why else do you think they're here? Not much more fun working here than doing time here, if you ask me. And some of them hang around for a while, too. Take Mr Harker – he's been here longer than Bookworm."

A sudden thought creased Adam's brow. "What about Mr Pitt? What happened to him?"

"Now that's a mystery," Doughnut admitted. "I've been through every page of these books, and I've never been able to find it. We reckon he must have torn it out. Wouldn't want us laughing at him, would he?"

"No talking in class!" Miss Roderick barked. With a roll of his eyes, Doughnut returned to his work.

As much as he tried to concentrate on *Betrayals*, the silent copying soon bored Adam. Over Paintpot's shoulder, he saw that she had slipped a sketchpad under her exercise book and was drawing a picture of a boy. Adam watched, fascinated, as Paintpot carefully shaded in dark hair and brought a pair of twinkling, mischievous eyes into life.

Finally the siren put an end to their misery and Miss Roderick abruptly dismissed them. Adam was almost out of the door when a cry made him turn around.

"Hey!"

Mouthwash had snatched Paintpot's sketchpad from

her and was displaying her drawing of the boy to the other prisoners as they walked past.

"Check this masterpiece out!" he laughed.

"Give it back!" Paintpot protested. "It's just a doodle!"

"Doodle my foot!" crowed Mouthwash. "It's Lover Boy, isn't it? It's Luca D'Annunzio."

The prisoners around them froze; there was an audible intake of breath. Doughnut glanced over towards Miss Roderick, but she was too busy telling off a girl for wearing lipstick to notice them.

"Shut up, Mouthwash!" Paintpot hissed, her face reddening. "You're not funny."

She made another attempt to grab the book, only succeeding in knocking it from Mouthwash's hands on to the floor – straight at the feet of the girl Adam had met in the Docking Port the previous night.

Tucking a strand of hair behind her ear, the girl knelt down and picked up the sketchpad.

"Ignore him," she said quietly to Paintpot, handing back the sketchpad. "It's a lovely picture. You're really talented."

The girl hurried away before anyone could reply, disappearing into the busy corridor outside. Adam watched her leave.

"Who is that?" he asked.

"Her name's Jessica," Paintpot replied, glaring at Mouthwash as she jammed her sketchpad underneath her arm. "I think so, anyway. It's the first time she's ever spoken to me. Why do you want to know?"

Adam shrugged. "No reason," he lied.

Doughnut checked to see that Miss Roderick was still looking the other way, then gave Mouthwash a swift dig in the arm.

"Ow! What was that for?"

"Paintpot's right – that wasn't funny."

Mouthwash rubbed his arm, a wounded expression on his face. The two of them began bickering loudly, and Adam decided to leave them to it while he accompanied Paintpot back to the prisoners' quarters. He waited until they were safely alone on the staircase before asking:

"What was all that about back there? Who's the boy in the picture?"

Paintpot blushed again and held her sketchpad to her chest. "His name is Luca D'Annunzio. He used to be a prisoner here."

"But he's not any more?"

She shook her head. "Not for a long time. Look, we shouldn't talk about him. If people hear us talking about him, we'll get into trouble."

"Trouble?" pressed Adam. "Why?"

"If you really want to find out more, go to the library and read the *Codex Treacherous*. I've said all I should."

"OK," said Adam. He gave Paintpot a gentle nudge. "Jessica was right, though. You are a really good artist."

A smile flickered over the girl's solemn face. "Thanks. Here." She handed him the pad.

"Don't you want to keep it?"

The smile broadened into a grin. "I've got others. See you at dinner."

Paintpot continued up the stairs towards the girls' quarters, leaving Adam to enter the boys' corridor on his own . . .

. . . Only to come running back in the opposite direction several seconds later, with Scarecrow and Jonkers hot on his heels.

"Not so hard now, are you?" Jonkers bellowed.

"Get back here!" added Scarecrow.

Adam hurtled down the steps three at a time, just managing to keep out of his pursuers' grasp. Where were the guards when he needed them? He leapt down to the ground floor and pelted along the empty hallway, heading for the front door and the safety of open ground. Behind him Scarecrow and Jonkers were still yelling threats, but they had lost the element of surprise and Adam was faster on his feet than they were. He yanked open the front door and ran outside.

Straight into a brick wall.

Adam crashed to the floor, Paintpot's sketchpad flying from his hands. Dazed, he looked up to see that what he thought had been a wall was actually another boy standing in the doorway, a craggy mountain of muscle and flesh topped with cropped dark hair. He stared down at Adam with utter contempt.

"You dozy chimp," the boy snarled. "Look where you're going, eh?"

"Sorry," said Adam, hurriedly getting to his feet. Glancing over his shoulder, he saw that Scarecrow and Jonkers had skidded to a halt and were reluctantly retreating back up the stairs. They were the least of his problems now – more boys had followed the first through the doorway and were crowding around him, all dressed in identical woollen greatcoats and with matching stern expressions.

"Sorry," Adam said hastily. "It was an accident. I don't want any trouble."

"You're bloody right you don't," the first boy retorted.

"Hang on a minute, Corbett."

The circle parted, revealing a much shorter figure wearing a peaked cap and a crisply ironed blue uniform. Though he was younger and a head shorter than everyone else in the corridor, the other boys stopped as he calmly picked up the sketchpad, which had fallen open at the page of Paintpot's drawing of Luca.

"I like a good picture," he said conversationally. Then he slammed the sketchpad shut and shoved it back into Adam's hands. "And this is nothing like one. I don't recognize your face. Who are you?"

For the third time in a matter of hours, Adam found himself outnumbered and on the defensive. This was worse than Scarecrow and Jonkers, though. Any one of this gang looked like they could make mincemeat out of him.

"I'm Adam," he said. "I'm new here. Who are you?"

A wave of deep chuckles greeted his questions. The young boy smiled thinly.

"You've got a lot to learn, sunshine. Let me introduce myself: my name is Major X, and this here is the Tally-Ho

Escape Committee. Seeing as you're new here, I'll give you a little bit of advice: if you want to do a nice peaceful stretch without any palaver, *stop drawing pictures of collaborators*. And remember our faces – because we'll remember yours. Come on, lads."

The Tally-Ho Escape Committee marched haughtily down the corridor after the diminutive Major, Corbett making sure that he banged into Adam on the way past. Adam waited until they were out of sight before trudging over to the mess hall, his heart heavy once more. His relief on making friends with Doughnut had been short-lived. Mr Pitt, Scarecrow and Jonkers, now the Tally-Ho . . . if life wasn't difficult enough, Adam was making a lot of enemies in a very short space of time. If he was going to have any chance of surviving this place, he told himself, he was going to have to watch his step.

CHAPTER TEN

Although Adam's first day on the Dial was the longest of his life, the next few weeks passed by with increasing speed. For all the idle hours in the dormitories and the yard, roll calls and mealtimes gave the days a routine, soon making them as familiar and mundane as a French or chemistry lesson. In a strange way, the sheer length of Adam's sentence also helped: there was simply no way his mind could grasp the prospect of spending nearly three centuries in prison. It was all he could do to get through one day, and then the next.

Mindful of Bookworm's warning about staying sane, Adam tried his best not to think about his home and his family and friends – especially not Danny. But in the middle of the night, when winter was reaching its icy nadir, it was hard to block out the images of his home and the people he loved. It was then that Adam allowed himself to cry, his shoulders shaking silently beneath his blanket.

Despite such dark moments of unhappiness, Adam was coping better than many of the inmates. Distressed prisoners could be found in most corners of the prison: shedding tears of shame during roll call; rocking back and forth in the chapel pews; staring numbly into space for hours on their bunks. A week into Adam's sentence, a boy ran amok in the mess hall during dinner time, smashing plates and throwing chairs while screaming unintelligibly. He was jumped on by three large guards and promptly manhandled towards the exit.

"That's the last we'll see of him," Mouthwash said sadly. "He'll be dosed up in the infirmary until the day he gets out."

As the boy clung on to the doorway, snarling and spitting at the guards, Adam realized he knew him. It was Carstairs, the know-it-all from the *Quisling*. Adam watched, shocked, as the boy's fingertips were peeled from the door frame and he disappeared with an anguished yell into the night.

Following the *Quisling*'s crash landing, the Docking Port was closed off to inmates, and over subsequent days the prison echoed with the sound of welding and hammering as repairs began on the zeppelin. With the Dial's only airship out of action, there was no way to return to Earth to pick up supplies – placing great strain on the prison's food stores, which were housed in the granary store and the allotments behind the mess hall.

Adam didn't need more reasons to dread mealtimes. The food was shockingly bad: an endless cycle of scalding-hot stews, blackened lumps of potatoes and mouldy bread. At first he pushed away his meal half-finished, and was shocked to see the rest of his table descend like vultures on his leftovers. But as the days progressed and the temperature continued to drop, Adam began wolfing down his food out of sheer hunger. Even so, he felt increasingly tired and weak, and his stomach rumbled angrily through the night. How Doughnut managed to maintain his portly shape after decades of measly portions was a mystery. But then, there were a lot of questions about Adam's new friend that remained unanswered. The loss of the *Quisling* seemed to irk Doughnut in particular, and the curly-haired boy was chased away from the Docking Port several times for checking on the progress of repairs.

One afternoon Adam received an urgent message to go over to the library, where he found Doughnut struggling to carry several large boxes down to the cellar.

"Give us a hand, will you, mate?" he asked, glancing around the library. "These books are pretty heavy. And don't hang about, yeah?"

Adam ferried the boxes down the cellar steps, repeatedly overtaking Doughnut as the larger boy puffed and panted with the effort. They left the boxes in the corner of the cellar, draped under a sheet of tarpaulin. Doughnut remained tight-lipped about where his haul had come from, and despite his curiosity Adam knew better than to ask. The next day, however, he saw that several of the girls were showing off brand-new scarves as they swished around the Dial, and that the boys in the next dormitory had somehow got hold of a large net which they had stretched across the room for an impromptu game of volleyball.

Doughnut wasn't the only inmate guarding a secret. There were endless doorway conferences and impromptu councils of war, where delegates talked in whispers behind their hands. Chapel services provided an excellent opportunity to do business – the congregation's off-key singing and Mr Harker's energetic organ playing drowning out any private conversations. The first time Adam went to chapel he found the Tally-Ho assembled in a bulky row along the back pew, crowding around Major X as he held court. Despite their awkward first encounter, Adam couldn't help his gaze drifting over in their direction, earning himself a glacial stare from the head of the Escape Committee.

"I don't think the Major likes me very much," Adam remarked to Doughnut as they mooched out of the chapel afterwards. "He's a bit odd, isn't he?"

"It's not *all* his fault," the fixer replied. "The Tally-Ho's been going for thousands of years, and they're pretty heavy on tradition. They're named after the first Major's rabbit, Tally-Ho, who kept escaping from his garden back on earth. Before he can take charge, every Major has to learn all these regulations about how to dress, how to act – even how to speak. It's supposed to help maintain discipline."

"It doesn't make sense, though," said Adam. "If they're always trying to escape, why don't the guards lock them all up?"

"Give Mr Pitt half a chance and they would. But Mr Cooper won't let him."

"Why not?"

Doughnut shrugged. "Why bother? Even though most of us keep our heads down and do our time, there's always going to be *someone* crazy enough to try and break out. At least this way the guards know who to keep an eye on. He's clever like that, is Mr Cooper."

"OK," Adam said slowly. "In that case, why don't the Tally-Ho keep their gang a secret?"

"Because they're a bunch of poseurs," laughed Doughnut. He lowered his voice. "But they're also a *big* bunch of poseurs, so don't tell them I said that."

There was no way that Adam would do anything to put his friend in trouble – he was already indebted to Doughnut. On his second morning in the prison, Adam had awoken to find a woollen cap and a pair of gloves lying next to his bed. The fixer didn't say anything, but Adam knew who he had to thank. Standing up for Doughnut in the canteen had also helped Adam earn a measure of respect from the rest of the boys in their dormitory. At first the nicknames and the prison slang were like a foreign language, but as he became more familiar with life on the Dial he cautiously joined in with the jokes and the grumbles. The largest complaints surrounded the continued banning of Bucketball. Although no one had bothered to explain the game to Adam, it was clear that the inmates were itching to play it again.

"Someone had better hand those bloody infirmary sheets back," Mouthwash muttered as he squinted at a gift from Paintpot – a painting of a rolling green pasture filled with flowers, now hanging on their dormitory wall. "I don't care how much it's annoying the goons – I need to play a few rumbles."

"It's too cold to play now, anyway," said Doughnut. "They'll back down when spring comes."

"Like you care," came a sly voice from a lower bunk. Caiman's head emerged like a turtle from a shell. "When was the last time you did any exercise?"

Doughnut raised his middle finger by way of reply, and rolled over in his bed.

Given that Scarecrow and Jonkers' vendetta against Adam had died down to glares and rude gestures across the exercise yard, he had decided that Caiman was the most annoying prisoner on the Dial. Caiman treated his bunk like a sniper's nest, only raising his head to take bitter potshots at the others. According to dormitory legend, he suffered from vertigo so badly that he had browbeaten his bunkmate into switching beds so he could be closer to the floor. Caiman didn't appear overly grateful for that – in fact, he didn't seem capable of a nice word about anything or anyone. If any of the other inmates had complained so incessantly, Adam knew that one way or another they would have been sorted out. Why Caiman was treated with such patience was a mystery.

The Dial's other great hate figure was less of a puzzle.

Every day, usually in the middle of the afternoon, the loudspeakers cleared their throats of feedback and a high-pitched voice gleefully delivered messages to the inmates – usually a combination of taunts, admonishments and punishments. The announcements were broadcast from a small radio station perched on top of the guards' quarters. Adam recognized the announcer from his bedroom radio and quickly grew to hate his nasal tones. He wasn't alone – every time the boy spoke, the prisoners spat on the ground.

"Who is that?" Adam shouted finally, over the jeering din.

A dark look crossed over Doughnut's face. "That's Echo. The little runt finished a three-hundred-year sentence last year – only he liked it so much round here he asked to stay on to help the guards. Now he hides away up in the Radio Station, lording it over us and sucking up to Pitt and Cooper. What a toad."

It was the angriest Adam had seen the affable fixer look. He tried to change the subject, but they slipped into an awkward silence that lasted until the mocking sneers came to an end.

With Major X's warning about Luca D'Annunzio still fresh in his mind, Adam waited a couple of days before following Paintpot's advice and sneaking over to the library. Bookworm's eyes narrowed at the mention of the *Codex Treacherous*, but the librarian said nothing as he led Adam up one of the spiral staircases to a glass cabinet on the first floor, whereupon he produced a key from his pocket and unlocked the door. Reaching inside, Bookworm pulled out a large official-looking file and handed it to Adam.

"Here you go," he said, wrinkling his nose. "Although I've no idea why you'd want to read it. The *Codex* isn't allowed out of the library, so tell me when you've finished with it."

As Bookworm shuffled away, Adam carried the heavy book over to a reading desk and thumped it open. He pulled off his gloves and tried to rub some life into his cold fingers. The *Codex* was filled with typewritten reports, brisk summaries of the Dial's most infamous inmates: the liars and the thieves, the double-crossers and the backstabbers. But when he reached the page with Luca's name at its head, Adam saw that the rest of the report had been torn from the binding. On the facing page, someone had written, in an elegant, mocking scrawl:

They seek him here, they seek him there,
The daft goons seek him everywhere,
But he's long gone, the only true traitor,
Luca D'Annunzio – the Collaborator!
V. Mix

Adam scratched his head. It was hardly the first graffitied book he'd seen – but there seemed something very deliberate about the damage here. What terrible crime had

Luca committed that made people want to cover it up? He wondered about asking Bookworm, but then he wasn't sure he knew the librarian well enough to show interest in such an unpopular inmate. Instead he carefully placed the *Codex* back into the cabinet and went downstairs to tell Bookworm he was finished.

Still immersed in thought as he crossed the walkway back to the prisoners' quarters, Adam nearly missed Jessica hurrying out of the infirmary, a yellow trustee's armband wrapped around her sleeve. He had seen her a couple of times in the classroom since the incident with Paintpot's drawing, but no matter how many times he tried to catch her eye or give her a friendly smile, she kept her head down and sat on the other side of the room. Now he waited for her outside the dormitories, but as she stepped down from the walkway a shadow crossed her face at the sight of him.

"Hi!" Adam called out. "Do you remember me? You gave me my uniform the night I first came here. I'm—"

"I know who you are," Jessica said abruptly. "I don't want to sound rude, but I'd really appreciate it if you stayed away from me."

"What?" said Adam, taken aback. "Why? What's the matter?"

"Nothing's the matter. And I'd like it to stay that way. Why are you waiting for me?"

Adam shifted uncomfortably. "I don't know. I didn't mean any harm by it. I guess I thought maybe we could be friends?"

Jessica looked down at her feet. "I'm sorry, Adam, but I don't want to be your friend. My life's horrible enough without being chased around by someone Mr Pitt thinks is trouble. Please – stay away from me."

Before he could reply she hurried past him into the prisoners' quarters, her long hair falling over her face, masking her expression from Adam.

CHAPTER ELEVEN

If Adam had known how his day was going to turn out, he wouldn't have bothered getting out of bed at all.

He had awoken to find the Dial in a state of feverish excitement. It was film night – when, once a year, the guards brought over a projector from their quarters and let the inmates watch an old black-and-white movie. Adam's delight was only slightly tempered by the knowledge that it was his dormitory's turn for slopping-out duty. After lunch and dinner, they had to head to the kitchen at the back of the mess hall to scrub the encrusted pots and pans clean, a chore that left hands pink from the boiling water and covered in a film of sour grease. By common agreement, slopping out was one of the worst jobs on the Dial.

Even so, after dinner the boys attacked their chores energetically, keen not to miss a second of the film. Adam was wrestling with a particularly stubborn black mark on a saucepan when something heavy and wet thudded into the back of his neck. He spun round to see a damp rolled-up cloth on the tiles by his feet. There was a snigger from over by Mouthwash's sink.

"You missed a bit!" the boy called out.

Gloopy liquid dripped down Adam's neck. "Oh, you're going to pay for that, mate!" he said, with a grin.

Snatching up the cloth, he soaked it in the grimy water in his sink, bunched it up and hurled back at Mouthwash, who ducked neatly out of the way. Before long there was a crossfire of wet missiles flying through the air, splattering and squelching as they exploded against the walls. Only Caiman refused to join in, pointedly turning his back and continuing to scrub his pots.

Adam had Doughnut in his sights and was winding up a shot when his foot stepped into a puddle on the tiles. Slipping mid-throw, Adam watched in horror as his cloth veered away from its target, arcing in slow motion towards a tower of dirty plates stacked up on the sideboard. The cloth connected with the heart of the stack, knocking the plates to the floor, where they smashed into pieces with a deafening crash.

There was a shocked pause.

"Uh oh," said Doughnut.

There wasn't even time to sweep up the pieces before the door flew open and Mr Pitt strode into the kitchen, a cane clenched in his hand, his baleful eye sweeping over the shattered plates.

"What in damnation's going on here?" he barked.

As one, the inmates looked down at their feet. Mr Pitt strode over to Doughnut and jammed the butt of his cane underneath his chin, forcing his head up until they were eyeball to eyeball.

"I'm assuming you've got some food stuck in your ears," said Mr Pitt, "because you haven't answered my question. You're not going to make me repeat myself, are you?"

Even though Doughnut was trembling, he stayed silent.

"It's not his fault, sir," a voice piped up from the other side of the kitchen. Mr Pitt broke off from Doughnut and strode over to Caiman.

"You got something to tell me, sonny?"

"I said, it wasn't Doughnut who broke the plates, sir. It was Wilson."

Mr Pitt grinned wolfishly, baring his yellow teeth. He turned to Adam. "Wilson!" he said, in an almost comradely fashion. "I was beginning to worry about you. You'd kept your nose clean for a whole week."

"But, sir," protested Adam, "it was an accident!"

"Come, come, Wilson," Mr Pitt said amiably, patting him on the back. "Let's not fall out again. Mop out the chapel every day this week, starting right now. I'll be checking to make sure you're doing a thorough job – and if I'm not satisfied, you'll spend next week doing the latrines. Understand?"

Adam nodded slowly.

Mr Pitt raised a single, quivering eyebrow.

"Yes, *sir*," Adam corrected himself.

"You're walking a fine line, Wilson," Mr Pitt said ominously. "A very fine line." The guard turned on his heel and strode towards the door, calling out as he did so: "You're a lickspittle, Caiman. Don't think that shopping Wilson is going to curry any favour with me."

They waited until the sound of Mr Pitt's footsteps had faded away before letting out their breath. Accusing eyes trained on Caiman.

"Good one, idiot," Doughnut said sarcastically.

"Don't have a go at me," Caiman shot back. "Someone had to tell Pitt, or we'd all have ended up in the punishment cells. You think I'm going back in there again? You ask me, Adam should have owned up."

He was drowned out by a chorus of boos and whistles from the rest of the boys. Wounded, Caiman slunk back to his washing up.

"That lad's starting to do my head in," Adam muttered to Doughnut.

"Forget about him," the fixer replied. "He's not worth it. Come on. I'll show you where the cleaning cupboard is."

Ten minutes later, Adam found himself struggling over the walkway towards the chapel with a heavy bucket of water, a large mop banging insistently against his side. As the icy water slopped over the side of the bucket, once again he found himself grateful for the gloves Doughnut had given him.

As evening drew in, lights were flicking on around the prison – except for Wing XI, which was bathed in darkness. The Commandant's residence was a surprisingly modest building – a lone tower with a crooked spire, linked to the neighbouring Re-education Wing by a covered walkway a hundred metres above the ground. No matter how times he had sneaked a glance towards the tower, Adam had never seen any movement or signs of life inside. Given the shadowy nature of the Dial's head, Adam couldn't help wondering whether the Commandant had been made up – an invention of Mr Cooper's, perhaps, a bogey man to help keep the inmates in line. But there was nothing imaginary about the respect in both the guards' and the prisoners' voices whenever they mentioned the Commandant's name. They certainly didn't question that there was someone up there.

As Adam neared the chapel, the sound of excited giggles drifted over through the gloom from Wing VII, where the rest of the inmates were queuing to enter the theatre above the classrooms. Of all the nights he had to get into trouble, Adam thought glumly, it had to be film night. He struggled through the chapel doors, splashing water over his trousers, and stumbled inside.

The chapel was a narrow room with high ceilings, illuminated by a blazing forest of candles. It was modestly decorated, with few of the ceremonial flourishes Adam remembered from churches back home: there were no shining stained-glass windows, no intricate stone carvings, not even an altar. There were only banks of empty wooden pews and a row of confession boxes running along the left-hand wall, awaiting their next penitent arrival.

With a sigh, Adam dunked his mop in the bucket and

began dragging it across the church floor. It looked like no one had cleaned this place in years, and the water in the bucket quickly turned brown with grime. Adam was looking for a drain when a grating sound caught his ear. He frowned. All the inmates and the guards would be watching the film – why would anyone else be here? Tightening his grip on the mop, Adam crept forward in search of the source of the noise.

He was startled to see that in the gloom beyond the last confession box, a flagstone was moving magically across the floor, revealing a black hole beneath. A dirtied face popped up from below the ground. It was Corbett, the giant Tally-Hoer. He wiped the back of his hand across his face and took in a couple of long, deep breaths.

"I can't believe I'm missing the film to spend time digging in this stinking hole with you," he complained back beneath the surface. "I see that while we're down here, Major X is putting his feet up and watching the flick."

There came a muffled reply from below him.

"Too right," said Corbett. Glancing around the chapel, he caught sight of Adam watching him.

"You!" he hissed. "What are you doing here?"

Adam held up his the mop. "Punishment duty," he replied. "I've got to clean the floor."

"Then go and do it somewhere else!" Corbett said angrily. "And keep your bloody trap shut, or you'll be eating through a straw for the rest of the year. You catch my drift?"

Adam nodded dumbly. His eyes flashing with a final warning, the Tally-Hoer lifted the flagstone back over his head and disappeared from view. Determined to put as much distance between himself and the confession boxes as possible, Adam hurried to the other side of the chapel, only to round a pillar and find another boy sitting quietly in the front pew.

"Excuse me?"

As the boy looked up, Adam couldn't help but stare. Beneath his cap, the boy's face was submerged beneath a swathe of bandages. Slits had been cut for his mouth and his nostrils, allowing him to breathe, and two eyeholes revealed a pair of dark-brown eyes.

"Oh, sorry," Adam said hastily. "I didn't mean to—"

"It's all right. Sit down if you like."

Adam wanted to finish his mopping and get out of the chapel before he bumped into anyone else, but saying no seemed somehow rude. He put down his mop and took a seat on the pew.

"You didn't want to watch the film?" he asked.

The boy shook his head. "I prefer places when they're quiet," he said. "The other kids don't want me around, anyway. The bandages spook them."

"What ... erm..." Adam began hesitantly, "I mean ... what happened to you?"

"Gas fire," the boy replied. "I was carrying gas canisters over to the *Quisling* when one of them went off. I got caught in the flames."

He lifted up his left hand, which was covered in a patchwork of angry burns and scars. Adam swallowed, unsure how to respond. The bandaged boy chuckled and waved his hand. "Don't worry about it. No one ever knows what to say."

As Adam shifted uncomfortably in his seat, the boy gazed off into the middle distance. "What's the point in watching a film anyway?" he said quietly. "You might pretend you're somewhere else for a couple of hours, but when it's over we're still stuck here."

"A couple of hours is better than nothing," Adam replied. "That's why I like sleeping. Sometimes I dream I'm back at home with everyone and even though I'm not really, it's still nice to feel like that."

The bandaged boy nodded. "I have the same dream over and over again," he said. "I'm digging my way out of the Dial, only not through soil, but fresh air. I'm in some kind of . . . sky tunnel, I guess, that takes me far above the prison and all the way up to the warphole. I climb so close to the warphole that I can stick my head through and there's this amazing feeling, like when you stop holding your breath and all the air rushes into your lungs, and the light is so bright that it hurts my eyes and. . ."

He tailed off.

"And then?" Adam asked.

"Then I wake up," the boy said flatly. "Here. And I can't breathe again."

In the silence that followed, Adam became aware of the

loudspeakers crackling into life, and Echo's hateful voice announcing:

"Apparently a certain troublemaker isn't watching the film tonight. He should watch his step, or I bet things are going to get even nastier for him. This one's for him. . ."

Adam silently seethed as a scratchy record began to play. It was bad enough missing the film without Echo mocking him. The bandaged boy shook his head.

"I go on too much," he said. "I should get back to the infirmary. See you around."

The bandaged boy slipped past Adam in the pews and padded softly out of the chapel. As he watched him leave, Adam suddenly realized that he hadn't asked the boy his name.

He had only just picked up his mop again when the chapel doors crashed open and a platoon of guards came hurtling inside, their boots drumming on the flagstones. Mr Pitt was at their head, a barking German shepherd loping along at his side. To Adam's horror, the guards headed straight behind the confessional boxes, where Mr Pitt knelt down and prised up Corbett's flagstone, shining a torch down into the tunnel.

"Get out of there, you horrible little vermin!" he screamed. "I've got two punishment cells with your name on them!"

Adam watched open-mouthed as the two Tally-Hoers were hauled out of the tunnel and marched away. Corbett flashed him a vicious stare as he was bundled past.

"You dirty little—"

A guard cuffed the burly Tally-Hoer around the back of the head, cutting him off mid-insult. The men exited the chapel amid wounded protests and dragged feet, the doors slamming conclusively behind them. As the candles flickered in the sudden gust of wind, Adam picked up his mop and dolefully returned to his chores.

CHAPTER TWELVE

After the excitement of film night, sullen clouds closed in over the Dial. With the *Quisling* still too damaged to fly to Earth for supplies, the food rations were reduced again, until the scant portions could no longer satisfy even the meagrest of appetites. Mealtimes took on a violent edge: the inmates guarded their portions warily, aware that a stray breadcrumb or a spilled blob of soup could spark an argument with the person sitting beside them. After the fourth fight had broken out, extra guards had to be posted to the mess hall during mealtimes.

Adam kept out of trouble, taking particular care to steer clear of the Tally-Ho and their grim huddles in the exercise yard. Following their capture in the chapel, Corbett and his accomplice had been given a week in solitary – and judging by the filthy looks Adam was getting, it was clear that the Tally-Ho were pinning the blame squarely on him.

On the final day of his own punishment detail, Adam helped Doughnut stash away another mysterious consignment of boxes – this time in an empty attic room above the prisoners' quarters – and then mopped the chapel until night fell, determined not to give Mr Pitt any excuse to dole out further chores. With aching muscles, he hauled his mop and bucket back across the bridge towards the mess hall. Guards were briskly patrolling the perimeter wall, training searchlights at the slightest movement in the darkness.

Adam hummed a happy pop song to himself as he walked, careful not to let his mind wander. It was easy to get spooked crossing the chasm at night, especially when passing the Re-education Wing. There was a chilly atmosphere to the brooding, windowless structure, an ice cube down the back on a boiling summer day. Late at night, the inmates told hushed horror stories of what took place within its walls, of troublesome inmates who had been dragged there in secret by the guards, who used the machinery to wipe their minds completely, reducing them to a state of vacant obedience. Though the tales made Adam shiver, when he recounted them to Bookworm all he elicited was a reedy laugh at the implausibility of it all. Wherever possible, Adam heeded the librarian's advice and tried not to think about it.

No guards were keeping watch outside the mess hall; inside, the benches and tables formed an army of still silhouettes in the gloom. Adam navigated his way over to the cleaning cupboard and gratefully returned the mop and bucket for the final time. He was closing the door when a rattling noise in the canteen stopped him in his tracks.

"Hello?" he called out. "Anybody there?"

There was no reply, only a choked sob. His pulse beating a little quicker, Adam crept over to the canteen, pushed the door open and flicked on the light switch. And stared.

"Jessica?"

The girl looked up, her eyes wide with fright. She was standing beside a large fridge, her hand resting on the heavy padlock securing its doors.

"What are you doing here?" asked Adam. "If the guards catch you they'll punish you for sure!"

"I thought there might be some food," Jessica said, gesturing uncertainly at the fridge, "but it's locked away. . ."

"The guards aren't stupid. There'd be a riot here if it wasn't." Adam peered closely at Jessica's wan features. "Are you all right?"

"I'm fine. It's just—"

She passed a hand across her forehead, and collapsed to the ground.

"Jessica!" Adam cried out.

He ran over and knelt by her side, lifting her head off the tiled floor. Jessica stirred hazily.

"What's wrong?" Adam asked.

"I don't know," she breathed. "I felt dizzy for a second."

"You need someone to look at you. I'll take you to the infirmary."

"No! Don't take me there!" Jessica clutched Adam's arm. "I know how dirty that place is. People only get sicker there. I'll be better after a night's sleep, I really will."

She climbed unsteadily to her feet as Adam hovered

next to her, waiting to grab her if she fell. They walked awkwardly out of the mess hall together, and called back the walkway to take them to the prisoners' quarters. Adam was afraid that at any moment a patrolling guard would stop and interrogate them, and he didn't relax until they were standing back outside Wing II.

Jessica gave him a weak smile. "Sorry to cause such a fuss," she said. "I wasn't thinking straight. I'll be OK in the morning."

She walked slowly up the stairs towards the girls' rooms, glancing back shyly over her shoulder before disappearing from sight. A resolute look came over Adam's face, and he hurried back to his dormitory. He found Doughnut sprawled out on his bunk, lazily playing cards with Mouthwash. Adam pulled the fixer to one side.

"What's up?" asked Doughnut.

"I need a favour," Adam said softy. "A friend of mine's ill. She needs food – proper food, not the rubbish they serve up here. I know you can get stuff other people can't. Can you help me?"

"I wish I could. Everyone's on at me to get them food, but I've got a problem with supply right now."

"Please, Doughnut. This is serious."

Doughnut chewed his lip thoughtfully.

"OK," he said finally. "I'll help you." He grabbed Adam's arm, his amiable features suddenly serious. "But you tell anyone about this – *anyone* – and me and you are finished. You're on your own."

"I won't say a thing. I promise!"

The fixer shrugged. "What's a promise worth in a prison full of traitors? I've told you how it is – the rest is up to you."

"Can we get the food now?"

Doughnut shook his head. "Too many guards around," he said. "Later."

After lights out Adam lay impatiently in his bunk, fully clothed beneath the sheets, waiting for the whispers and sniggers to die down around him. Eventually the room went quiet, and as the boys fell asleep their deep, even breaths rose and fell in time with one another, until it felt as though the room itself was sighing with contentment.

There was a movement in the darkness: a large black silhouette carrying a knapsack rose silently from Doughnut's bunk and, gesturing to Adam, crept towards the door with surprising stealth. Adam pushed back his sheets and followed suit, wincing at every creak of the floorboards beneath his tread. Caiman stirred in his bunk as he passed, but didn't wake up.

Outside their dormitory, Doughnut turned right, heading deeper into the heart of the building. They ghosted through the corridors like draughts of air, alert for the burly footsteps of the guards. Doughnut led Adam down a flight of backstairs to a door, where he produced a bulky key ring from his pockets. Selecting a worn iron key, he slipped it in the lock, opened the door, and ushered Adam into the room beyond.

They descended into a dank cellar, where water seeped across the flagstones and the atmosphere was stained with damp. Doughnut picked up an oil lamp from a shelf and lit it carefully, casting a pale glow over the cellar.

"Nice place," Adam said dryly.

"The goons tend to give this place a swerve. Good job, too."

"So what are we doing here?"

Doughnut shone a light over a rotting wooden chest against the far wall. "Give me a hand with this." As they heaved the chest away from the wall, the fixer explained:

"Believe it or not, when I first came here all the other guys thought I was a loser. People wouldn't hang out with me, kept making fun of me. So I spent all my time exploring the Dial, from the cellars all the way up to the roofs. I bumped into the Tally-Ho a few times, and had to do some pretty fast talking to stop Major X setting his boys on me. I got caught by the guards too, and did some time in solitary. But it was worth it – I know this prison better than anyone, mate. Which is how I know what's behind here."

With the chest cleared out of the way, Adam saw that it had been concealing a small black hole in the wall behind it.

"See, prisoners have been trying to dig their way out of here for centuries," explained Doughnut. "No matter how much time the guards spend combing the prison for old tunnels, they can't find all of them. This was the first one

I ever found – and the best. It's how I started my business. Now everyone knows who I am, and if they think I'm a loser, no one'll say it to my face. Follow me."

Holding the lamp out in front of him, Doughnut got down on his hands and knees and crawled into the tunnel. After a brief pause Adam followed, staying low to avoid banging his head on the ceiling. The space was cramped to the point of breathlessness – there wasn't even enough room to turn round. The light from Doughnut's lamp flickered over the walls, picking out the wooden struts inserted in the tunnel to guard against cave-ins.

As he wriggled forward, rocks biting into his knees and palms, Adam felt a draught of cold air whipping across his face. It was coming from a long fissure in the left-hand tunnel wall. Adam stopped and pressed his face against it, taking in a deep lungful of fresh air. As he looked out through the hole, he found himself staring into a deep, desolate black. Adam swallowed and licked his lips nervously. They were on the edge of the chasm in the centre of the Dial. Above his head, the outline of the walkway was visible as it bridged the abyss.

"Come on, mate," Doughnut called back softly. "No time for sightseeing."

The tunnel curved to the left, skirting around the edge of the chasm. Adam wasn't sure how long they had been underground – it might have been five minutes, it might have been an hour – but already his back was aching and the musty air inside the tunnel was making him dizzy. Only the fact that Doughnut continued without complaint stopped Adam from suggesting they turn back.

Just when he thought that the tunnel was never going to end, the ceiling changed from jagged rocks to smooth flagstones. Doughnut stopped, and turned out his lamp. He twisted round to look back at Adam.

"Not a word from now on," he whispered. "Just watch me, and do what I do. OK?"

Counting the flagstones above his head, the fixer reached up and lifted one into the air, before pushing it to one side. He hauled himself up into the room above with Adam following close behind, grateful to escape the tunnel. They had come out into some kind of storage room, filled with crates stacked on top of one another. From upstairs there came the sound of laughter and clinking glasses, and scratchy gramophone music.

Doughnut quietly prised open the lid of the nearest crate and stared inside, his eyes lighting up. Looking over his shoulder, Adam saw that the crate was packed with food: cans of tuna, packets of biscuits and tinned peaches. After months of lumpy potatoes and thin gruel, the sight made Adam's mouth water.

"What is this place?" he whispered.

"The pantry below the guards' quarters," Doughnut whispered back. He gave Adam an amused look. "What, did you think that they were eating stew too?"

As they rummaged through the crates, filling up Doughnut's knapsack with food, Adam felt like a bank robber rifling through a vault filled with gold ingots and precious jewels. He was adding a jar of honey to their haul, stifling a triumphant chortle, when the door at the top of the stairs opened. Doughnut grabbed Adam and hauled him down behind a giant sack of flour. A light bulb flicked on. Peeping out from behind the sack, Adam saw a skinny boy with glasses enter the pantry, a look of disdain etched on his sallow face.

The door opened again, and a man's voice barked down: "Make sure you get enough beer, Echo! I don't want to have to send you back down there again."

"Yes, sir!" the boy called back, a wheedling tone to his nasal voice. "Back as quick as I can!"

Echo waited until the guard had gone before rifling through a small crate on the floor. Watching the boy greedily stuffing chocolate bars into his pockets, Adam had a strong urge to rush out and throttle him. Did he not know that the other children on the Dial – his former friends and roommates – were slowly starving? Or did he simply not care? Seeing Adam's fists clench, Doughnut shot him a warning glance and shook his head. Adam had to sit and watch as Echo picked up a case of beer bottles and carried them upstairs, humming a jaunty tune to himself.

As the door closed, Adam realized that he had been holding his breath.

"Close call," he whispered.

"Too close," Doughnut replied softly. "Let's fill up this

sack and get out of here. We can't take too much, or the guards'll know someone's been down here."

Above their heads, the party was in full swing: the laughter became more raucous, and feet stamped on the floor in time with the music.

Finally Doughnut's knapsack was full, and he gave Adam the thumbs up. They were just about to lever themselves back into the tunnel when the room was engulfed in sirens.

CHAPTER THIRTEEN

Immediately the laughter upstairs ceased, and footsteps thundered across the floor above Adam's head. Doughnut hurled the knapsack through the hole into the tunnel and ushered Adam inside, before diving down after him and dragging the flagstone back over their heads.

Seconds later the pantry door crashed open, and a pair of footsteps marched into the room. "Who's there?" a young man called out.

Doughnut grabbed Adam, frantically motioning at him to stay still. Adam held his breath, willing his heart to stop pounding so loudly. There was the click of a rifle being cocked, and the tread of jackboots got closer and closer, until the guard was standing right above their heads.

"Oi!" another voice barked. "What do you think you're doing down here?"

At the sound of Mr Pitt's voice, Adam's blood froze.

"I was on my way out with the others, sir," the guard replied, a quaver of fear in his voice. "Thought I heard a noise down here, so I came down to check."

"Attention! Attention!" Echo's breathless voice erupted from hissing loudspeakers, penetrating down into the cellar. "Suspected breakout in the exercise yard! All guards to Wing VI! Repeat: all guards to Wing VI!"

"Well?" Mr Pitt roared at the guard. "You heard him! If you're not in the exercise yard in the next minute I'll put *you* in the punishment cells. Understand me, boy?"

"Yessir."

The young guard ran out of the pantry and slammed the door behind him. Doughnut wiped a hand across his brow with relief.

"That's a bit of luck," Adam whispered. "I thought we were done for."

"We still might be," replied Doughnut, "unless we're back in our beds by the time the guards do the rounds. Let's get out of here."

As they scrambled away, the siren burrowed down into the tunnel like a drill, reverberating around the cramped surroundings and battering Adam's skull. He crawled on through the tunnel, not caring any more about the musty air or the rocks scraping his scalp. They emerged back in the cellar beneath the prisoners' quarters, barely catching their breath before moving the chest back over the hole in the wall. Doughnut unlocked the cellar door and looked up the stairs.

"Coast's clear," he reported. "The guards should be down in the exercise yard, so if we're lucky we'll make it."

The two friends raced up through the building, past

dormitory doors bulging with animated chatter. As they mounted the final flight of stairs, Adam pressed Doughnut back into the shadows as a guard stomped along the corridor above them, his rifle in his hands.

The sirens had abated by the time they burst back into their dormitory, panting as they closed the door behind them. The rest of the room had gathered by the windows and were looking out towards the exercise yard. Caiman shot Adam a sly look.

"Where have you two lovebirds been?"

"Leave it out, Caiman," Doughnut replied wearily. "What's going on outside?"

"Can't really tell from here," reported Mouthwash. "Obviously the goons thought someone was trying to make a run for it. We thought it was you. Where've you been?"

"Nowhere," Doughnut said shortly. Pressing the knapsack into Adam's hands, he said quietly: "You take that, mate. Anyone asks what it is, tell them to shove off."

Adam smiled. "Cheers, Doughnut. I owe you one."

The fixer smiled. "Doesn't everyone?" Stifling a bone-cracking yawn, he collapsed on to his bunk and curled up. "I'm knackered. Turn out the lights, will you?"

Within seconds Doughnut was sleeping soundly, the wooden slats beneath his bunk bed creaking as he snored. Adam's mind was still churning following their breathless escape, and he lay awake for longer, clutching the precious knapsack. When he did finally fall asleep, he dreamed that he was back at the disused skate park near his home. Danny was standing on top of one of the ramps, staring accusatorily at Adam. As the silhouette of the *Quisling* appeared behind his friend, Adam tried to shout a warning, but no sound came out of his mouth.

The next morning, even the tense atmosphere of the mess hall couldn't dispel Adam's good mood. He polished off his lumpy porridge in double-quick time, scanning the tables around him. Through the throng, he caught sight of Jessica sitting alone at the far end of another table. Adam picked up his knapsack and skirted round the edge of the room towards her, careful not to catch the eye of any of the watching guards.

"How're you doing, Jessica?"

She looked up warily from her food, only to break into a slight smile at the sight of Adam.

"Better this morning. Thanks for asking." Jessica lifted her spoon out of her porridge, letting its contents slop back into her bowl meaningfully. "Even this doesn't taste quite as bad as usual."

Adam slipped into the seat opposite her. "I've got something better than that," he whispered, passing the knapsack under the table. "Take this, and whatever you do don't show anyone else."

Jessica cautiously opened the flap and looked inside the knapsack, her eyes widening with shocked delight.

"This is for me?" she breathed. "Thank you! But how . . . where. . .?"

Adam pressed a finger to his lips, winked, and walked back to his table. He sat down, whistling happily to himself.

"I take it your friend liked her present," Doughnut said slyly.

"*Our* present," corrected Adam.

"Eh?"

"I saved a bit for us as well."

The fixer clapped him heartily on the back.

"Good man!" he exclaimed. "I'll get word to Mouthwash and Paintpot and we'll have a little picnic."

They congregated that afternoon in a cellar beneath the chapel, sitting cross-legged on the flagstones as they merrily munched their way through sandwiches and packets of crisps. Mouthwash arrived late and out of breath.

"Where've you been?" asked Adam.

"Having a chat with old Harker. He doesn't half go on a bit." Settling down beside them, Mouthwash plucked a half-eaten sandwich from Doughnut's hand, ignoring the fixer's cry of indignation. "Seems last night was a false alarm – a guard got jumpy and thought he saw something. Mr Pitt's blaming Harker for the mess, and has spent the last hour screaming at him. I almost feel sorry for the poor goon."

Adam knew what he meant. Mr Harker was the most amiable of all the guards, and seemed to spend almost as much time being told off by Mr Pitt as the prisoners did. Adam had wondered whether there was some bad blood between them, but the simple truth appeared to be that

Pitt was a natural bully who couldn't help seizing upon any weakness – wherever he found it.

"I don't know why the guards are so obsessed with prisoners trying to escape," Paintpot said quietly. "Only the Tally-Ho are crazy enough to still think that they can make it over the wall. No one ever gets out of here."

But there had been one notable exception to that rule, and everyone in the cellar knew it – even if no one mentioned his name. Adam thought back to the library, and V. Mix's mocking poem in the *Codex Treacherous*: *But he's long gone, the only true traitor, Luca D'Annunzio the Collaborator!* He chewed thoughtfully on his sandwich.

"Any of you guys heard of a prisoner called V. Mix?"

Paintpot shook her head. "Doesn't ring any bells."

"And she should know," Mouthwash butted in. "Paintpot's been here longer than any of us."

The dark-haired artist glanced at Adam. "Why are you asking?"

"No real reason," replied Adam. "Thought I heard someone talking about them the other day."

"If it's bugging you, go to the library. They've got a big register there with all the people who've ever done time here. You'll know soon enough if there's a V. Mix or not."

"Good call," said Mouthwash, taking a giant bite out of his cheese and pickle sandwich. "After all, the library's Wing V, isn't it?"

He nudged Adam jovially, unaware that the latter had paused. Even though their simple meal was the finest, most delicious feast Adam had ever tasted, silently he seethed with impatience as his friends lingered over the remaining morsels. Finally he was able to make his excuses and hare over to Wing V.

As usual, the library was deserted – its vast collection of books slumbering in the quiet. Bookworm was fast asleep behind a desk, his mouth wide open and his feet propped up on two volumes of the *Encyclopaedia Britannica*. Adam crept past him and into the warren of shelves, where he stopped to think.

What if Mouthwash had stumbled across the truth – and that V wasn't an initial at all, but code for the library? Maybe Mix wasn't another prisoner but the author of a book. As he inspected the shelves, Adam saw with a sinking heart that the volumes weren't arranged alphabetically, but by reference numbers. Or, more accurately, reference letters: LX, LXI, LXII. . .

Adam slapped his forehead with exasperation. Of course! It wasn't "Mix", it was "MIX" – roman numerals for 1,009! It was a coded reference to a particular book! Picking up the trail of numerals, Adam plunged deeper into the library, until the aisles got narrower, the books reeked of mould and mildew, and warped shelves sagged under the weight of their burdens.

Finally he located the right aisle, dragged over a rickety ladder and clambered up to the top shelf. Swaying uncertainly on the highest rung, Adam thumbed the spines of MVII (*The Penitent Prisoner*) and MVIII (*Terrible Tales from The Re-education Wing*) before finally alighting upon MIX. He pulled out the book, his hands shaking with excitement. It was a hefty red volume entitled *The Dial Cookbook*, filled with page after page of handwritten prison recipes: Stir Fry; Lamb with Thyme; Canned Chicken. Not what Adam had been expecting. He fanned the pages and turned the book upside down and shook it, but no secret notes fell out. Maybe "V. Mix" hadn't been code after all. Dispirited, Adam was about to close the book when a particular recipe caught his eye. It was tucked away near the back of the book, and written in the same flowing handwriting as the mocking poem in the *Codex Treacherous*:

Volcano Chilli
This explosive concoction will burn
more than the roof of your mouth!

As he scanned the list of ingredients beneath the recipe's cheerful introduction, Adam frowned. The Volcano Chilli was made up of a mixture of chemicals and fertilizer – nothing that could be eaten. In fact, he was fairly sure he was looking at a recipe for a home-made bomb.

"What are you doing here?"

Adam jumped, dropping the cookbook to the floor with a thump. Bookworm was standing at the end of the aisle, sleepily rubbing his eyes.

"Just browsing," Adam replied weakly.

The librarian picked up the book and inspected its

spine. "Unusual choice," he said wryly. "As far as I know, no one's ever taken this book out before."

"Really?" Adam's ears pricked up. "How do you know?"

"I've had a long time to memorize the books here. And I always try to remember the ones no one else cares about." Bookworm paused. "I'm not going to be around here for ever, though. This place is going to need someone to look after it when I'm gone. What about you?"

"I don't think I'd be up to it," Adam said quickly.

"Really? You're in here almost as often as I am. Did you find what you were looking for in the *Codex Treacherous*?"

"Not really." A thought occurred to Adam. "Is there another copy anywhere?"

"Of the *Codex*?" Bookworm scratched his head. "There's a set of official records in the guards' quarters, but they're off-limits to inmates. Why – what's wrong with mine?"

"Nothing," said Adam, climbing down from the ladder. "Listen, I've got to go – I'll see you later."

Bookworm held up the cookbook. "Don't you want this?"

"Maybe next time!" Adam called back, hurrying away down the aisle. He didn't want to encourage the librarian into any further investigations. Although the *Dial Cookbook* had raised more questions than answers, there was definitely something going on: certainly suspicious, and possibly dangerous. This was Adam's mystery – and his alone.

CHAPTER FOURTEEN

To the immense relief of the Dial's inhabitants, winter began reluctantly releasing its icy fingers from around the prison's throat. No longer were the walkways booby-trapped with frozen puddles, nor the inmates' stale morning breath collecting in frosty clouds above their bunks.

As his dormitory prepared for roll call one daybreak, Adam saw the sunlight streaming in through the window and decided to leave his cap and gloves on his bunk. He walked down to the exercise yard in a happier mood than he had for a long time. It felt as though the sun was warming him from the inside out. Although life on the Dial was far from easy, Adam was slowly adapting. With the only copy of Luca D'Annunzio's record locked away in the guards' quarter, his quest to learn more about the infamous inmate and his escape had quickly reached a dead end. Any time Adam had tried to broach the subject with Paintpot she had only reddened and looked away, and he didn't want his friend to think that he was deliberately trying to embarrass her.

Two weeks after Adam had discovered the *Dial Cookbook*, the guards had carried out an impromptu search of the dormitories, amid rumours that bags of fertilizer had gone missing from the allotments. But if an inmate was trying to cook up some "Volcano Chilli", he or she managed to escape detection. Maybe Adam should have mentioned it to someone, but there was no telling who he might have ended up betraying – and if there was one thing of which Adam was sure, it was that he didn't want anyone calling *him* a collaborator.

Following the morning roll call, Mr Cooper delivered one of his familiar cautionary speeches before breaking into a benevolent smile.

"It has now been four months since I brought to your attention the robbery of sheets from the infirmary," he declared, "and I am disappointed that no one has come forward to return the stolen items. However, following an appeal from some of the more senior inmates, we have agreed that the crime was the act of a lone foolish inmate, and that punishing the entire prison population serves little purpose. For that reason, we have decided to lift the ban on Bucketball."

A cheer went up from the crowd, and several prisoners started clapping. Behind the head warder, Mr Pitt glowered, a picture of frustrated violence.

"Let it be clear, though," Mr Cooper continued, holding up his hands for silence. "Any more thefts of this nature, and we will remove Bucketball privileges for the rest of the year. If you refuse to think of the consequences that will befall you if you are caught stealing, I would encourage you to consider the harm you may bring to your fellow inmates. That is all."

As the guards cleared the yard, the inmates surfed back to their quarters on a wave of excitement, friends gesturing at one another to ensure that they'd be on the same team at game time. Back in his dormitory, as the rest of the boys changed into shorts and T-shirts, Adam disappeared beneath his bunk, reappearing with the copy of Bookworm's *Inmate's Handbook* that he had decided to borrow from the library during his first miserable week on the Dial. As he flicked through the pages, he came across a short passage devoted to Bucketball:

> *Down the centuries the game of Bucketball has become one of the Dial's most singular and beloved features: a pastime dreamt up within the prison's walls. As far as we know, it is played nowhere else in existence. During the game two teams compete for the possession of a ball, with the aim of carrying it to their opponents' end of the exercise yard and placing it in a bucket known as the "goal". The team with the most number of buckets at the end of the game wins.*
>
> *For those who have never witnessed an actual game of Bucketball, it should be noted that its simplicity on paper is deceptive. Indeed, Bucketball is a game more notable for its lack of rules than its actual rules:*

tactics and team numbers are left entirely to partici-
pants, and there is no time limit – games (individually
known as "rumbles") stop when the sides are simply
too tired to continue. Though this does lead to a cer-
tain amount of roughhouse behaviour (e.g., headlocks,
rabbit punches, throttling), all competitors are urged
to adhere to the highest levels of sportsmanship. To this
end, three golden rules have been set in place:

1.) No hair-pulling
2.) No eye-gouging
3.) Handshakes all round afterwards

Given the massed numbers of players and the
anarchic nature of play, it is perhaps unsurprising that
there have only ever been four recorded buckets in the
history of Bucketball. The other few thousand games
have all ended 0-0, with the moral victors generally
determined by the side boasting the fewest number of
trips to the infirmary.

As Adam closed the book, Mouthwash burst into the
room.

"Heads up, lads!" he said. "Game's going to start in ten
minutes. You want to borrow a spare kit, Adam? You're not
a real inmate until you've played a rumble."

"I guess," Adam replied dubiously. He glanced over at
Doughnut. "Are you coming?"

Doughnut stretched out on his bunk and yawned lazily. "Count me out. While you chumps are getting your heads bashed in, I'm putting my feet up." He winked at Adam. "Got some business negotiations to take care of, anyway."

Adam quickly changed into his borrowed kit, then jogged outside and joined the inmates making their way over to the exercise yard. It looked as though almost everyone in the prison had turned out for the game. The tiered benches on the sidelines were overflowing with chattering people. Even the guards had turned out in force, including Mr Cooper – though to Adam's relief, Mr Pitt was nowhere to be seen. The two teams were already filing into position, each forming a protective line in front of a bucket placed at opposing ends of the yard.

As he threaded his way through the crowd, Adam noticed Jessica talking to Corbett by the fence. The Tally-Hoer towered over her, his meaty legs and arms covered in tangled black hair. Looking more closely, Adam saw that Jessica's back was pressed to the fence, and there was a tense expression on her face.

"Adam!" she called out, with a desperate wave. She smiled gratefully as he walked over. "Are you playing today?"

Adam nodded, mindful of Corbett's hateful gaze burning a hole in the back of his neck. "Yeah. I thought I'd give it a go."

"You'll be great. Good luck!"

"You're going to need it," Corbett added in a growl. He stalked off towards the benches, where a knot of

Tally-Hoers had gathered to watch the game. Adam gave Jessica a sidelong glance.

"Was he bothering you?"

"No more than usual," she replied. "I think he likes me. He'll get bored and leave me alone eventually." A shy smile flickered over her lips. "Thank you for asking, though."

"No problem. And if you ever want to—"

"They're just about to start. Go on!" Jessica propelled him gently towards the teams. "Try not to break anything!"

Grinning, Adam jogged on to the field of play and took up position by Mouthwash's shoulder. He guessed that there had to be at least forty people on each side. Here and there, Adam was surprised to see girls in the line-up, doing warm-up stretches as they tied their hair back into ponytails.

He nudged Mouthwash. "*Girls* play this game?"

The other boy giggled. "Don't let them hear you say that, or you're dead meat. There's been quite a few good girl 'Ballers down the years. I remember one a few decades ago – Daisy, I think her name was – giving Major X a right old going-over. We had to peel him off the floor. The lad got so embarrassed he hasn't played a game since."

A cheer went up from the sidelines as a guard carrying a battered leather football stepped into the centre of the yard. The guard hurled the ball high into the air, then beat a hurried retreat as the inmates stampeded towards it. Caught on his heels, Adam was jostled by his own teammates as they ploughed past him into the giant melee. The ball vanished from view beneath a maelstrom of whirling fists. With a roar,

Corbett reared up from the centre of the scrum, red-faced with anger. The Tally-Hoer had opponents hanging off either arm – he roared again as he tried to shake them off.

It didn't take long for Adam to realize that the *Handbook* had been right: Bucketball was less of a game, more of a legitimized riot. Occasionally one team would get hold of the ball and try to pass it to one another, but it wasn't long before the ball-carrier was dragged to the floor and everyone dived on top of them. Weakened by months of no exercise and a poor diet, Adam was soon gasping for air. He was moving on sheer exhilaration. For the first time since he had landed on the Dial, Adam felt free. Again and again he caught his breath just so he could throw himself into the fray, barely feeling the opposition elbows as they burrowed into his ribcage, or the blows glancing off his head.

Adam had just wriggled out of one scrum when he heard a scream of excitement go up from the sidelines. He turned in time to see the ball squirt out from under the pile of bodies and roll straight towards him. Cheered on by the crowd, Adam picked up the ball and barged a girl out of the way while fending off another boy with a hand to the face. Suddenly, there was daylight ahead of him. Adam accelerated away from the pack, the ball tucked safely under one arm, pursued by shouts of dismay from the opposing team. His heart pounding, he saw that there was only one smaller boy standing between him and the bucket, and Adam had all the momentum. He was odds-on to score and the crowd knew it, their screams reaching a crescendo.

Adam was lowering his shoulder, readying to charge into the final defender, when a foot caught his. His legs tangled up with each other, and suddenly he was skidding headlong across the gravel. The ball flew from Adam's grasp and away across the yard, which now rang to the sound of booing. Adam lay on the ground, coughing in a cloud of dust.

A hand patted him roughly on the back of the head. "Hard luck, butter fingers," said Corbett. Kneeling down, the Tally-Hoer grabbed Adam's ear and hissed into it: "That's for getting me nicked in the chapel, rat. And if you don't want your legs broken, stay away from my girl!"

With that, Corbett lumbered away after the ball, which had been swallowed up by a scrummage near the sideline. Adam slowly picked himself up and began brushing the gravel from his skin and clothes. His elbows were red-raw from where he had scraped them, his lip was swollen, and blood was running down his left knee.

On the other side of the pitch, Mouthwash disentangled himself from a brawl and jogged over to him. "Bloody hell, mate. You all right?"

Adam nodded gingerly. "Guess so. What happened?"

Mouthwash grimaced. "You were clean through, but Corbett managed to get back and trip you up."

"What was the booing about?"

"Tripping's not exactly banned, but no one likes to see it. Corbett's such an ape. You want to stick around and try to get some revenge?"

Adam shook his head. "I think he's won this one. I'd better get this blood off me. I'll see you later."

He patted Mouthwash on the back and hobbled off the pitch, trying to ignore the sympathetic round of applause the crowd gave him. It didn't matter how close he had come to scoring – he still felt humiliated. A boy with a bucket and sponge ran along the sideline towards Adam and began washing the blood from his legs.

"Not bad for a first go," he said admiringly. "Keep this up and you'll get some proper Bucketball scars."

"You don't have to sound quite so happy about it," Adam replied sourly. He looked up to see Jessica hurrying towards him, her face creased with concern.

"I saw what happened," she said. "Are you OK?"

"I'm fine!" Adam replied in a cheery voice, trying not to wince as the physio scraped the gravel from his elbow.

"Don't let Corbett get to you," she said quietly, squeezing his arm. "You were the best player out there – you'll get him next time."

She stayed by his side for the rest of the rumble, watching as the game petered out into a series of weary punch-ups. When the whistle finally went, Corbett saw the pair of them together and immediately stalked back to the prisoners' quarters, refusing to shake hands with anyone. Suddenly Adam's cuts and bruises didn't hurt quite so much, and he reflected that maybe Bucketball wasn't such a bad game, after all.

CHAPTER FIFTEEN

Adam woke up the next day to find his joints aching and his limbs as stiff as tree trunks. One game of Bucketball had made him feel like he'd gone twelve rounds with Mr Pitt. To make matters worse, he had a lesson that morning. Adam spent two torturous hours shifting uncomfortably in a wooden chair, silently cursing both the volume of *Betrayals* in front of him and Mr Harker's tired pleas for the inmates to stop talking. When the siren eventually rang for lunch time, Adam had to resist the urge to go back to bed. The weather may have improved on the Dial, but food was still too scarce to risk missing a mealtime.

Adam was slurping up the dregs of a particularly watery carrot soup, the *Inmate's Handbook* propped open in front of him, when Doughnut waddled up to his table.

"All right, mate," he said. "Listen, do you like music?"

Adam shrugged and pushed his empty bowl away. "Why – downloaded anything good recently?"

"Come with me, funny man. There's something I want to show you."

Picking up his book, Adam followed Doughnut out of

the canteen and over to Wing VII, where they walked past the classrooms and headed upstairs. Having missed movie night, it was the first time Adam had entered the theatre, and he found himself standing in a surprisingly vast, airy hall. Dust sparkled in the afternoon sun as it poured through the high, arched windows. The curtains on the stage had been drawn back, revealing a group of inmates perched behind a collection of musical instruments – violins and cellos, trumpets and horns, even a large grand piano. The only other onlookers aside from Adam and Doughnut were Major X and two Tally-Ho cronies, who were plunged in conversation in a corner of the hall.

"Pretty cool, isn't it?" said Doughnut. "At the end of every summer we put on a show up here, play music, do sketches – stuff like that. Even the guards come to watch. Mr Cooper's the biggest fan of them all."

"Where did all the instruments come from?"

"The guards brought them over from Earth. See, they've got to give us *something* to do, or we'd all go completely nuts. And a harp's not much use in a prison break."

Adam glanced at his friend. "That's how you got hold of stuff for people, isn't it? It must be! You brought it over on the *Quisling*?"

"The penny drops," said Doughnut, amused. "Only taken you half a year."

Adam frowned. "But how? You can't leave the Dial."

"I can't. But then I'm not a trustee. Or a goon."

"The *guards* help you bring things over?"

Doughnut laughed. "How else could I do it? I'm a fixer, not a magician. Mate, everyone will do a deal with you in the end – as long as you know what to offer them."

"What the hell do you think *you're* doing here?"

Startled, they turned round to find Major X glaring at them, his hands on his hips.

"I'm just showing Adam the orchestra," explained Doughnut. "No drama."

The Major trained his gaze upon Adam. "I thought after Bucketball you'd have got the message that you're not welcome around the Tally-Ho."

"Hey!" Doughnut protested. "Leave him alone! What's your problem?"

"We're tightening security," snapped Major X. "We think someone around here's not on the level."

"Well, you don't have to worry about either of us, do you?" said Doughnut. "I'll vouch for Adam. And if that's not good enough for you, you can forget me getting any more shovels for you."

The Major glowered at the fixer, barely managing to bite back an angry retort before stalking off.

"Ignore him," Doughnut murmured. "He thinks every-one is a rat."

For all his friend's reassurance, Adam couldn't help feeling a bit uncomfortable. He nodded at the orchestra on stage, who were carefully tuning up their instruments.

"So are these guys any good, then?"

125

"They've been playing together for years, my friend. Watch and learn."

Major X stepped up to the conductor's podium and tapped a baton sharply on a music stand, silencing the musicians. He raised his arms into the air. Adam waited expectantly.

"Here we go," said Doughnut.

With a flourish the Major swept his arms down, and the orchestra burst into life. It was the loudest noise Adam had ever heard – a deafening racket that assaulted his eardrums and made his head hurt. He wasn't sure what was worse – the onslaught of screeching violins, the sullen plink-plonk of the piano, or the discordant farts of the brass. At the back of the orchestra, Mouthwash thundered away on a pair of large drums, oblivious to any sort of rhythm. No one appeared to even be playing the same piece of music.

Adam stared at Doughnut, who was merrily tapping his foot on the floor. The fixer looked back quizzically.

"What's up?" he shouted over the din.

"What's up?" Adam yelled incredulously. "They're rubbish!"

Doughnut nodded. "Absolutely terrible," he shouted back cheerily. "Sounds like someone's set a zoo on fire."

If the orchestra were aware of their musical shortcomings, it didn't seem to bother them. They continued to lustily parp, bang and fiddle away, broad grins plastered across their faces. In front of them, Major X was a flurry of activity, weaving intricate patterns in the air with his baton. As he watched the conductor, Adam was suddenly aware that the other Tally-Hoers had vanished. They weren't amongst the musicians, and the only way out of the hall was past Adam. Slowly, things began to fall into place.

Adam tapped Doughnut on the arm. "One thing about this racket," he shouted, "you can't hear a thing over it. I mean, you could do *anything* up here, and the guards wouldn't have a clue. I reckon you could even dig a tunnel."

"What did you say, mate?" Doughnut cupped a hand to his ear, a mischievous glint in his eye. "I can't hear you."

Adam grinned. Now that he understood what was going on, he could relax and enjoy the mayhem. If anything, the orchestra got worse the longer they carried on – completely ditching any pretence of playing their instruments properly. Adam burst out laughing when a boy playing the trombone lost his slide, causing havoc amongst the brass section as he searched for it on the floor.

After an hour of ceaseless racket, Major X held up his hands for silence. His brow was drenched in sweat, and his hair was plastered to his forehead. He tossed his baton wearily to one side.

"Excellent rehearsal, ladies and gentleman," he said. "It's going to be a top-notch show this year, I can tell. But to make sure, we're going to have to put in lots of practice. Let's meet up again at the same time tomorrow, when Mr Corbett will be taking over the conducting duties."

As Major X led the musicians out of the hall –

studiously avoiding eye contact with Adam – their ranks had been swelled by the two missing Tally-Hoers, whose faces were now streaked with dust. Wherever they had gone while the orchestra had been playing, they had been busy.

Adam and Doughnut left the empty theatre and wandered over to the exercise yard, where they sat on the sunlit benches with Mouthwash and Paintpot and played cards. Doughnut was flourishing yet another winning hand when Adam sat up and swore loudly.

"What's wrong?" asked Paintpot.

"I left the *Inmate's Handbook* in the theatre," he replied. "Bookworm will kill me if I lose it."

Adam hurried out of the yard and back across the walkway towards Wing VII, muttering to himself under his breath. As he climbed the stairs, he became aware of music floating down from the theatre – not the painful clatter of the orchestra, but a soft, sad piano melody. At the top of the stairs, he stopped and looked towards the stage.

The hall was now completely empty, save a girl sitting at the grand piano. It was Jessica. She was completely immersed in the tune, her head bowed low as her fingers drifted across the keys. Adam felt like he was intruding upon something private, as though he had accidentally opened someone else's diary. Spotting his book lying on a nearby windowsill, he crept over and picked it up, only to knock into a chair on his way out. Jessica looked up, startled. At the sight of Adam, her cheeks flushed.

"What are you doing spying on me?" she snapped.

"I'm not spying!" protested Adam. He held up the *Inmate's Handbook*. "I forgot this. I didn't know you were here."

"Oh." Jessica looked down at the piano, her long hair falling in a tangled waterfall over her face.

"You're really good," said Adam, cautiously approaching the piano. "At least I think you are. I don't really know much about classical music."

"It's *Für Elise*," Jessica replied. "By Beethoven."

"It sounded nice. A bit sad, though."

"I used to play on my mum's piano. It reminds me of home."

"I didn't see you up here earlier," said Adam. "Why don't you play with the orchestra?"

Jessica shrugged. "I prefer to play on my own."

"You should really think about it. For their sake – they're bloody awful."

There was an awkward pause, and then Jessica finally smiled. "Why are you so nice to me, Adam?" she asked, quietly tapping a piano key with a finger. "I haven't always been very nice to you."

Adam took a seat next to her on the piano stool. "I don't know what it is," he said slowly. "You're not like the rest of them. Everyone around here just gets on with stuff and acts like it's all normal, but it's not. It's crazy, and sometimes I think you're the only other person who feels the same way. And that's . . . I don't know . . . kind of nice."

"I'm sorry I was rude to you," Jessica said. "It's just that when people try to talk to me I end up hating them because they don't understand. Everything about this is so wrong, Adam: don't you see? These monsters have kidnapped us and locked us up and sentenced us to hundreds of years in prison. I feel like I'll go mad if I spend another week here, let alone another. . ."

Her voice trailed off.

"Hey, it's going to be all right," said Adam, gently touching her shoulder. "You'll get through it. I promise."

He leaned forward and kissed her. For a brief second, their lips touched, and then Jessica pulled away. She scrambled up from the piano stool and fled across the hall.

"Wait, Jessica!" Adam called after her. "I'm sorry! Come back!"

But she disappeared down the staircase without looking back, leaving behind only the accusatory echo of her fleeing footsteps.

CHAPTER SIXTEEN

Though Adam would never have believed it when he was shivering beneath his blanket in the depths of midwinter, conditions on the Dial only worsened with the onset of summer. As the blazing red sun scaled higher into the sky, the barren landscape beyond the prison walls cracked under its cruel inquisition. Within the Dial, the air curdled with the smell of sweat, and the walls of the prisoners' quarters seemed to close in around them. The inmates squabbled constantly, the pettiest disagreements and smallest imagined slights sparking fights. Beneath the latrines at the edge of the exercise yard, flies rose in great clouds from the manure heap, and the stench was so thick it had a physical quality.

By midday, the fierce heat sent the prisoners retreating inside their quarters, leaving the luckless guards in the watchtowers to maintain their parched vigil. The sun didn't relax its grip until late afternoon, when the inmates emerged into the light to stretch their legs in the exercise yard and play the occasional rumble of Bucketball.

Conditions were at their most bearable just after daybreak, making the eight o'clock roll call an unexpected highlight of the day. One morning, as the prisoners were waiting for the Wing II gates to open, Adam was scanning the crowd for a friendly face when he noticed Major X standing apart from the rest of his men, looking out over the chasm. He was bareheaded, in a grudging concession to the heat, revealing sandy hair combed into a neat side parting. Realizing he was being watched, the Major caught Adam's gaze and gave him a sharp look.

"Heads up, dozy!"

Adam turned to see Doughnut waddling towards him. Even this early in the morning, the fixer's chubby face glistened with sweat, and his uniform was stained with damp patches underneath the armpits. He dabbed at his forehead with a handkerchief.

"All right, Doughnut. How's it going?"

"Peachy." The fixer nodded meaningfully up at the sun. "Going to be a right scorcher today."

"Any chance you could get your hands on an ice cream or two?"

Doughnut sarcastically patted his pockets. "Looks like I'm all out. Maybe if you asked Mr Pitt nicely?"

The walkway gates creaked open, and the prisoners began trooping across to the exercise yard.

Finely tuned to the mood of the Dial, Adam soon became aware of a subtle change in atmosphere beneath the normal chatter. A rumour was rustling among the inmates like wind through the trees, passed on with winks, nods, and raised eyebrows. The air was taut with anticipation. Major X marched impassively at the heart of the throng, hands thrust into his pockets.

Adam tugged Doughnut's sleeve.

"What's going on?"

"I guess there's a run on. Crazy fools."

"A run?" Adam hissed, his eyes wide. "What, now?"

"If I were you, mate," Doughnut murmured, "I'd keep your voice down and your questions to yourself. You're not the Tally-Ho's favourite inmate, and they can get a bit testy with people who give the game away."

Adam swallowed and hurriedly looked down at his feet. As the procession reached the other side of the walkway and filed into the exercise yard, he tried to look as nonchalant as possible, cracking stupid jokes and chatting with Doughnut. But for some reason his stomach muscles had clenched like a fist, and his pulse was racing. In six months on the Dial, Adam had never had prior knowledge of an escape attempt. He wondered which prisoners were making a break for it – whether it was anyone he knew.

"You want to repeat that?"

Adam looked up to see Corbett and Fletcher – respectively, the largest and the second-largest members of the Tally-Ho – squaring up to each other, each with a fistful of the other's shirt.

"I *said*," Fletcher repeated through gritted teeth, "go and stand somewhere else – you stink so bad you're making my eyes water. Are you deaf as well as stupid?"

Corbett snarled and hurled a punch at Fletcher. Within seconds the two boys were rolling around in the dirt, surrounded by a mob of screaming inmates. The guards hastily elbowed their way forward, only to find themselves sucked into the melee, and in the confusion it took them a couple of minutes to drag the combatants apart. Corbett and Fletcher were unceremoniously dragged to opposite sides of the yard, still spitting insults at each other. Flashing the two Tally-Hoers dark looks, Major X cleared his throat and called for order.

"Enough of the nonsense, lads," he shouted. "Let's get into line and get this roll call over with. It'll be noon at this rate, and I'm bloody hot enough as it is."

Adam had to hand it to the Major – when he spoke, people listened. Immediately the prisoners began shuffling into the roll call formation: eight rows of inmates, one behind the other. As he took his place in the third row, at the far left-hand end of the yard, Adam noticed a sizeable gap between the prisoners standing next to him. Wondering why they didn't move up, he flashed Doughnut a questioning look.

"Not a word," Doughnut breathed back. "They're doing a covering run. Some of the lads must have done a runner during the fight."

Adam glanced around the flat gravelled expanse. There seemed no room to hide behind the tiered benches, and every side of the enclosure was surrounded by high wire fencing with barbed wire running around the top. Even the latrine doors at the edge of the yard were wide open. If some of the inmates had managed to hide themselves away, he hadn't the faintest idea where they could be.

The guards had begun walking along the front row of the prisoners, counting heads. As they reached halfway, Adam heard footsteps racing along the space between his row and the row behind him. Two boys were running down from the right-hand end of the line – the end that had already been counted. They skidded into the gap close to Adam, breathing heavily. Both whipped off their caps and stuffed them into their shirts, presumably to stop the guards spotting that they had already counted them. Adam stared straight ahead, barely daring to blink. He didn't breathe again until the guards had passed them. To his reflief, they barely gave the two runners a second glance. Maybe it wasn't that surprising. After weeks, months and years of counting heads, Adam thought, all the prisoners must look the same.

With the counting at an end, the head guard nodded at Major X, who snapped to attention and saluted. The guard was just about to give the order to dismiss when the siren wailed again, and with a plummeting heart Adam saw a group of officers striding across the bridge towards the exercise yard. They were led by two unmistakable figures, one rotund and flabby, the other lean and wiry: Mr Cooper and Mr Pitt.

"Uh oh," whispered Doughnut.

As the officers entered the exercise yard, the guards snapped to attention and saluted. Major X broke away from the prisoners' ranks and walked forward to greet Mr Cooper.

"Good morning, sir," he said stiffly. "I didn't think you were inspecting us this morning."

Mr Cooper nodded. "I thought we'd pay the prisoners a surprise visit. Like to keep you on your toes, Major. Has the roll call been taken yet?"

Major X saluted briskly.

"Yes, sir. All present and correct, sir."

"Really?"

As Mr Cooper raised an eyebrow, Adam felt Doughnut tense up beside him.

"He's on to 'em," the fixer hissed, out of the corner of his mouth.

Mr Cooper did seem strangely amused by the brief exchange. He folded his arms and tapped a finger against his cheek. Then he glanced at Mr Pitt.

"Apparently the roll call has been taken."

"Apparently so, sir."

"According to Major X, the prisoners are all present and correct."

"All due respect, sir, but Major X is a lying little toerag."

"Would you be so good as to check for me?"

Mr Pitt saluted, and then marched past the inmates and straight over to the latrines at the end of the yard. To audible gasps, he kicked over one of the toilets and dropped down through the large hole beneath on to the underground manure heap. Swatting the flies away from his face, Pitt raised aloft his bayonet and began stabbing downwards into the dung.

Mr Cooper eyed Major X with interest.

"Anything you'd like to tell us?"

Indecision flashed across the Major's face. Then he stepped forward and called out to the manure heap.

"Game's up, lads. Better come on out before you get skewered."

There was a movement amongst the steaming piles of waste to Pitt's left, and two boys rose up like zombies from the grave, their hands held aloft in surrender. They were smeared from head to toe in brown. Pitt grabbed them by the scruff of their necks and hauled them back up on to the exercise yard. As the boys were ushered at bayonet length across the exercise yard, a terrible smell filled Adam's nostrils, making his stomach heave. There were groans of revulsion around him.

Doughnut shook his head in awe.

"Crazy fools," he said once more.

As the two prisoners were herded across the bridge and towards the punishment cells, the murmurs died down until the yard was swathed in silence. Mr Cooper gave Major X a knowing smile.

"*Now* we're all present and correct."

By way of reply, the Major clicked his heels together smartly and stood to attention. Then he brought his hands together and began a slow handclap – a tribute to his men's honourable failure. At first the Major was alone, but then Corbett and Fletcher joined in, and then the rest of the Tally-Ho, and then the rest of the prisoners, and the clapping speeded up and swelled until the exercise yard rang to the sound of a riotous ovation. The smile on Mr Cooper's face faded. Adam found himself clapping furiously, his heart swelling with pride, and he was still shouting and applauding long after the failed escapees had disappeared from view.

Afterwards, Adam felt strangely drained, as though he himself had taken part in the failed escape. He went back to his bunk to get away from the stifling heat, his eyelids drooping shut almost immediately. He woke with a start to find a blade biting into his neck and a pair of strong arms pinning him down to the bunk. Adam looked up to see Corbett's grim face staring at him.

"I wouldn't say anything if I were you, sunshine," Corbett whispered. "I might slip and slice you open."

Out of the corner of his eye, Adam could see the Tally-Ho Escape Committee lined up against the far wall of his dormitory, their arms clasped behind their backs. Major X was pacing up and down in front of them, his footsteps beating a tattoo on the floorboards. Eventually he came to a halt and looked at Adam.

"Four months our lads have been planning that. We went through the plans over and over again. Fixed every minor detail. They were *foolproof*."

The knife bit deeper into Adam's throat, cutting off his attempted reply. Major X ran a hand through his blond hair.

"Do you have any idea the sort of pluck needed to hide in the manure heap at the height of summer? To lie completely still, breathing in that disgusting stink, feeling it in your mouth and in your ears and up your nose. Do you have any idea?"

Adam slowly shook his head.

"No, you wouldn't. The guards were too busy breaking up Corbett and Fletcher to see those lads getting in there – I was watching. But then Pitt turns up and tries to turn them into pincushions. He couldn't have found them by chance. Someone told him. You saw Cooper's face when he was talking to me. He *knew*. Someone told him. There's a rat in the ranks, and I've got a nasty feeling it's you. And if you can't persuade me otherwise, Corbett here's going to slit your throat."

CHAPTER SEVENTEEN

"I'm waiting."

Adam's first thought was that this was just a sick prank, the Tally-Ho trying to intimidate him. No matter what the Major said, they wouldn't really kill him – they couldn't! Then he looked up at Corbett. The older boy's eyes were grim, and his face was glistening with sweat. If Adam didn't know better, he would have said that Corbett was nervous.

"It wasn't me!" squeaked Adam.

Major X raised an eyebrow.

"Oh, sorry to bother you, then," he replied sarcastically. "You're going to have to do a bit better than that."

"I'm not a rat! Honest!"

The Major pulled a chair up to Adam's bunk and sat down.

"Listen carefully," he said, his voice low. "Ever since you showed up here, we've been having problems. Guards smirking like they know something we don't. Mr Pitt turning up every time we're close to breaking out. Now some of our papers have gone missing – maps, plans, diagrams. And every time I turn around, there you are. Watching.

Eavesdropping. Sticking your nose in. I've been in this place long enough to know when there's a rat running around it, and everything's pointing to you."

Adam was desperate to protest his innocence, but it was hard to think with a blade digging into his throat, Corbett's rank body odour overpowering his senses, and the rest of the Tally-Ho lined up in the background like a firing squad. What could he say that would change their minds?

"Ask Doughnut, if you don't believe me!" he tried desperately. "He'll tell you I'm not a rat!"

Major X snorted.

"Doughnut? That boy's too busy thinking about his next meal to spot an informer. I couldn't give a monkey's what he says." He leaned in closer. "You're starting to try my patience."

There was an exclamation of surprise from behind the Major. Adam's eyes flicked up to see Jessica's slim frame in the doorway.

"What's going on?" she asked slowly.

Major X quickly rose from his chair and saluted her.

"Tally-Ho business. It doesn't concern you."

Jessica took a step into the room and peered over towards Adam's bunk. "What are you doing to Adam? Oh my God, is that a *knife*?" Her hand flew to her mouth.

"Don't worry, Jess—" Corbett began hastily, before the Major waved him silent.

"Listen, you really shouldn't be here," Major X continued

calmly. "We've got some important business to discuss, and we don't need any girls turning up and getting all emotional."

"All emotional?" Jessica echoed incredulously. "Well, why don't you calm me down by taking that knife away from his throat and telling me what's going on here?"

The Major made a small noise of exasperation. "If you must know, we're looking for an informer."

"And you think it's *Adam*? That's a ridiculous idea! Of course it's not him!"

"All we're asking him to do is prove it. This may look a little rough to you, miss, but you can't be too careful with rats."

"Rats indeed!" Angrily tossing her hair out of her face, Jessica strode over to the Major and poked him in the chest. "You boys and your little gangs. You stride around this place thinking you're so honourable and heroic, but you're nothing but bullies. Let me tell you one thing. If *anything* happens to Adam I'll run straight to Mr Cooper and tell him you're responsible. You'll be in solitary for a year – unless you're planning on slitting my throat too."

Adam couldn't tell who was more stunned – himself or Major X. It was as though Jessica was a different person.

"I'd never harm a girl," the Major replied bashfully. "Wouldn't dream of it."

"Well, I guess you're leaving then, aren't you?"

Jessica gave him a challenging stare. The Major looked thoughtful for a second, and then came to a decision.

"Tally-Ho!"

Adam felt the grip around his throat relaxing, and Corbett stood up and folded his knife. He spread out his hands helplessly and tried to say something to Jessica, but she turned her back on him.

As his men filed out of the quarters, the Major called out to a small blond boy cowering by the door. "Bosworth? When I tell you to keep a lookout I mean it. You and I are going to have a serious discussion when we get back to HQ."

Bosworth blanched and scurried out of sight. Major X looked back at Adam, setting his hat carefully atop his head.

"Just because you've been saved doesn't mean I think you're on the level. If you are a rat, I'll find out. Trust me on that."

The Major spun on his heel and marched past Jessica out of the room.

Doughnut chewed slowly, his eyes closed, hands behind his head, savouring every second the chocolate lasted in his mouth. Finally, with great reluctance, he swallowed.

"Bit of a close shave, that," he said eventually, inspecting his fingers for stray specks of confectionary.

"Close shave?" Adam repeated incredulously. "They nearly slit my throat!"

It was early evening, and the pair were stretched out on a small slanting patch of roof on top of the prisoners' quarters, their backs gently warming on the slates. Sandwiched between two higher sections of rooftop that hid it from prying eyes, this was Doughnut's private paradise. The only access point was a skylight in a cupboard that nobody ever used, and from here the careful observer could poke his head over the incline and view the whole of the Dial – from the guards keeping watch in the towers to the tiny figures charging around the Bucketball pitch. The wind had been picking up since mid-afternoon, and as he looked over the desert Adam could make out a dust cloud dancing across the horizon.

"Nearly," Doughnut acknowledged. "But not quite – thanks to Jessica. Didn't think she had it in her."

Neither had Adam. If anything, he had been more stunned by the shy girl's intervention than the Tally-Ho's ambush. He was still staring open-mouthed at Jessica long after the Escape Committee had left his dormitory.

"How did you get in here?" he managed finally.

Jessica pointed at the yellow trustee band around her arm. "I'm on official duty. A boy's fallen ill on your corridor; I'm supposed to help take him to the infirmary."

"Lucky for me," Adam said ruefully.

"Ignore those creeps," said Jessica, with a sudden fierceness. "You're not a rat. You're more honourable than they'll ever be."

As she turned to leave, Adam scrambled up from his bunk. "Listen, about the other day, in the theatre. . ."

With a smile, Jessica pressed a finger to his lips.

"I know," she whispered. "And I'm sorry too."

She walked out without another word.

Now Adam propped himself up on one elbow, the stiffening breeze blowing his fringe into his eyes.

"The Tally-Ho weren't serious, though, were they? I mean, I know they go on about escaping and stuff, but they're not *that* bad. You haven't heard of them, you know. . .?" Adam made a slicing gesture across his throat with his finger.

Doughnut frowned. "I couldn't say for sure. There are rumours – there are *always* rumours on the Dial. It's true that lads who fall foul of the Tally-Ho have a nasty tendency to have accidents afterwards."

"Accidents?"

"Tripping down flights of stairs, falling out of second-floor windows, bookcases toppling over on to them. They go to the infirmary and when they come out they're very careful about who they talk to. Draw your own conclusions. Don't you want to eat that?"

Adam wordlessly passed the square of chocolate back to his friend. Though he knew how generous Doughnut had been to share such precious contraband with him, Adam's stomach was still churning from his encounter with Major X, and the sweetness only intensified his nausea.

Doughnut popped the chocolate into his mouth and settled back with a contented smile on his face.

"It's rough on you, mate, but it's got to be done," he said. "Even though this place is supposed to punish treachery, you can always find a goon who'll be grateful for the odd bit of helpful information. Imagine if a bunch of prisoners escaped on your watch – would you want to explain that to Mr Pitt?"

"Not really."

"It's hard to blame them. And given the fact that every single prisoner here is a traitor, people have got to know that if they try and sell anyone out there's going to be consequences. If it weren't for the Tally-Ho going round threatening to slit people's throats, it'd be chaos."

"I've got no problem with the Tally-Ho trying to track down a rat," Adam complained, "I just wish they didn't think it was me. Everything I seem to do in this place goes wrong, and. . ."

Doughnut had stopped listening. He was looking out over the walls of the Dial, shielding his eyes from the sun. Following his gaze, Adam saw that the dust cloud was no longer troubling the distant horizon but churning through the air towards them.

Doughnut stood up and brushed the back of his trousers. "Time to go."

"What's up?"

"Sandstorm. We don't want to be outside when that hits. Jesus, it's coming in quickly."

Even as he spoke, the sky began to darken and the sirens broke into a wail, calling the inmates indoors. The Bucketball players hared towards the gates, and the guards began a hasty descent from the watchtowers. Doughnut had hurried over to the skylight and was already lowering himself back inside. Adam knew that he should follow suit, but as the sandstorm closed in on the walls and filled his vision, he was transfixed by the way it writhed and thrashed about like a wounded animal. The screeching wind was so loud it hurt his ears.

Adam was turning to go when he saw Mr Pitt striding defiantly along the perimeter wall, shrouded in a long leather jacket with an upturned collar. Adam scrambled across the tiles and peered over the edge of the roof in time to see a second, smaller figure emerge from the opposite direction on the wall. A prisoner, Adam was sure – although the whirling clouds of sand stopped any chance he had of identifying him. Mr Pitt came to a halt directly beneath Adam and nodded briskly at the inmate.

"What are you doing?" Doughnut shouted, his head poking up through the skylight. "Come on!"

The sandstorm had begun a full-frontal assault on the Dial, lashing one giant handful of sand after another at Adam, stinging his eyes and clawing at his skin. He tried to cover his mouth with his sleeve, but it was already filled with grit and his throat was burning. Through his tears, he saw the inmate hand a sheaf of papers over to Mr Pitt, who tucked them inside his coat and patted the prisoner on the arm. Whatever they said to each other was lost amidst the squall.

A violent gust of wind suddenly took hold of Adam, threatening to drag him off the roof. Grabbing hold of the slates, he turned and crawled blindly back in the direction of the skylight. It was impossible to see or hear anything now. The world was just sand and wind. Adam was wondering if he'd ever manage to find a way down when a pair of pudgy hands grabbed hold of his arm and pulled him through the skylight to safety.

As he lay coughing in a heap on the cupboard floor, winded by the impact of landing, Adam was certain of one thing: Major X's suspicions had been correct. There was a rat on the Dial, all right.

CHAPTER EIGHTEEN

Adam didn't tell anyone else about the clandestine meeting he had witnessed on the perimeter wall. He supposed that he could have gone to Major X, in the hope that telling him would help to clear his own name, but there was no guarantee that the Tally-Hoer would believe him. And anyway, with the memory of Corbett's knife pressed against his throat still fresh in his mind, Adam didn't particularly feel like cooperating with the Major.

But why he didn't tell Doughnut, or Mouthwash, or Paintpot was another matter entirely. For reasons he couldn't quite explain, the matter of the rat had become personal for Adam – the same kind of feeling that had driven him to try and find out more about Luca D'Annunzio. In the crammed dormitories and bustling corridors of the Dial, where there was never any space or privacy, there was something life-affirming about a secret, about owning something you didn't have to share.

As the summer progressed, the preparations for the upcoming show intensified. Everyone seemed to have a role, whether it was acting or singing, sticking up posters advertising the performance, or making streamers with which to festoon the hall. A newcomer to the prison might have been surprised by the feverish anticipation, but Adam had been inside long enough to appreciate how an event like this – something different to the everyday routine – raised morale. Every afternoon, strangled strains of music emerged from above the classrooms, as insistent as they were out of tune. Whenever possible, they were timed to coincide with one of Echo's broadcasts, drowning out his sneering pronouncements – much to the amusement of the other inmates. Following his latest run-in with the Tally-Ho, Adam didn't watch the rehearsals again, but that didn't stop him from glancing up to the theatre windows from time to time, wondering what sort of perilous activity was being cloaked behind the racket.

There were only two weeks to go before the show when the prisoners were summoned to a special roll call in the exercise yard. Mr Cooper stepped forward, a broad smile on his face as he declared:

"I am pleased to announce that repairs on the *Quisling* have finally been completed! This afternoon will see its first voyage since the accident, and all prisoners and guards are invited to the Docking Port to wave it off."

His announcement garnered a mixed reaction: some clapped and cheered, relieved that the airship could finally go back to Earth for desperately needed supplies; others folded their arms and said nothing, aware that the *Quisling* would not return with food alone. There would be more prisoners; more misery; the walkway would continue to revolve around the Dial.

Doughnut tried hard to disguise his glee, but Adam knew that the fixer needed the *Quisling* functioning more than anyone.

"I bet you'll be going to wave it off this afternoon, won't you?" he teased at lunch, in between mouthfuls of cold stew. "Make sure you take a hankie."

"I bet *everyone* will be going this afternoon," countered Doughnut. "I know Mr Cooper said we're 'invited', but you just try not going. You'll be off to the punishment cells before you know it – prisoner or guard."

Sure enough, when the sirens sounded later that afternoon, the inmates trooped across to Wing I as one, sweat dripping down their backs as they congregated in the oven-baked air. They were herded through the docking area into a cordoned-off section of the landing strip, the *Quisling* rearing up above their heads like a black, leathery beast. Men in overalls scurried around the airship's gondola, checking the guide ropes and making last-minute adjustments to the engines before take-off.

Back in Adam's dormitory, the sound of a single dripping tap echoed around the room. The only movement was a ripple of notepad pages in the breeze stealing in through the window.

Then Adam rolled out from beneath his bunk bed.

He knew that what he was doing was crazy. But if Doughnut was right, and everyone in the prison would be down on the landing strip, then the guards' quarters would be empty. Which presented Adam with the perfect opportunity to find the copy of Luca's missing record.

He hared out of the dormitory and along the empty corridor, then down the backstairs to the cellar housing Doughnut's secret tunnel. Earlier in the afternoon, he had taken the precaution of removing the correct key from the fixer's bedside table as he dozed; now he slipped it into the lock and opened the door. The cellar was as dank and forbidding as ever, and the rotting wooden chest covering the hole was difficult to shift alone. But Adam's mind was made up – there was no time for second thoughts. He reckoned he had an hour at most before the *Quisling* went through the warphole and the prisoners returned to their quarters. Heaving the chest to one side, he squeezed through the gap into the tunnel, aware of the ceiling closing in around his head once more. Adam crawled onwards, past the small fissure overlooking the chasm, following the curve of the walls. It felt as though he was moving much more quickly than he had the time he'd accompanied Doughnut, and it wasn't long before he reached the smooth flagstone ceiling that heralded his arrival beneath the guards' quarters.

Taking a deep breath, Adam reached up and pushed the loose flagstone to one side, then pulled himself out of the tunnel and into the pantry. The air was cold and still. Ignoring the lure of the crates of food, Adam hurried up the stairs and inched open the pantry door into the guards' quarters. The corridor was empty, silence ebbing from the surrounding rooms. Doughnut had been right – the guards had also been ordered from their rooms to watch the *Quisling*'s return flight.

Thankfully, none of the doors were locked. Adam supposed the guards had no reason to worry about anyone breaking into their building. Fighting the urge to fill his pockets with valuables and scrawl graffiti on the walls, he worked his way up from the ground floor, past the games room and the kitchen and the bedrooms on the second floor. On the third floor, he stopped outside a door with the words "Records Office" painted in black lettering on the pane of glass.

Adam hurried inside the sun-dappled room, grateful that the windows didn't look out on to any of the watch-towers on the perimeter wall. The walls were lined with metal filing cabinets filled with bulging reports on current inmates – and, in their own cabinet, the notorious denizens of the *Codex Treacherous*. Thankfully, the records were listed alphabetically. Adam quickly located Luca D'Annunzio's file and pulled it out. He began to read:

D'ANNUNZIO, LUCA
EARTH CRIME: Stealing money from his mother,
                  and then blaming it on his
                  brother.
VERDICT: Guilty of high treason
SENTENCE: 436 years

PRISONER NOTES:

- A popular inmate, D'Annunzio quickly rose to second-in-command of the Tally-Ho Escape Committee, sharing the position with the prisoner known as Caiman.

- Unbeknownst to the Dial's authorities, D'Annunzio and Caiman spent 150 years digging a tunnel to the Docking Port. They planned to wait until the Quisling was timed to leave during a Bucketball game, taking advantage of the lax security to crawl through the tunnel to Wing I.

- However, minutes before the Quisling was to depart, the escapees' tunnel was discovered by guard Hector Pitt, whose pursuit inadvertently caused a cave-in. Caiman was pulled free from the tunnel's debris, but D'Annunzio was nowhere to be seen. It transpired that he had sent Mr Pitt a letter that morning giving details of the escape. The only sensible conclusion is that D'Annunzio made his way through the tunnel to Wing I early and stored himself aboard the Quisling, which took off before the authorities could stop it.

- A thorough search of the aircraft on its return to the Dial revealed no trace of the inmate, and D'Annunzio has never been seen again.

- Inmate Caiman was sentenced to six months in
solitary as punishment for his role in the plot. A
harsh sentence was considered necessary in light of
his co-conspirator's escape.

- Though the prisoner's successful escape should
have damaged the Dial's reputation, D'Annunzio's
betrayal of Caiman has made him a hate figure
amongst other inmates. Now reviled as a
"collaborator", D'Annunzio's actions have - if
anything - worked to the regime's advantage.

- After a thorough investigation, Chief Warden
Frederick Cooper concluded that Hector Pitt had
not colluded with D'Annunzio and aided his betrayal.
Exonerated, Mr Pitt was promoted to Assistant Chief
Warder on account of his bravery and forthright action.

ADDITIONAL INFORMATION
- D'Annunzio's brother Nino is also imprisoned on
the Dial - for stealing money from their father
and blaming it on his brother. Although they were
transported to the Dial on the same voyage, the
two brothers share a mutual loathing and have
never acknowledged their relationship. Nino is not
considered to pose any sort of similar threat of
escape.

Adam's brain was struggling to take it all in. So *that* was why Luca was hated – he had betrayed his friend to escape. No wonder Caiman was so bitter. But it still didn't explain why the *Codex* in the library had been damaged – unless it wasn't anything to do with Luca's escape at all, but the mention of his brother. Had Adam stumbled across a trail Nino D'Annunzio had been laying? Was it Nino who had written the recipe for "Volcano Chilli"?

Adam was replacing the report in the cabinet when a noise from the corridor made him freeze.

Footsteps.

CHAPTER NINETEEN

Adam dived behind the filing cabinet and pressed himself against the wall. The footsteps reached the door of the Records Office – not the brisk march of a guard's boot, but a softer, more considered tread – then paused for a brief second before continuing onwards. Further down the corridor, a door creaked, and the footsteps died away.

Adam let out a long, quiet breath. Who could it be wandering the corridors? Everyone was supposed to be on the landing strip! Whoever it was, they had put Adam in a tricky situation. He couldn't hide in the Records Office for ever – he was going to have to risk creeping downstairs. Adam cursed himself for his recklessness.

Adam opened the door as slowly and quietly as possible. He had one foot outside when the sound of violins came screeching out from a room further down the corridor. He jumped, his breath catching in his throat. The deafening noise offered the perfect cover for Adam to flee down the stairs. But instead he found himself irresistibly drawn in the opposite direction – towards the music. He tiptoed down the corridor and pressed his face against a crack in the half-open door. Then he looked inside.

The room beyond was large and airy. Through the large window in the facing wall, Adam could see all the way to the landing strip, where the *Quisling* was still moored to the ground, surrounded by a vast crowd of inmates. Echo was sitting with his back to Adam, at a desk with a series of large dials and a small upright microphone. A record was crackling loudly on the turntable at his shoulder – as it faded out, Echo leaned towards the microphone and exclaimed, in his grating nasal tones:

"Good afternoon, everyone! So glad you could all make it!"

Adam didn't think he had ever hated a stranger like this before. He remembered the last time he had seen Echo – when the boy had been greedily filling his pockets with chocolate bars, seemingly oblivious to the inmates' hunger. And now here he was, the guards' lapdog, mocking the prisoners with whom he had once been friends.

Over on the landing strip, men had begun untying the guide ropes as the airship's motors growled into life. The *Quisling* rose uncertainly into the air, its engines spluttering and choking before bursting into a full-throated roar. Despite himself, Adam couldn't help but marvel at the sight of the huge zeppelin lifting off the ground.

"And there it goes!" crowed Echo. "Let's hear it for the *Quisling*, and all the guards who've helped restore it to its former glory!"

If there was any response from the inmates on the

ground, it didn't carry up to the radio station. Echo flicked off the microphone and leaned back in his chair with satisfaction, as a loud whirr signified the siphoning of the Dial's electricity to the Commandant's Tower – and its warphole machine. There was a loud crackle from the tower to Adam's left, and then a bolt of power shot out from a window on the top floor up into the sky, where it exploded like a firework. The *Quisling* banked in the air, setting a course towards the churning mass of the warphole.

By the time the airship had been swallowed up by the vortex, Adam was no longer watching. He had backed away along the corridor and was creeping down the stairs as quietly as he could. With the *Quisling* gone, it wouldn't be long now before the prisoners would be back. Adam descended through the guards' quarters to the cellar, before hurrying back into the tunnel. This time, however, there was a smile on his face – a smile of exhilaration, of a risk rewarded, of a mission accomplished.

The flight of the *Quisling* – and the extra helping of pudding doled out at dinner in celebration – seemed to have a galvanizing effect on the inmates. That evening, Mouthwash started a giant wrestling match in the dormitory, which ended with the roommates leaping off the top bunks like monkeys on to one another. Adam was too preoccupied with his day's discoveries to join in. Doughnut didn't seem in the mood either, so the two of them played chess in a quiet corner of the room, the fixer sucking on a boiled sweet as he calmly took piece after piece.

It was nearly ten by the time the *Quisling* returned, the Dial descending into darkness as the electricity was funnelled up to the Commandant's Tower, where the mysterious warphole machinery opened the vortex. Adam left his depleted army on the board and went to the window to watch. About twenty minutes elapsed before the new inmates appeared outside the Docking Port, bug-eyed with bewilderment, their faces stained with tears. They shrank under the pressing of the guards, jumping at every shouted command. As he watched them stumble across the walkway, Adam thought back to his first night, when he had been numb with shock and every second had been a new nightmare. It had been nine months ago; it might as well have been a lifetime.

"Poor sods," he murmured.

Doughnut didn't bother to look up from his chessboard. "Save your sympathy. This won't be the last time you see a new batch of prisoners. Let's carry on with the game." The fixer slid his queen along the board, taking Adam's rook and checking his king. "Didn't see you on the landing strip earlier. People were asking after you."

"I was there," Adam said casually, moving his king to safety. "Must have missed you in the crowd, that's all."

"Oh yeah? Then where did all the dust come from?"

Adam blinked. "What?"

"When you turned up for dinner your back was covered in dust. Most people wouldn't notice it, but I did – I got caught that way once, when I was younger and stupid and didn't know how to take care of myself. You weren't on the landing strip, Adam. You were in a tunnel."

"So what if I was? What's it to you?" said Adam defensively.

"What's it to me?" Leaning over the chessboard, Doughnut whispered sharply: "You were in the tunnel I showed you, weren't you? If you get caught, that'd wreck everything!"

"But I didn't get caught, did I?"

"Listen here – I've been holding your hand from the first second you got into this place. Never asked for anything back. But I told you to stop digging stuff up about Luca, and you didn't listen to me. Bookworm told me about you creeping around the library, looking through the *Codex Treacherous*. And now you're using my tunnels behind my back, and you won't even tell me why. I'm *this* close to turning my back on you."

"Don't worry about me," Adam retorted. "I can take care of myself."

"Yeah, you know it all, mate," Doughnut said sourly. He slid his queen in line with Adam's king.

"Checkmate," he said, and walked out of the room.

CHAPTER TWENTY

The frosty relations between Adam and Doughnut showed no signs of thawing: at mealtimes, the fixer pointedly sat at another table, and the two boys avoided eye contact every time they bumped into each other in the dormitory. Even though a part of Adam wanted to apologize, an indignant voice in his mind complained that it was all Doughnut's fault, and insisted that *he* should be the one who tried to patch things up first.

Despite his bruised feelings, Adam couldn't deny that his life was far less interesting for the fixer's absence. Three days after the argument, he wandered down to the exercise yard in search of a Bucketball rumble, only to find the gravel playing area empty. The only inmate in sight was a small figure standing by an easel and canvas on the top tier of benches. It was Paintpot. The dark-haired girl had turned her back on the view over the perimeter fence and was squinting thoughtfully at the surrounding wings of the prison.

"What's going on?" asked Adam, climbing up to the bench and taking a seat next to her.

"Not much," Paintpot replied, squeezing thick blobs of paint on to a wooden palette. "Thought I'd finally get around to painting the Dial."

Adam laughed incredulously. "You've been here all this time, and you've never painted the prison?"

Paintpot shook her head. "I see enough cell doors without painting them too," she murmured. And then added, with an awkward shrug: "But I finish my sentence next month, so I figured . . . why not?"

"You're getting out?" Adam sat up. "That's great news!"

"Yeah, I suppose," she said uncertainly. "I shouldn't really say anything. You don't want to make someone who's just starting their stretch feel worse about it."

"Like me, you mean? Don't worry about that. We can't all stay here for ever." Adam followed the artist's gaze over towards the grim edifice of the Re-education Wing. "But aren't you nervous about going in there? Letting them mess with your mind?"

"Nervous?" Paintpot laughed softly. "I can't wait, Adam. I can't wait until I'm back home and all of this is a bad dream. I can't wait to get my life back."

A thoughtful silence descended upon the yard. Adam sat back and watched as his friend sketched out the prison in pencil before daubing the image with oil paints, humming softly to herself as the buildings of the Dial slowly unfurled across the canvas. Paintpot carried on well into the evening, until the light began to fade and shadows crept across the yard like inky fingers. Adam helped her pack up and carry the easel and canvas back to Wing II, where they parted on the stairs outside the entrance to the boys' quarters.

He noticed the silence straight away – the absence of noise louder in his ears than any alarm. The doors to the dormitories were all flung open, but there was no one inside the rooms. It was as though the boys had been called away to some ghostly roll call. Adam had a sudden, unsettling premonition of what it might be like to be alone on the Dial, stranded in no-time for eternity.

As he hurried along the corridor towards his dormitory, he heard the first faint murmur of voices. The noise grew louder and more animated until Adam rounded a corner and walked straight into the vast crowd of boys gathered outside his room, jostling one another and standing on tiptoes as they competed for a view inside.

Adam blinked with surprise. "What the hell—?"

He elbowed his way through the throng and into the dormitory, which was overflowing with boys: some sitting cross-legged on the floor; others perched on the window ledges; still more sandwiched next to each other on the bunk beds. The air was thick with sweat and anticipation. Conversations bubbled like excited kettles. A pair of paraffin lamps draped a gossamer veil of light over the dormitory, the gloom broken only by the occasional intrusion of a searchlight through the window as it continued its unceasing rounds of the prison.

A space had been cleared at the far end of the room, where Major X was waiting solemnly behind a desk, flanked by the upright figures of Corbett and Fletcher. Caiman was sitting in a chair next to the Tally-Hoers, his arms folded and his face drenched with disdain.

"Adam! Over here!"

Mouthwash was waving at him from his bunk, where the talkative inmate was crammed next to Doughnut and the rest of the boys from their dormitory. Adam threaded his way towards them and wormed into a seat by Mouthwash, who shouted down the groans of protest from the other prisoners on the bunk. Doughnut looked away, refusing even to acknowledge Adam's appearance.

He had barely sat down when Major X produced a gavel from his pocket and rapped it sharply on the desk in front of him. Immediately the room subsided into an expectant hush.

"Right, listen up," said the Major. "For the last few weeks the Tally-Ho have been convinced that there's a rat amongst the inmates. We've been trying to hunt him down – and today, we think we've found him." He turned to the surly boy seated beside him. "This is your court martial, Caiman. How do you plead?"

The accused snorted. "Go take a running jump."

Fletcher leaned over and gave the boy a meaty clip around the back of the ear. "Show the judge some respect," he growled.

"It's all right, Fletcher," Major X said briskly, ignoring

the sniggers in the room. "We'll put that down as 'not guilty'."

Adam was speechless. For weeks he had been the Tally Ho's prime suspect, subject to the dark threats and accusations of the Major's men. And all along it had been Caiman?

"Calling Corbett for the prosecution!"

As the hulking Tally-Hoer stepped forward, Adam's eyes were drawn to the top bunk behind him, where the bandaged boy from the chapel was sitting alone in the shadows. Even though the room was heaving with inmates, no one had chosen to sit next to him. The boy leaned forward as he watched, clearly intrigued by proceedings.

"Tell the court martial what happened earlier today," Major X instructed his henchman.

Corbett coughed. "Not much to tell," he said. "I got this note saying that if I wanted to know who the rat was I should go talk to Caiman. I went to his bunk to find him but he wasn't there. Then I saw this sticking out from under his pillow."

Corbett dug a folded sheet of paper from his pocket and spread it open on the desk in front of the Major.

"It's a page from one of our escape plans," he said. "One of the pages that went missing." Corbett jabbed a burly finger at Caiman. "That little scumbag must have nicked it!"

"Thank you, Corbett!" Major X called out, above the hubbub that greeted the accusation. "You can stand down now."

He waited for Corbett to stomp back to his position before continuing: "So now you all know why we're here. Usually we'd sort this out ourselves, but since the accused used to be a member of the Tally-Ho, he's got the right to a proper court martial." He glanced across at Caiman. "What have you got to say in your defence?"

"Nothing!" Caiman retorted. "I've got nothing to say to any of you. This is a joke! I've never seen that piece of paper before in my life. Someone must have put it there. Who sent you this note, anyway?"

Corbett shrugged. "Dunno. It didn't say."

"See what I mean? I'm being framed, and you idiots are believing every word of it!"

With a curl of his lip, Caiman sat back and refused to speak again, ignoring all of the Major's questions. Angry mutters rippled through the audience; many of them had been on the receiving end of the accused's sharp tongue over the years and were only too happy to believe the charges against him. Adam should have been watching the proceedings with glee. After all, from the first moment that they had met, Caiman had taken every opportunity to pick on him, to needle away at him, to shop him in to the guards. But something was nagging at Adam, like an itch just out of reach. The evidence against Caiman was flimsy, but it was more than that, something only he knew. . .

"I wouldn't want to be in Caiman's shoes," Mouthwash whispered. "He's in for a right old kicking."

Adam barely heard him. His brow knotted as he desperately searched his memory. At the front of the room, Major X had lost patience.

"Right, Caiman, have it your way," he declared. "The accused isn't going to defend himself. Is there anyone here who'll speak for him?"

Eyes glanced down at shoes; heads shook vigorously.

"In that case," Major X continued, raising his gavel into the air, "on the basis of what we've heard today, and without any contradictory evidence, I can only declare Caiman g—"

"Wait!" Adam cried.

The gavel froze in mid-air. Major X frowned. "Who said that?"

"What are you playing at?" hissed Mouthwash, elbowing Adam in the ribs. "Keep out of it!"

"I can't!" Adam whispered back. "Something's not right here. And I think I've worked out what it is."

"Well?" Major X said impatiently, shielding his eyes as he looked out over the crowded dormitory. "Who interrupted me?"

Clearing his throat, Adam stood up and raised his hand, aware of every pair of eyes in the room swivelling in his direction. Further along the bunk, he heard Doughnut sigh. The Major gave him a hard stare.

"I'd have thought you of all people would have been best off keeping your mouth shut," he said ominously.

Adam pushed his way to the desk, anger pulsing through his veins.

"Yeah, because you called me a rat too, didn't you? Forgot to mention that in your little speech."

"You were one of our suspects," Major X said icily. "What's your point?"

"My point is that you were wrong about me, and you're wrong about him." Turning to face the crowded room, Adam declared loudly: "Caiman's not the rat, and I can prove it."

The dormitory exploded into uproar. Major X hammered his gavel on the desk, but no one took any notice. Corbett and Fletcher had to stride around the room shaking boys into silence before any sort of order could be restored.

"That's a big claim you've made there, Wilson," Major X said, visibly seething. "Can you back it up?"

"About a week ago I was up on the roof and—"

"Up on the roof? Doing what?"

"Just clearing my head," Adam said quickly, not looking at Doughnut. It didn't matter that they had fallen out – he wasn't going to drag anyone else into this. "Anyway, I was up there when that sandstorm hit. Before I went back inside, I saw a prisoner meeting Mr Pitt on the perimeter wall and giving him a load of papers. I'm guessing they were the rest of your escape plans."

"Really?" Major X didn't look convinced. "And did you see who this prisoner was?"

Adam shook his head.

"So how do you know it wasn't the accused then?"

"Caiman?" Adam laughed. "Up on the perimeter wall?"

There was a strangled cry behind him. Mouthwash jumped to his feet. "Of course it couldn't be Caiman, Major!" he exclaimed. "He's terrified of heights – everyone in our dormitory knows that! He gets the shakes just looking out of a second-floor window. Caiman'd never make it up to the perimeter wall. Adam's right – he can't be the rat!"

The resulting clamour threatened to rattle the dormitory's windowpanes in their frames.

"Order, order!" raged Major X, hammering away with his gavel. "Why didn't you tell us about this before, Wilson?"

"Why bother? You wouldn't have believed me, would you?"

"Who says I do now? Have you got anyone who can back up this story?"

Adam's breath caught in his throat. He had been so excited to have worked out that Caiman was innocent, he had forgotten that, on its own, his word might not be enough.

"Yeah, I can back him up," came a voice from the back of the room. "I was on the roof with him."

Adam didn't need to turn round to identify the speaker.

"Doughnut," said Major X, through gritted teeth. "I should have known. And did *you* see Mr Pitt meeting a prisoner on the wall?"

He couldn't have – Doughnut had been inside when the sandstorm hit. Adam had been on his own.

"Yes," Doughnut replied firmly.

"You're sure?"

"Hundred per cent."

"Then in light of this new evidence, I can only declare Caiman innocent of all charges," the Major said, with a shake of the head. "Case dismissed." He banged the desk a final time.

The crowd burst into applause, submerging Adam beneath a sea of handshakes and claps on the back. Even the bandaged boy banged the ceiling in appreciation. Major X shoved his way out of the dormitory, with Corbett and Fletcher in grim attendance. Only Caiman remained seated, his expression unchanged.

Adam waited until the congratulations had died down and the crowds had melted back to their own rooms before seeking out Doughnut, who had returned to his bunk and was flicking through a comic.

"Listen," Adam began hesitantly. "Thanks. For, you know, backing me up. I know you didn't see them."

"No, but you did," Doughnut replied evenly. "You wouldn't lie about something like this – that's not your style. Surprised you took the risk for Caiman, though. He's a first-class idiot."

"He's also innocent," said Adam. "It's not nice to be accused of something you didn't do – trust me."

Doughnut watched as Caiman sloped past them back

to his bunk, disappearing beneath his blanket without a word.

"If you think he's going to thank you for helping him, you're in for a long wait."

"That's all right," Adam replied, with quiet satisfaction. "I've got plenty of time."

CHAPTER TWENTY-ONE

It seemed to Adam that, no matter how hard he tried to keep his head down on the Dial, trouble tracked him down like a sniffer dog. One way or another, he had fallen out with almost every prisoner he had met. Despite their successful defence of Caiman, he and Doughnut still hadn't made up properly, and judging by the murderous looks Corbett flashed at him in the week following the court martial, Adam's actions had only worsened his standing amongst the Tally-Ho.

But one shadow loomed larger over Adam than any other. Mr Pitt appeared to be on a one-man mission to make his life as uncomfortable as possible. If a plate was dropped in the mess hall, if a comb went missing from a dormitory, if a half-dug tunnel was found in a cellar, then Adam was always to blame. When a boy and a girl started whispering furtively to each other during a morning roll call, it was Adam who was singled out for talking and made to wait behind. He watched forlornly as the rest of the inmates trooped out of the exercise yard, leaving him alone with Mr Pitt. The warder briskly lit up a cigarette.

"No excuses, Wilson?" he asked archly. "No whining protestations of innocence?"

"No, sir," Adam replied evenly.

"That's not like you. Are you feeling all right, son? Coming down with a bout of manliness?"

"No, sir," Adam replied again.

Mr Pitt marched up to him until their noses were almost touching. With every inhalation, the burning end of his cigarette glinted like the eye of a malevolent beast.

"You're a toad, Wilson," whispered Mr Pitt. "A warty little toad, hopping from one stinking pond to the next. One of these days, you're going to drown in your own muck. And I'm going to be there to watch."

Adam turned his face to one side, trying to escape the warder's stale breath. Gazing at Adam through his filmy eye, Mr Pitt dropped his cigarette to the floor and ground it beneath his foot. He patted Adam on the cheek, too hard to be a friendly gesture, then strode off towards the walkway.

"Kitchen duty for a week," he called out over his shoulder.

Adam watched him leave with barely concealed hatred. After months of persecution, the seed of fear that Mr Pitt had planted in Adam's soul had grown into something blacker and harder. He was still fuming later that day, when he returned from the mess hall to hear Mr Pitt's stentorian bark coming from the side of the prisoners' quarters. Peering around the corner, Adam saw that

the guard had backed two inmates up against the wall –
the boy and the girl who had been whispering during roll
call.

"I thought I'd seen some squalid sights in my time here,
but this one takes the biscuit!" Mr Pitt yelled. "To catch the
pair of you sucking on each other like leeches in the shadows – and so soon after I had eaten! Did you think I wanted
to see that? Well, did you?"

"No, sir," the girl replied, in a faltering tone.

"No, sir, indeed," said Mr Pitt. "This is a prison, not
a Mexican bordello! Perhaps my memory fails me, but I
thought the rules explicitly stated that this kind of disgusting fraternization between inmates is strictly forbidden.
Does my memory fail me?"

The boy mumbled a reply.

"Correct, Barker, it does not. . ."

Aware from bitter experience that Mr Pitt was just
warming up, Adam backed away from the corner of the
building, only to see Mouthwash heading towards him
across the walkway. The inmate was struggling with a large
bucket that he was holding at arm's length, and there was a
wooden clothes peg clamped over his nose.

"That's a good look for you," Adam said dryly.

"Go boil your heb," Mouthwash replied, his jaws moving like pistons as he chomped furiously on his chewing
gum. "You try smellib bis."

He lifted up the bucket, sending a swell of foul odour
over Adam: a smell of sewers and toilets, of rotten eggs and

fish and worse. Adam's stomach churned as he peered into the green mess.

"That's *gross*!" he exclaimed, holding his nose.

"Why d'you think I'b got thib peg on by nobe?" Mouthwash replied.

"What is it?"

"I gabe Mr Harker some chat, and he mabe me clean out a blocked sewer. There's years of scub here."

"I can see that. Where are you taking it?"

Mouthwash jerked his head towards the perimeter wall. "Going to chuck ib ober there."

Looking down at the revolting slime, Adam was struck by a sudden delicious thought.

"Don't worry about that," he said. "I'll take it."

"You whab?"

"Give it to me. I'll sort it out for you."

Adam carefully took the bucket of slops from his bemused friend's grasp. Mouthwash removed the peg from his nose, and took in several grateful gulps of fresh air.

"God, that was minging. I never thought old Harker could be so cruel." He held out the peg. "Want this?"

Adam shook his head.

"I probably don't want to know what you're going to do with that, do I?"

A smile played across Adam's lips. "I'll see you later, mate."

He turned and walked away, carrying the bucket as if it were a landmine, desperately trying to avoid any of the slime splashing on to his clothes. Even though he tried to hold his breath, the stench from the bucket still seared his nostrils.

"This place is getting to you!" Mouthwash called out after him. "You're going nuts, mate!"

Adam hauled the bucket into the prisoners' quarters, disregarding the looks of disgust and loud protests from the other inmates. He laboured up the staircase to the second floor, where he darted inside an empty storage room facing out towards the mess hall. Still retching at the ghastly smell of the sewage, Adam balanced the bucket on the window sill and opened the window.

Cast in the glow of a summer's afternoon, there was a certain grave beauty about the Dial's burnished brickwork. But Adam only had eyes for the patch of ground directly below him, where Mr Pitt's oily hair glistened in the sunlight as the warder continued to scream at the two inmates.

Adam didn't even think about it. He pushed the window further open and tipped over the bucket, sending a waterfall of green scum cascading through the air and down on to the guard's head.

"AAAARGH!"

Mr Pitt's shocked bellow echoed around the Dial. He staggered like he'd been shot, stinking gloop covering him from head to toe. Barker and his girlfriend took one look at each other and scampered away to safety. Clawing the sewage from his eyes, Mr Pitt reeled blindly back towards the walkway, shoving away a guard who had run over to help him.

As the second guard looked up towards his window, Adam ducked inside the room – but not before their eyes had met. He dropped the bucket with a clang and sprinted out of the room, bounding down the stairs as the first news-flashes began transmitting along the Dial's communication channels. Drawn to the window by the yelling, inmates were laughing and pointing at Mr Pitt, tears of laughter rolling down their cheeks.

Adam's dormitory was empty; he hared inside and jumped into his bed. He lay there for a few seconds, barely able to believe what he had just done, then burst out laughing. Who was the toad in the muck now?

From the moment he had taken the bucket from Mouthwash, deep down Adam had known there was no way he was going to get away with it. The fact that the guard had seen him at the window only set it in stone. But the prospect of a spell in the punishment cells left him strangely untroubled. Even a month in solitary would be worth it, just for Mr Pitt's agonized screams.

So as the other inmates gossiped and giggled over dinner, Adam kept his own counsel and waited. In some ways, it was almost a relief when Mr Harker approached their table.

"Hello, sir," Doughnut greeted him cheerily. "What's up?"

The guard ignored him. "Wilson," he said, his face stony. "Come with me."

"What's going on?" Doughnut asked.

"It's nothing," Adam told him, although his nerves had begun to tingle with trepidation. He followed Mr Harker out of the mess hall, through an honour guard of loud whispers from the other tables:

"What do they want him for? Caught tunnelling, was he?"

"I heard he was the one who threw that gunk on Pitty. . ."

"No! *Him?* I heard Scarecrow boasting that he did it."

"Well, if you listen to idiots like that. . ."

As they passed the Tally-Ho's table, Corbett started humming the funeral march, prompting laughter from his friends. Adam was surprised to see Major X nudging his giant companion into silence, before giving Adam a little nod of respect.

Outside, the Dial was unnaturally quiet, as though everyone in the prison was holding their breath. Mr Harker marched across the walkway towards Wing IX, pointedly rebuffing Adam's attempts to talk to him.

The guards' quarters were housed in a rambling, three-storey building topped by a lone tower rising up from one corner of the roof. Two men were standing guard at the front door, rifles slung over their backs. As he reached the gate at the end of the walkway, Mr Harker unlooped a key from a chain on his belt and unlocked it. He led Adam past the sentries and into a narrow hallway inside the building. Through a half-open door, Adam caught a glimpse of a recreation room, where a couple of guards were engrossed in a game of snooker. One of the men paused in the middle of his shot and stared at Adam. The look on the guard's face – not one of anger, exactly, but bordering on apprehension – unnerved him.

Before Adam could say anything, Mr Harker grabbed him by the shoulder and ushered him up the staircase at the end of the corridor. At the third floor, past the radio station and the Records Office, the stairwell closed in upon them, and the steps became twisted as they wound their way up the tower. Adam became aware of his heart pounding against his ribcage, his earlier exhilaration replaced by a sinking dread. At the top of the staircase, Mr Harker pushed the door open and waited for Adam to enter the room beyond before closing it firmly behind him.

Mr Pitt was standing at his desk, his back turned to Adam. The warder had cleaned himself up and changed into a new uniform without a speck of dirt or hint of a stain upon its sharp creases. He didn't move or say a word.

Adam coughed nervously. "You wanted to see me, sir?"

At the sound of his voice, Mr Pitt's shoulders began trembling. For an astonished second Adam thought that the warder had started to cry, but when the warder whirled round he saw that Mr Pitt was shaking with rage.

"Wilson," he said raggedly. "You . . . little. . ."

"Sir?" tried Adam.

Mr Pitt stepped up and punched Adam in the face, the force of the blow sending him reeling backwards. The attack was so sudden that there wasn't time to try to defend himself, or strike back, or even feel afraid. Adam was aware of another blow hitting him in the head, and the smack of the floorboards against his back. Mr Pitt's sovereign rings gave a warning flash as they hurtled towards Adam's face, and then the lights went out.

CHAPTER TWENTY-TWO

Even unconscious, there was no respite for Adam. A feverish gallery of faces flashed through his mind: his mum and dad, Doughnut, Jessica; all of them shaking their heads with sorrow and disapproval. Then Adam was back at the skate park near his home. He was chasing after Danny, trying to say he was sorry, but his friend was walking ahead of him and it felt like Adam was trying to run through treacle. Eventually Danny stopped and turned around. He pointed at Adam, laughing, and as Adam turned round he saw to his horror that the ground beneath him had turned into a watery current, dragging him backwards towards the Dial's chasm, which had appeared with a great yawn in the middle of the skate park. With a despairing scream, Adam tumbled over the edge...

And then he was awake. Adam opened his eyes, immediately regretting it as a barrage of white light exploded in front of his vision. There was an agonizing throbbing in the back of his head, and his face felt puffy and sore. Even blinking hurt.

Squinting out of his right eye – his left wouldn't open

properly – Adam pieced together his surroundings. He was lying in a hospital ward, in the middle of a row of beds pushed up against whitewashed walls. All around him were children in varying degrees of discomfort: those with their limbs encased in plaster and hoisted into the air on pulleys; those with skin covered in angry red spots, who groaned in distress as they tried to resist the urge to scratch themselves. The cloying stench of antiseptic couldn't mask the smell of sickness and despair.

As Adam stirred, a pretty young woman in a white nurse's uniform appeared by his bedside and looked down at him.

"Oh, you're awake!" she said brightly.

He tried to reply, but the words poured from his mouth in a slurred, soupy mess.

"Don't worry, love," the nurse said, checking his pulse rate against the watch pinned to her dress. "We gave you something to help you sleep. Don't try to speak just yet."

As she continued to count his pulse, a voice boomed out across the ward like a gunshot. "What have we here?"

At once the nurse stepped back, her eyes fixed dutifully on the ground. A burly woman with arms like rolling pins barrelled up to Adam's bedside, with the violent intent of a boxer approaching the ring. She was dressed in a blue uniform, her hair tightly pinned beneath a flowing headdress. Her skin was lined and weathered, a tuft of black hair visible in the light as it dangled from her chin.

"This is Adam Wilson, Matron," the younger woman said meekly. "He was admitted yesterday evening."

"Well, give me the report, Nurse Waters!" barked Matron.

"As you can see, he's been beaten up quite badly. There's severe facial bruising, swelling around the left eye, and he's lost a tooth. Probable concussion, too, I'd imagine."

"We'll see about that." Matron reached down and grabbed Adam by the chin, twisting his face left and right. He winced as lightning bolts of pain shot through his skull. Eventually the woman let go, wiping her hand on her uniform as though Adam were infectious. She turned to Nurse Waters.

"He can stay here for the time being, but I want him out of here by the end of the week. Don't waste too much medicine on him, and no visitors – this little monster is under caution for provoking a guard." She leaned in so close to Adam that the hairs on her chin almost tickled his nostrils. "You come anywhere near me with a bucket, young man," she hissed, "and you'll regret it."

With a final warning glare, the matron stormed out of the infirmary. Nurse Waters waited until she was halfway out of the door before sticking out her tongue at her superior's back.

"Don't listen to that old dragon," she whispered to Adam. "Everyone knows she's got a thing for Mr Pitt. I'll make sure you're taken care of. Are you in a lot of pain right now?"

Adam nodded.

"Let's see if I can give you something to help with that."

Patting his hand, the nurse produced a needle from a surgical tray and injected him in the arm. Immediately Adam felt the pain in his face begin to ease, and he slipped gratefully back into unconsciousness.

It was the middle of the night when he woke again. The harsh overhead lights had been turned off – now slender candle flames wavered in the draughts. As he lay there, still and numb, Adam had the unsettling feeling that he was being watched. Cautiously turning his head, he recognized the bandaged boy sitting in a rocking chair by the window, his small frame wrapped in a tatty dressing gown. The boy seemed to be staring straight at Adam, his expression unreadable beneath the swathes of dressing. Before Adam could try to speak, the boy stood up and walked silently out of the ward, nodding at Adam as he passed his bed.

Over the next couple of days, Adam began to understand why many of the inmates considered a spell in the infirmary to be a blessing in disguise. The ward was steeped in a blissful lethargy, the patients soothed to sleep by a lullaby of soft moans and painkillers. Nurse Waters was the beloved queen of the ward, dispensing kindness and relief in equal measure. At one point, half dreaming, Adam confused her for an angel, and was rewarded with a tinkling laugh of delight.

On his third day in the ward, Adam was roused from his stupor by the ward's excited greeting of the lunch time trolley. He looked up to see Jessica handing out the meals, her trustee armband wrapped around her sleeve. When she saw Adam's bruised face, her hand flew to her mouth.

"Oh, Adam!" she gasped. "Look what he did to you!"

Adam tried to force a smile, even though the gesture made his face ache.

"It's not that bad, is it?" he mumbled.

Jessica caught herself. "No, no . . . it's just a shock, that's all. I heard what had happened, but . . . I mean, I thought even Mr Pitt couldn't be cruel enough to. . ."

"Trustee!" boomed Matron from across the ward. "Less dilly-dallying! Give him his meal and move on!"

"Take care," Jessica whispered. "I'll be back if I can."

She squeezed Adam's hand as she passed him his meal, then hurriedly wheeled her trolley away. Later in the afternoon, Adam got up to go to the toilet, and inspected himself in the mirror. He could see why Jessica had reacted the way she had – the entire left side of his face was a swollen purple mess of bruising.

In the early evening, when the ward had quietened down, another familiar figure slipped in through the entrance. It was Doughnut. The portly fixer glanced left and right before awkwardly sidling up to Adam's bedside and pulling up a chair.

"All right?" he said.

Adam smiled weakly. "Doughnut! I'm not allowed

any visitors, you know. You'll get into trouble if they catch you."

"I'll be OK. I gave Nurse Waters a new pair of stockings to keep an eye out for me."

"I should have guessed." Adam paused, then added meaningfully: "It's good to see you, mate."

"Yeah." Doughnut shifted uncomfortably in his seat. "Look, I'm sorry about all that stuff between me and you. I shouldn't have given you such a hard time about that Luca stuff."

"Forget about it," Adam said. "It wasn't your fault – I was being an idiot. If it hadn't been for you I'd have been done for months ago."

The fixer gave him a wry look. "Have you looked in a mirror recently? You look pretty done for now, if you ask me."

"You know what I mean."

Doughnut glanced over at the maudlin huddles in the beds around them. "Lively here, isn't it?" he remarked. "What time's the party starting?"

"This is better than any party I've been to," replied Adam. "The beds are comfier, and you get more food. Don't hear any news, though. What's going on outside?"

"It's great, mate. Everyone's still buzzing."

"Buzzing? Why?"

Doughnut laughed and clapped him on the shoulder. "Because of you, idiot! You're the talk of the prison! No one's *ever* had the guts to get Mr Pitt like that before. And to top things off, he's in all sorts of bother now."

"What do you mean?"

"When they found out how badly he'd beaten you, Mr Cooper suspended him. Pitt's confined to the guards' quarters until further notice. Bookworm reckons there's a chance they'll kick him out for good. If that happens you'll probably be made King of the Dial."

Adam lay back on his pillow. He wasn't sure what to think. After nearly a year of fights and arguments, the constant struggle to fit in, it felt surreal imagining other inmates cheering his name. But what would happen if Mr Cooper did decide to send Mr Pitt away? The Assistant Chief Warder would come after him for sure.

From somewhere on the ground floor of the infirmary came a shrill blast of a whistle. Doughnut got up from his chair.

"Time's up," he said. "I'll see you when you get out, yeah?"

"Count on it," Adam replied.

Doughnut crept out of the ward, silently slipping a bar of chocolate under Adam's pillow before he left.

The lazy rhythms of infirmary life lulled Adam into a state of happy lethargy. He spent most of his time dozing in bed, fanned by the warm breeze floating in through the open windows. His bruises lost some of their angry glow, and the swelling in his face began to subside. Every afternoon he closed his eyes and listened to the faint strains of the orchestra as they persevered with their discordant charade above the classrooms. Twice more Doughnut managed to slip back into the ward to keep Adam updated with Dial gossip – with only days to go until the summer show, excitement was apparently reaching fever pitch.

In the middle of his final night, Adam was awoken by the insistent nagging of his bladder. He crept out of bed and past the elderly nurse on duty, who was fast asleep in her chair. In the corridor beyond, a warm late-summer breeze drifted in through the open window. The bandaged boy was sitting beside it, playing a sad tune on a harmonica. He stopped playing at the sight of Adam.

"Hello again," he said.

"Hi," Adam replied uncertainly. "I ... erm ... needed the toilet."

The boy chuckled. "Don't have to explain to me. I'm not Matron."

"Why are you up?"

"Why not? I've spent enough time here asleep."

Adam drew cautiously nearer. "Aren't you going to get into trouble? The nurses don't like it if we're up in the middle of the night."

"They don't care," the boy replied nonchalantly. "The exits are all guarded. Most of us aren't in a fit state to get out of bed, let alone start digging tunnels. What's the worst that could happen?"

"I saw you at the court martial the other night."

The boy nodded. "I saw you, too. Quite an impressive performance. Can't keep out of the spotlight, can you?"

"It's not on purpose," Adam said ruefully. "Trouble follows me around here."

"I know the feeling," the boy replied. "It seeks me here, it seeks me there, trouble seeks me everywhere. . ."

Adam started. He would recognize that phrase anywhere. Suddenly he was back in the library, staring at a mocking poem in the *Codex Treacherous*. All sorts of thoughts and possibilities began flashing through his mind.

"Nino?" he breathed. "Nino D'Annunzio? Is that you?"

The boy blinked with surprise. When he spoke again, there was amusement in his voice.

"Afraid you've got the wrong brother," he said. "I'm Luca."

CHAPTER TWENTY-THREE

Adam gaped at the bandaged boy as he sketched out an extravagant bow, his eyes twinkling with delight.

"Surprised?" asked Luca.

Adam was too shocked to reply. All this time, all these years, and all along Luca D'Annunzio had been walking round under everyone's noses. The Dial's most infamous escapee had never even left the prison!

"Unbelievable!" Adam managed finally. "But . . . how . . . why?"

Luca glanced up and down the corridor, then took Adam by the arm. "Perhaps we should continue this conversation somewhere else," he said softly. "The walls have ears, and all that."

Adam allowed himself to be led up the staircase to the top floor of the infirmary, where a corridor came to an end at a forbidding set of swing doors. Above the doors, a hand-painted sign warned: "Infectious Disease and Hysteria Ward. No Unauthorized Admittance." Luca walked nonchalantly through the swing doors, and into a long, gloomy room with a row of beds running alongside each wall. None of the patients stirred beneath their blankets as they walked past. As Adam covered his mouth with his hand, he noticed that the floorboards were stained and the walls grimy with dirt.

"It stinks in here," he whispered. "Where are the nurses?"

Luca shrugged dismissively. "Downstairs putting their feet up and having a cup of tea, probably. The kids up here have either lost their minds or got something pretty nasty that the nurses are scared of catching. So they drug the patients and stay away from the ward. That's why it's the best place to hide in the whole prison."

"But aren't you worried that you might catch something?"

"If it happens, it happens," Luca replied breezily. "I can't worry about everything."

He pushed through another set of swing doors into an icy, deserted room where the beds were draped in cobwebs and thick layers of dust.

"This room's been empty since poor Cowley died of pneumonia," Luca continued. "Everyone reckons it's haunted. And it is, I guess – by me."

The final bed in the left-hand row had a heavy green curtain pulled around it, discouraging any closer inspection. Luca slipped through the curtain and jumped on to the empty bed beyond. As Adam looked on, the bandaged boy reached up and pulled down a hatch set into the ceiling. A rope ladder tumbled down to the bed from the hidden room above them.

"Very handy," Adam remarked.

"Years before they closed this ward, I got chickenpox and was stuck in this bed," Luca explained softly. "I spent a week staring up at the hatch, wondering what was above it. Thinking about that took my mind off the itching. Anyway, before they discharged me I made sure I had a look around, and made some alterations to make getting up here easier. You never know when you might need a hiding place."

He scampered up the rope ladder and disappeared through the hatch, leaving Adam to make slightly more laboured progress after him. Pulling himself up into the room, Adam found himself in a musty attic nestled in the gables of the infirmary. The roof sloped sharply down on both sides of the room, forcing him to stoop every time he strayed from the centre. In the facing wall, a door with an inlaid window led out on to a narrow balcony. The room was sparsely furnished: two battered armchairs spilling stuffing out on to the floor; a wooden school desk; a large wicker basket; and a cracked mirror above a mantelpiece covered in candles. The desk and the walls were submerged beneath sheets of paper covered in diagrams labelled in Luca's sweeping handwriting.

Standing on his tiptoes, Adam looked through a grimy circular window out over the Dial – from the distant expanse of the exercise yard to the ominous edifice of the Commandant's Tower and the Re-education Wing to his left. Despite the warmth of the evening, the air was chilly in the attic, and draughts of cold air gnawed at Adam's ankles.

He shivered, imagining what this room would be like in winter.

Luca began unwrapping the bandages from around his head, gradually revealing a mischievous face with an olive complexion and tousled dark brown hair. It was as though Paintpot's drawing had come to life before Adam's eyes.

"If I had known how much of a pain it was going to be dressing up like a mummy every day," he declared, tossing the bandages on to one of the armchairs, "I'd have chosen a different disguise."

Running a hand through his tangled hair, Luca picked up a box of matches and began lighting the candles on the mantelpiece. As the light played across the boy's face, Adam saw that Luca was about the same age as he was – even if, like so many other inmates on the Dial, there was a world-weary edge to his movements that suggested a life lived far in excess of his age.

"It's a pretty good disguise, though. Especially your hand." Adam peered down at the scarred skin on Luca's right hand. "Is that make-up?"

"I wish," grimaced Luca. "I knew that if I was going to pull this off then my disguise had to be convincing enough to stop people asking too many questions, so I crept down to the kitchens one night, turned on a stove and ... well, you know."

"You *burned* your own hand?" Adam asked incredulously.

"You're looking at me like I'm crazy," said Luca. "Maybe

you're right – maybe I am. How are you supposed to stay sane here? If you sit there quietly and just wait for three hundred years to go by, isn't that more crazy than doing anything you can to get out? Even if it means burning your own hand?"

Adam rubbed his face. "I don't understand any of this," he confessed. "What are you doing up here? Everyone thinks you escaped years ago!"

"I know what everyone thinks," said Luca, plumping himself down into one of the armchairs. "I'm a collaborator, right? The most hated prisoner ever to do time?"

There was a bitter edge to his voice. Adam looked away.

"It's because of Caiman," he said quietly. "It's because you betrayed him."

"I didn't betray him!" Luca replied fiercely. "It was the other way round! Caiman was the collaborator, not me!"

"What?"

"The morning we were supposed to escape, something happened to me, something so important that I decided that I was staying. I tried to get word to Caiman, but he was busy finishing off the tunnel. Afterwards, when I heard that Pitt had somehow rumbled us, I knew something was wrong. Seeing as everyone else had been at the Bucketball game and thought I'd escaped, I decided to hide up here. That night I broke into the punishment cell wing – got as far as Caiman's window when I heard him and Pitt talking. Seems they'd had a deal; in exchange for selling me out, my 'friend' was going to get smuggled back to Earth. I guess Caiman figured it was safer that way – he always was a coward.

"Problem was, I never showed up. They both came to the wrong conclusion: that I'd double-crossed Caiman and made an early run for it. Pitt did his nut and threw Caiman in solitary. But neither could risk anyone finding out the truth about what had happened, so they got together and blamed it all on the person who wasn't there. Me. Pitt got a promotion; Caiman got everyone to feel sorry for him, and make sure no one thought he was the rat."

"But you *were* there!" Adam exclaimed. "Why didn't you say something? Why didn't you tell people he was lying?"

"And blow my cover?" Luca shook his head. "It doesn't matter what people think about me. I don't exist. I'm a ghost. I can walk around the Dial without making anyone suspicious." He gestured at the sheets of paper stuck to the walls. "I can plan. I've learned my lesson, Adam. This time I *will* break out, and no one's going to double-cross me."

"I won't say a word," Adam said solemnly. "You can trust me."

"I know," replied Luca. "You proved that at Caiman's court martial. And when you tipped that gunk over Pitt. No one would ever do that unless they were on the level – or as crazy as me." He grinned. "But how on earth did you find out about Nino? I thought if I tore out my entry in the *Codex* no one would find out. After all, it's not like he's going to tell anyone."

"There's a copy of the report in the guards' quarters," said Adam. "I sneaked in and read it."

"Really?" Luca's eyes came alive. "You took a hell of a risk there. How did you manage it?"

And so Adam explained the trail he had followed, from Paintpot's picture to the *Codex Treacherous* and on to the *Dial Cookbook*. Luca listened intently, a look of growing admiration upon his face.

"I've got to hand it to you," he said finally. "After all these years I never thought anyone would be able to track me down."

"Not even your brother?"

Luca said nothing, shifting uncomfortably in his armchair.

"Nino's still on the Dial, isn't he?" asked Adam.

"Yes. Though he hasn't been called Nino for a long, long time."

"What happened between the two of you? Why did you fall out?"

"Have you got a brother?"

Adam shook his head.

"Then you wouldn't understand. It's complicated."

Luca abruptly stood up and walked over to his desk, which was covered with a hand-drawn map of the Dial, overlaid with a complicated network of arrows. Adam peered over his shoulder.

"What are the arrows?"

"Wind currents," Luca replied. "I've been measuring them for years."

"Why?"

"Because with their help, I'm going to break into the Commandant's Quarters, turn on the warphole, and get the hell out of here."

"What?" gasped Adam. "No one's ever got inside the Commandant's Quarters! How are you going to do it?"

"Remember when we talked in the chapel, and I told you about my dream?"

Adam frowned. "The one about the sky tunnel?"

"Exactly!" cried Luca. "It was trying to tell me something. Other prisoners keep trying to escape by digging tunnels, but they're going the wrong way. They need to go straight to the warphole! They need to go up, not down!"

"OK," Adam said slowly. "So you're going to dig a tunnel through the *air*?"

"Well, no. That's impossible." Luca grinned. "I've got the next best thing, though. Look!"

He dragged Adam over to the corner of the attic, and what appeared to be a pile of junk: a battered wooden crate and some metal cylinders covered in a jumble of ropes and white sheets.

"Those are the sheets from the infirmary!" Adam exclaimed. "It was you who was stealing them last year!"

Luca nodded.

"But why?"

"Can't you see?" Luca said gleefully. "I'm making a balloon!"

Adam stared dumbly at the patchwork of roughly sewn sheets. "You're going to try to fly in *that*?"

"I know she doesn't look much now, but when she's inflated she'll be a beauty, I'm telling you!" Luca gestured at the plans adorning his walls. "I've thought it all through," he said proudly. "I stitched the sheets together to make the balloon, used a crate as a basket, and filched some gas canisters and a burner from the Docking Port so I can power the thing. The wind usually blows north across the Dial. So if I inflate the balloon out on the balcony there, with any luck it'll carry me straight to the Commandant's Tower!"

"What about the guards?" asked Adam. "They'll shoot you down if they see you."

"They'll be too busy at the granary store."

"Why?"

Luca grinned. "Because I'm going to blow it up. You read the recipe for Volcano Chilli, didn't you? I've spent a year making up enough explosive to bring down a building. And while Mr Cooper and his men are putting out the fires, I'm going to fly to the Commandant's Tower, turn on the warphole machine and go home. Piece of cake."

Adam had listened with mounting incredulity. For all Luca's certainty, his plan made Major X's plots seem the height of common sense.

"So what do you think?" he asked archly. "Impressed?"

"Honestly?" Adam scratched his head. "I think you're nuts."

"It's not that far-fetched," Luca muttered, crestfallen.

"I'm not trying to be rude," Adam said hastily. "It's just – it sounds really dangerous."

"Like I say," he replied, "I can't worry about everything."

Luca's energy was infectious. They talked through the night, going over the plan until the candles burned low and the sky reddened with the onset of dawn. As Adam slipped back through the hatch into the infectious diseases ward, he had almost been convinced that it could work.

Almost, but not quite. Slipping back into the comfort of his bed, Adam fell asleep instantly – and in his dreams, he saw a burning craft plummeting towards the ground, exploding over the Dial like a firework.

CHAPTER TWENTY-FOUR

The next morning, Adam awoke with a start to find the matron looming over his bedside. When she gleefully announced that he was to be immediately discharged, he couldn't hide a twinge of disappointment.

"No use pulling faces," Matron snapped. "You've been lazing around far too long as it is. There are children here who are genuinely ill, you know. I won't waste any more time on a malingerer."

Behind the burly woman's back, Nurse Waters rolled her eyes. Adam grinned.

"Think that's funny, do you?" Matron barked, looming threateningly over Adam.

"No, Matron," he replied hastily.

"You ask me, Mr Pitt had the right idea about you," she said hoarsely. "Sometimes a firm hand is the only thing that some children understand. If your smart mouth gets you back in here, don't expect me to look after you."

Matron straightened up and stomped away, her thick tights bunching around her stocky legs. Adam glanced over at Nurse Waters.

"She really doesn't like me, does she?"

"I think it's more that she really likes Mr Pitt," the nurse whispered back. "They make a lovely couple, don't they?"

Adam laughed. "What are you doing here?" he asked, before he could stop himself. "I mean, you're different to all the other guards. You're not mean like they are."

Nurse Waters sighed, and then sat down at the edge of his bed. "There was a boy," she said hesitantly, looking down at her hands. "A boy I loved very much. He said he loved me too, but all the time he was telling lots of other girls the same thing. Everyone knew but me. When I eventually found out I was very hurt and very angry, and although I tried to move on the pain wouldn't go away." She grimaced. "I wrote to a problem page in a magazine about how betrayed I felt, and a week later a strange letter came through my door. It was from the Commandant, offering me a job here. Before I knew it, I had signed a contract to work on the Dial for a hundred years. Too late, I realized it was a terrible mistake."

That sounded very familiar to Adam. "I'm really sorry," he said sympathetically. "How long have you got left to go?"

"Ninety-eight years," the young woman replied. For a second Adam thought Nurse Waters was going to cry, but instead she suddenly stood up, and when she spoke again her tone was light. "But it's not all bad news. We'll all get to leave one day – you and me. In the meantime, let's get you out of here before the dragon returns."

Adam climbed reluctantly out of bed and pulled his coarse blue uniform over his underclothes. With a final smile and a wave to Nurse Walters, he walked downstairs and out into the sunshine, where he took in deep lungfuls of fresh air. Nice as it had been lazing around the infirmary, it felt good to stretch his legs. As Adam crossed over the walkway back to the prisoners' quarters, he became aware that the Dial was curiously empty – no Bucketball rumbles disturbed the exercise yard, and the theatre was silent. Save the guards manning the perimeter walls, he was completely alone.

As he stepped down on to Wing II, Adam saw Mouthwash leaning by the entrance to the dormitories with his hands thrust in his pockets, his jaws working lazily on the ever-present chewing gum.

"All right, Adam," he said casually. "Didn't realize you were getting out today."

"Matron kicked me out." Adam looked around the prison, frowning. "Where is everyone?"

Mouthwash shrugged. "Probably preparing for the show. You coming back to our room?"

Adam nodded, and followed his friend into the building. As his eyes adjusted to the change in the light, he suddenly realized that they weren't alone. The hallway and the staircase were jammed with inmates lined up next to one another. At the sight of Adam, the crowd burst into a riotous cheer and began clapping and whooping so loudly it felt like the whole building was trembling.

"Here he is!" Mouthwash called out. "Three cheers for Adam! Hip hip!"

"HOORAY!" the crowd shouted back.

"Hip hip!"

"HOORAY!"

"Hip hip!"

"HOORAY!"

Adam was too dumbfounded to react. Everyone was here: his friends from the dormitory at the front of the crowd, leading the cheers; Jessica, smiling with secret pride halfway up the staircase; even Scarecrow and Jonkers were whistling appreciatively as they leaned over the first-floor bannister.

As the ovation continued, members of the crowd surged forward to shake Adam's hand and clap him on the back.

"Well done, mate. . ."

"We love you, Adam!"

"You legend! That'll teach Pitty!"

Adam was sinking beneath a tidal wave of good wishes, the press of the crowd threatening to knock him off his feet. A protective arm wrapped around his shoulders, propping him up.

"Give him a bit of room!" Doughnut called out. "He's only just out of the sick room, for Chrissakes!"

Grumbling, the crowd obeyed, shuffling backwards. Adam gave his friend a bewildered look.

"This is unbelievable! Did you organize this?"

204

Doughnut shook his head. "Wasn't our idea. It was his."

Adam was amazed to see Major X step forward from the crowd, his cap wedged under his arm.

"Only right we paid our respects," the sandy-haired boy said. "I know we've not always seen eye to eye, but everyone owes you a debt for putting Pitt under lock and key. I hope this means that we can bury the hatchet."

The boy extended his hand. Adam stared at it for a second, and then shook it with a broad grin. The crowd cheered again.

"Not sure I deserve all this," Adam said. "All I did was get punched."

"You took those punches for all of us," the Major said seriously. "I won't forget it."

With a crisp salute, he organized the Tally-Hoers into a bodyguard around Adam, shielding him from the press of the crowd as he walked up the stairs with his friends and back to their dormitory, where Doughnut firmly closed the door behind them.

"Welcome back, mate," he said, with a twinkling smile.

If Adam thought that his hero's welcome would be the end of the matter, he was in for a shock. In the space of a week, he had become the most famous person on the Dial. Inmates queued up to sit next to him at mealtimes, eagerly offering him extra portions of their food. Pretty girls circled around him like vultures, drenched in perfume, staring balefully at one another as they vied for his attention. The first time Adam tried to play Bucketball, his opponents refused to tackle him, forcing him to leave the field out of sheer embarrassment.

Having spent the previous months of his sentence as an anonymous sidekick of Doughnut's, he was utterly unprepared for this newfound popularity. Perhaps he should have basked in the attention; instead he found it suffocating. Like an escapee trapped in a guard's spotlight, Adam fled, making for the quieter parts of the prison where he could talk with his friends in peace.

One afternoon he was enjoying a cup of cocoa in the library with Bookworm when the door crashed open and a large figure strode through the gloom. It was Corbett, a black look etched across his face. Adam instinctively shrank back in his seat, but Corbett stopped several paces away, muttering something under his breath.

Adam leaned forward in his chair. "Sorry?"

"I *said*," Corbett replied, in a louder voice, "that the Major is overseeing the dress rehearsal for the show tomorrow, and he wants to know whether you'd meet him there."

"Um, yeah. Of course."

"Right. Don't keep him waiting, then."

Corbett walked away without another word. As the Tally-Hoer slammed the library door behind him, Bookworm chuckled. "It appears that there's still one person in this prison who doesn't think you're the bee's knees."

"You know what the weird thing is?" Adam said thoughtfully, cradling his mug of cocoa. "I kind of like him for it."

He finished off the dregs with a slurp and hurried over to the theatre. He found the stage swamped in competing musical acts, elbowing one another out of the way as they fought for rehearsal space. As Adam looked on, a chorus line of dancing girls crashed into a pair of scene-shifters, sending all of them toppling to the floorboards beneath a giant cardboard cut-out of a tree.

Corbett was leaning over the grand piano by the side of the stage, talking to Jessica as she slowly picked out notes with her index finger. Adam recognized the melody at once: it was the song she'd been playing when he'd tried to kiss her. When she shook her head in response to a question, Corbett slammed his fist down on the piano and stormed away past Adam.

"You can have her," the Tally-Hoer snarled. "I'm sick of the bloody tease."

Startled, Adam hurried over to Jessica.

"Are you all right?" he asked.

She smiled at the sight of him and nodded quickly. "I think Corbett's got the message – finally. It's nice that I've got the Dial's new hero looking out for me, though."

Adam laughed ruefully. "Don't believe the hype. I don't. You seen Major X?"

"He's backstage, looking even more self-important than usual," Jessica replied, playing a mocking trill on the piano.

"Thanks – I'll see you later."

If anything, the chaos was even worse behind the

scenes. Inmates hared backwards and forwards, clutching sequinned costumes and props; music sheets and spangly batons; juggling pins and magic cabinets. Major X stood in the shadow of the wings, his arms clasped behind his back. He shook Adam's hand warmly.

"Glad you could make it."

"No problem," Adam replied. "What's going on?"

"There was something I thought you might want to see. Follow me."

With a furtive glance left and right, the Major led Adam out of sight from the assorted acts to the edge of the wings, where two Tally-Hoers were leaning idly against the stage. At the sight of Major X, they snapped to attention and stepped to one side, allowing the small boy to drop down to the floor and prise off the wooden panel behind them. He gestured at Adam to join him; as Adam crouched down and peered into the dusty darkness beneath the stage, he saw that someone had knocked a gaping hole through the brickwork where the stage ran up against the right-hand wall of the theatre. A pulley system of ropes ran through the hole and into the pitch-black space beyond. In the distance, he could hear the faint sound of trowels digging into the earth.

"There's a blocked-up chimney that runs down the right-hand wall," the Major explained softly. "From here our men can climb all the way down to the bottom and start tunnelling out there."

Adam let out a low whistle. "Sounds like a big job."

Major X nodded. "The rest of the Tally-Ho thought I was crazy at first – it doesn't make sense, trying to start a tunnel up near the roof. It's taken us five summer shows to dig it, and we've nearly been sprung a few times. But now we're only inches from breaking through to the outside. Tomorrow night – after the interval, while all the guards are watching the show – we're making a break for it."

Adam got back to his feet, brushing the dust from his knees. "Good luck with that, Major. Do you want me to keep watch for you or something?"

"Keep watch?" Major X laughed. "I want you to come with us."

Chapter Twenty-Five

Adam gazed blankly at the Major. "What did you say?"

"I asked you whether you wanted to come with us. To escape."

"But I'm not a member of the Tally-Ho!"

Major X clicked his tongue with impatience. "I'm well aware of that, Adam. But if anyone's earned a ticket out of here, it's you."

The strains of "Climb Every Mountain" were floating back from the stage. Adam tossed a feather boa off the back of a chair and sat down, his brow knitted in deliberation. Although he had witnessed other inmates attempting to escape the Dial, the thought of doing it himself had never occurred to him. Yet the idea of breaking out through the prison walls, of taking his first free steps for nearly a year, was undeniably strong.

"Hang on a minute," he said, looking up at the Major. "Say we make it outside. What then? What happens if there's nothing out there?"

"Then we stick it out for as long as we can." The sandy-haired boy knelt down beside Adam. "Don't you see? The warphole is a distraction. Getting home is a distraction. The only thing that matters is getting out of this prison. Every time someone tries to jump the wall – whether they make it or not – the guards become a little less powerful, lose a little bit more of their authority. That's why, as long as there's a Dial, there'll be the Tally-Ho."

"What about my friends?" pressed Adam. "I don't want to leave them behind. Can they come with us?"

Major X shook his head. "It's going to be a difficult enough journey as it is, Adam, and timing's going to be tight. No disrespect, but I don't think Doughnut can even fit into our tunnel."

A freckled face popped out from the wings. "Goon on the prowl!"

"Listen, Adam," the Major said urgently, "whether you come with us or not, we're going tomorrow. Sleep on it and send me word, OK?"

Adam nodded. The boys shook hands, and Adam threaded his way back through the stage, where five different performances were simultaneously reaching a crescendo. Seeing his pensive expression, Jessica stood up from behind the piano and looked as though she was going to call out to him, before changing her mind.

His mind in turmoil, Adam sought the peace and quiet of Doughnut's hiding place on the roof of the prisoners' quarters. As he lay on the warm slates, his thoughts drifted back to Danny. Adam wondered what his friend was up to at that moment – whether he'd found a new school to go to, whether he'd made up with Carey and they were back together. Then, with a pang, Adam remembered that back on Earth not a second had elapsed since his capture. Danny was probably still sitting at the skate park, moodily staring out into space. The thought didn't reassure Adam in the slightest.

He waited until it was dark before he came down from the roof and returned to his dormitory. Doughnut and Mouthwash were sprawled out on their bunks, working their way through a pile of chocolate bars that had been left for Adam by a shrill blonde girl called Shelley, who was proving to be the loudest and most determined of his new admirers.

"Hope you don't mind," Mouthwash said, tossing a wrapper to one side. "We got peckish, and it's not like you're going to run out any time soon."

"Haven't seen you about today," Doughnut added casually. "Word was that Major X was looking for you. What did he want?"

"Nothing," murmured Adam, hurriedly climbing into his bunk. He was still feeling guilty about the Major's offer, and the last thing he wanted to do was tell his friends about it. He turned and faced the wall, but he was still awake long after the lights had gone out and the rest of the dormitory was asleep.

The day of the summer show dawned brightly, with a tangible air of excitement amongst the performers and the audience alike. The inmates were rowdy and restless during roll call, while breakfast was on the verge of descending into a full-on food fight until the guards stepped in. Only Adam stayed quiet, the bags under his eyes visible as he played with his porridge. He knew that he had to give the Major an answer. If he said yes, this could be his last morning on the Dial, the last morning with his friends.

"You going to eat any of that, or you happy stirring it?"

Adam looked up to see Doughnut pointing at his porridge.

"Mmm?"

"Jesus, you've been away with the fairies for a day now. Anything you want to talk about?"

Adam looked around the table – at Mouthwash gabbling through another supersonic flight of fancy, and Paintpot doodling something into a notepad, and back to Doughnut, whose face was shadowed with concern – smiled, and then shook his head.

"No thanks," he said. "It's all right."

After his friends had finished their meals, Adam scrawled a message to Major X on a piece of paper – "Sorry, can't make the show this evening. Good luck" – and passed it to one of the junior Tally-Hoers on his way out. He walked out of the mess hall feeling instantly sunnier.

Adam spent the rest of the day messing about with his friends, watching from the sidelines as a particularly exuberant rumble of Bucketball descended into a mass brawl. That night they joined the crowds milling around outside the theatre. Having only visited the hall during rehearsals, Adam was impressed to see it packed to the rafters with inmates. He didn't need to count heads to see that the entire population of the Dial had turned out. At the back of the auditorium, a row of chairs had been set out upon a raised platform: guest of honour seating for Mr Cooper and his guards. Even Caiman was present, albeit sitting alone in the corner. Adam was sorely tempted to stand up and let everyone know he was a liar and a collaborator – but since there was no way of doing that without blowing Luca's cover, Adam had to bite his tongue. He wondered how Luca was getting on in his room above the infirmary. How long would it be before the granary went up in flames, and a small balloon set off on a perilous journey towards the Commandant's Tower?

Amid a hubbub of excitement, the curtain jerked upwards, revealing a girl standing alone in the centre of the stage. It was Shelley. Adam slid low in his seat, trying to block out the muffled sniggers of his friends as the girl sang "My Heart Will Go On" directly to him. The song seemed to have even more verses than he remembered, and it took an age before Shelley took her bow and an inmate in a magician's cape walked on to the stage with a flourish.

As choirs followed comedians, and ballet dancers gave way to belly dancers, Adam couldn't shake the nagging feeling that something was wrong. He swivelled round in his chair, and looked at the row of guards. They were watching a unicyclist career across the stage with undisguised amusement, nudging one another and whispering. Adam frowned as he spotted an empty chair in the middle of their row. Mr Pitt was missing, unsurprisingly, but he wasn't the only one. . .

Adam nudged Doughnut, who was sucking contentedly on a mint.

"You said that Mr Cooper loves this show, right?" he whispered.

"Yeah – he's always here."

"Well, he's not here now."

"Maybe he got delayed."

"The first half's nearly over!"

"Shh!" someone hissed behind them.

Adam looked again at the empty chair. He stood up.

"Where are you going?" asked Doughnut.

"Need the toilet. Be back in a second."

Shuffling out of his row to a chorus of tuts and grumbles, Adam stole up the aisle and down the staircase leading to the classrooms. As he passed a window, he stopped and looked out over the empty prison, which looked eerily beautiful bathed in the milky moonlight. His ears picked up a stifled cough; looking down into the darkness below, Adam caught sight of a group of uniformed men gathered by the doorway beneath him. There was a low growl as a German shepherd strained on its leash. At the head of the guards, Mr Cooper checked his watch. There was a polite cough next to him.

"Are you sure you don't want us to go up now, sir?"

asked the man with the German shepherd. "Rex is getting a bit reckless."

"Not yet," Mr Cooper replied. "I want to make sure all of the Tally-Ho are in that tunnel before we collar them."

Adam gasped and drew back from the window. He had to warn Major X! Racing back up the stairs, he re-entered the theatre as the unicyclist tumbled from his bike amid a cascade of juggling balls, to howls of laughter from the audience. As the prisoner picked himself up from the floor, there was a generous burst of applause, and the curtain came down for interval.

Adam forced himself to walk backstage as casually as possible, all the while searching out the Major. The Tally-Ho had congregated in a tight huddle, dressed in mining costumes with plastic pickaxes. In the centre of the huddle a tall woman with flowing black hair and a Show White costume towered over them. To Adam's consternation, Major X wasn't among them.

"Hey!" he called out, grabbing Snow White's arm.

Snow White whirled round angrily, revealing the rather disturbing sight of Corbett in a wig and women's clothing, thick red lipstick smeared across his face.

"What?" he snapped.

"Where's the Major?" Adam panted. "I've got to speak to him."

"He's busy," Corbett said meaningfully. "You'll have to wait."

"This can't wait!" Adam hissed. "The goons are on to you – you have to call it off!"

Corbett's face grew grimmer and grimmer as Adam explained. The Tally-Hoer swore under his breath, tapping his foot as he thought.

"Well, that's blown it," he said, glancing around pensively. "The Major's in the tunnel on his own, digging through the last few inches. I'd go and get him, but we're on stage in a minute."

"It's all right," Adam said. "I'll go."

Corbett's brow furrowed with thought. Eventually he nodded. "OK – but don't hang about."

He ushered Adam to the back of the stage and lifted up the wooden panel. Adam got down on to his hands and knees and crawled inside the stage, the panel slotting back into place behind him like a coffin lid. He scrambled over towards the chimney shaft, trying not to sneeze as the dust tickled his nose.

Above Adam's head, there was a tramp of boots upon the stage and then a roar of laughter from the crowd.

"Why, there's seven little chairs here!" Corbett said in a falsetto voice, to more laughter. "Must be seven little children!"

The Tally-Ho had set up a complicated system of ropes and pulleys that ran through the hole in the wall down into the chimney shaft. Adam grabbed hold of the rope and began shimmying down it, hand-over-hand. The rope swayed dangerously as he descended, and he was relieved to get to the bottom of the shaft and feel solid ground beneath his feet.

The tunnel began in the left-hand wall of the chimney base, a dark worm winding through the earth. Adam didn't have time to feel afraid – he clambered inside and began wriggling towards a light flickering up ahead of him. As he crawled, the wooden slats supporting the burrow closed in over his head, and the air became closer. Major X was at the end of the tunnel, working at the earth with a trowel by the light of a candle.

"Major!" Adam called out. "You've got to get out of here! The goons are coming!"

The boy awkwardly shifted round. His face was streaked with mud and sweat. "What? They can't be!"

"Cooper's on his way!" Adam shouted. "We've got to go!"

"Dammit!" cursed the Major, hurling his trowel into the dirt.

They had barely begun their return journey when the wooden slats started to tremble around them. Fragments of earth pattered on Adam's head like raindrops.

"What's going on?" Adam hissed.

"Cave-in!" Major X cried. "Move it!"

Adam scrabbled furiously along the tunnel on his hands and knees, the Major right behind him. The earth was coming down on them more heavily now, clouding the way ahead. Back at the tunnel face, the candle winked out, plunging them into darkness. Caught up in the maelstrom of dirt, Adam crawled blindly onwards, trying to fight the rising tide of panic within him. He couldn't die in this way – buried alive, his body entombed beneath the Dial like some grim fossil.

Then, gloriously, the lip of the tunnel appeared in front of him. The chimney shaft – and safety – was only centimetres away. As the roof of the Tally-Ho's tunnel came down like a guillotine of earth, Adam turned and grabbed the Major's shirt, and dived for freedom.

CHAPTER TWENTY-SIX

Mr Cooper's room was a surprisingly homely study on the second floor of the guards' quarters: the walls covered with bookshelves and black-and-white photographs; the floor muffled in thick carpet; an agreeable clutter of antiques and china plates. The Dial's Chief Warder was standing behind his desk, looking down at the two boys in front of him with an expression that was half amusement and half peevishness.

"Well?" he said finally.

Adam glanced at Major X. Both of them were covered in a grey coating of dust and rubble, but apart from a few cuts and bruises they were unharmed. It had taken the guards over an hour to haul them out of the chimney and out from under the stage. As Adam emerged back into the theatre, he started at the sight of Mr Pitt standing at the back of the hall, his arms folded in triumph. The Assistant Chief Warder was free again. Mr Pitt made no eye contact with the two inmates, but nodded curtly at a couple of guards as they offered him congratulations.

As Adam and the Major were escorted over the walkway, windows lit up across the prisoners' quarters, and there was an eruption of cheers and banging. The shouts were still ringing in their ears as they were led up to Mr Cooper's room and ordered to sit.

Major X cleared his throat. "I take full responsibility for the tunnel, sir. It was my work and my work alone. Adam here must have heard me digging – he didn't know anything about my escape attempt."

"You dug that tunnel all on your own?" Mr Cooper raised an eyebrow. "That would be some achievement, even for an inmate of your renowned industriousness."

"I've had a lot of time on my hands, sir. As I said, the tunnel was my doing and I am prepared to accept the requisite punishment for the act of escaping."

"I'm sure you are," Mr Cooper said wearily. "I'm not surprised to see you here, but I am disappointed to have to speak to you, Wilson. Given your recent experiences, I would have thought that you'd be more careful about observing the prison rules."

"All due respect, sir," Major X cut in, "but what Mr Pitt did to Adam was a stain on the reputations of all the Dial's guards. I can't believe you've let him out."

"What happened with Mr Pitt was extremely regrettable," Mr Cooper said firmly. "He has been given a final warning as to his conduct. I would also remind you that had he not informed me of your plans to escape, who knows what might have happened in that tunnel." His eyes flashed behind his glasses. "And you will speak only when I ask you to, Hawkins."

Adam wasn't sure which he found more surprising: the sudden hardness in Mr Cooper's voice, or the fact Major X had a surname. When the Chief Warder spoke again, his tone was mild once more.

"I can't allow past events to excuse actions in the present. Wilson, you were apprehended in an illegal tunnel in the act of escaping. Though Hawkins is no doubt labouring under the misconception that he is being somehow honourable, I don't believe a word of his story. Are you going to try to persuade me?"

Major X kicked Adam in the side of his foot, urging him to stay silent. He needn't have bothered. Even though Adam hadn't helped plan or dig the tunnel – and had turned down the chance to escape with the Tally-Ho – there was no way he was going to leave the Major to face the music alone now. When all was said and done, they were both prisoners in the same gruesomely unfair regime. They were on the same team.

"No, sir," he said firmly. "If you're going to punish the Major, then you have to punish me too."

Mr Cooper blew out his cheeks with exasperation. He picked up a photograph of two small children from his desk and examined it thoughtfully.

"My boys," he said, proudly showing the photograph. "It's been a long time since I saw them. A couple of hundred years, in fact. But they'll be waiting for me on Earth when I get back, just like your families will be. It doesn't mean I don't miss them both terribly, though. I wouldn't have spent so much time away if I didn't truly believe in the Dial, and the vital lessons it teaches. It's my *duty* to be here, don't you see? I'm not just here to punish you. I'm also here to help you, to teach you, to protect you. You play at escaping but you don't realize that this isn't a game. Aren't you aware how close you were to getting killed tonight? Don't you see that getting caught is the best thing that can happen to you?"

He was greeted with a resounding silence.

"I've had enough of both of you," the Chief Warder said finally, setting down his photograph. "A week each in solitary. And don't let me see you in here again."

The punishment cells were housed in a low, reinforced hut on Wing X: ten tiny rooms linked by a single corridor. Each cell was identical, measuring six small paces by six small paces, with a cot, a hand basin and a bucket, and a barred window high up near the ceiling. The walls were covered in scratches – tallies of days previous prisoners had spent locked up. Running his fingers over the indentations, Adam imagined the inmates who had been here before him: their histories of stubborn dissent and daring escape attempts, fights and backchat; brave, unrepentant children who paced and raged their way through their punishment. Inspired, Adam settled down to take his incarceration without complaint.

But as one day crawled silently into the next, Adam's resolution waned, and he soon found himself wishing that he'd followed the Major's lead and denied that the tunnel had had anything to do with him. His only human contact came twice a day, when a guard appeared at his door to give him a plate of food and exchange his bucket. No matter how much Adam cajoled or goaded him, the guard remained tight-lipped. Adam wasn't sure if there was anyone else locked up besides him and the Major, until one night the hut was shaken by a piercing howl from a nearby cell. Adam heard guards hurry down the corridor; bolts were drawn back and voices raised, then the dreadful silence folded back over his head.

Time quickly lost meaning. Adam stopped bothering to wash, preferring to curl up in his cot and watch the shafts of sunlight as they crept up his walls. It was a shock when his cell door finally opened and a guard beckoned him outside. Adam stumbled into the corridor, light-headed with the sudden movement. Three doors down he saw Major X appearing from his cell, stretching airily and shaking hands with his guard. The Tally-Hoer looked like he had spent a restful weekend in a hotel. He nodded at Adam.

"Morning," he said. "Enjoy your stay at the Chateau Stir?"

Adam stared at him dully, startled by the first words said to him for over a week. He allowed the Major to propel him gently along the corridor and out into the morning sunlight.

"Keep it together," Major X murmured in his ear. "At

least while the goons are watching us. Don't give them the satisfaction of looking like they've got to you."

"Easy for you to say," Adam replied. "That was awful. I don't know how you put up with it."

"I've had a lot of practice. The first time is always the worst – not that it ever becomes a laugh riot, if you get my meaning." As they passed a guard standing watch at the Wing X walkway gate, the Major laughed loudly and clapped Adam on the back. "Quite right – the food *is* better in there. We should get caught more often!"

Across the Dial, the rest of the inmates were standing in ranks on the exercise yard for roll call. To Adam's relief, he was allowed to head straight back to the prisoners' quarters. He returned to his dormitory to find a piece of paper tucked under his pillow, with a brief message penned in a florid hand:

Chapel. 1500 hrs. Come alone.

That afternoon, Adam slipped out of his dormitory and walked across to the chapel, where Luca D'Annunzio was sitting at the right-hand side of the back pew, thoughtfully scratching his neck beneath the bandages. He grinned as Adam approached.

"I hear you've been up to mischief again. At this rate you're going to become as infamous as me."

Adam shrugged and took a seat beside him. "It's going to take more than a week in solitary. What's up?"

225

"I've hit a snag," said Luca, dropping his voice to a whisper. "I had an accident with one of the gas canisters – dropped it while I was making some last-minute adjustments to my balloon. Unless I can replace the stupid thing, I won't be flying anywhere, and I'm running out of time before the big day."

"I'm sorry to hear that, Luca – but I don't know what I can do to help. I've no idea where the guards keep gas canisters."

"No, I didn't think you would," he replied. "But you know a man who does."

Adam sat back in the pew. "Ah. I get it."

"D'you think if we go and have a word with your pal Doughnut, you can persuade him to help me?"

"I'm not sure," Adam said slowly. "He's not your biggest fan."

"Well, I'm all out of options," Luca replied, rising to his feet. "Let's hope he's in a good mood."

They went to each of Doughnut's favourite haunts in turn, but the fixer was nowhere to be found. In desperation, Adam led Luca down to the laundry room beneath the prisoners' quarters, where the air was clouded with steam and soapy suds ebbed across the tiled floor. Two inmates were working away at a mangle, sweat dripping down their foreheads as they fed sheets through the machine. Doughnut was reclining like a Roman emperor across a pile of laundry bags, flicking through a comic.

Adam frowned. "What are you doing down here?"

Doughnut jerked his head at the mangle. "Got told to do the weekly laundry by Mr Pitt. He's even meaner than he was before he got locked up. And this is taking bloody ages, I tell you." He called over to the inmates at the mangle, "Why don't you guys take a break? You can finish the rest of the sheets later. I'll have your magazines for you next week."

The two boys nodded gratefully, and trudged out of the laundry. When they had shut the door, Doughnut got to his feet, his manner immediately businesslike.

"What's up?"

Adam nodded at Luca. "My friend here wants to ask you something."

The fixer carefully scrutinized the bandaged boy. "I've seen you around a few times, haven't I? Don't think I know your name, though."

"Probably not," he replied calmly, offering his hand. "Luca D'Annunzio. Pleased to meet you."

Doughnut face froze. "This some kind of joke?"

Adam shook his head slowly.

"But he escaped! On the *Quisling*! Years ago!"

"Twenty-two, to be precise," Luca interjected. "Only I didn't escape."

Doughnut's eyes looked in danger of popping out of their sockets. "You've been hiding on the Dial all this time?"

"Yup. The first decade was a bit slow, but after that things picked up."

The fixer folded his arms. "Whatever you've been up to, I don't want anything to do with a collaborator."

"You've got it all wrong, Doughnut!" Adam burst out. "Luca's innocent!"

He leapt into his story, telling his friend how he had tracked Luca down. At first the fixer seemed unconvinced, but when Luca took up the tale, outlining how Caiman had betrayed him, eventually Doughnut came round.

"I still can't believe it," he murmured, scrutinizing the swathes of bandages. "You had us all fooled."

"It wasn't that big a deal," Luca said modestly.

"I saw you at Caiman's court martial," Doughnut said suddenly. "You must have been annoyed when Adam and I got him off."

Luca shook his head. "I was pleased. I don't want to see anyone who's innocent being found guilty." He paused. "Now, if they court-martial him for betraying me, that'd be a different matter."

"I've said a lot of bad things about you over the years," Doughnut confessed. "Especially to Adam."

Luca nodded. "You weren't the only one." He offered his hand again. "No hard feelings?"

With a smile, Doughnut warmly shook the other boy's hand. "No hard feelings. Now, what can I do for you?"

The fixer listened quietly to Luca's story, then plumped himself back down on the laundry bags, his face creased in thought.

"Gas canisters. . ." he mused. "Now, the Docking Port

would be the natural place to look, but security there has got so tight we'd be bound to get caught, and there's no point checking the guards' pantry. . ." Doughnut punched a fist into his palm. "Got it! There's a storeroom upstairs where the guards keep all sorts of junk. Last time I had a search round there, I'm pretty sure I saw a couple of canisters. It's worth a look, at any rate."

"Upstairs?" Adam said excitedly. "Brilliant – let's go now!"

Doughnut shook his head. "It's not quite as simple as that, my friend. The storeroom's on the fourth floor."

"The fourth floor?" asked Luca. "But that's in the girls' dormitories! How are we supposed to get in there?"

Doughnut looked him thoughtfully up and down. "What size are you?"

Luca gave Adam a baffled glance.

CHAPTER TWENTY-SEVEN

"No way," Adam said firmly, folding his arms. "Not a hope in hell."

He was standing in a reading room deep in the bowels of the library, amid stacks of frayed and tatty books in desperate need of repair. A bookshelf in the corner had been pulled out, revealing two of Doughnut's large boxes, which were now spilling their contents on to the floor. The fixer had surfaced from the depths of one of the boxes with a triumphant smile on his face, and was holding up a blouse and matching woollen skirt.

"You should be grateful I've got something in your size," he said. "There aren't many girls as tall as you."

Adam shook his head. "This is insane. The guards'll spot us a mile off."

"They won't, you know," said Luca. He had already changed into a dark blue girls' uniform, and was now selecting a long, dark wig from the pile on the floor. "It'll be dark, and they won't be looking. Who's going to try to break *into* the prisoners' quarters?"

"If the guards don't spot us, the girls will," Adam maintained. "We're going to look like idiots!"

"I don't know what you're complaining about," Doughnut said mildly. "Corbett was dressed up as Snow White the other day, and no one had a problem with that."

"Corbett was taking part in a show, not a top-secret mission!" Adam retorted. "And he didn't look much like a girl to me. I still don't understand why we don't ask Paint-pot to get the canister for us."

"She's getting out in a few days," Doughnut said firmly. "Do you want her to risk getting caught? The goons would extend her sentence for sure."

"The fewer people who know about this the better," Luca added, adjusting his wig in the mirror. "The three of us is more than enough." He turned round to Adam, straightening his skirt. "How do I look?"

"Do you really want me to answer that?"

He thought about it for a second. "No," he said finally. "Probably best not."

In fact, Luca looked surprisingly convincing, and even Doughnut made a passable impression of a girl – if not the most graceful one. But as Adam struggled into his uniform and an ill-fitting blonde wig, he knew that he was going to stand out like a sore thumb. The shoes were the worst. Even the largest pair Doughnut could find pinched horribly at Adam's feet, and the small heels made him feel like he was on a set of stilts. Luca watched with undisguised amusement as Adam tottered about the storeroom.

"Not the prettiest girl I've ever seen, but you'll do," he

231

declared, glancing at his watch. "Dinner time will be over soon. We'd better get a move on."

The boys stashed their own clothes in the corner, then repacked Doughnut's boxes and emerged from the storeroom. Bookworm was sitting behind his desk at the reception, leafing through a large leather-bound book. He started at the sight of them; then a smile broke out across his face.

"Not a word," Doughnut warned. The librarian looked down at his book, his hurried cough failing to disguise a snigger.

They slipped out of the library and into the night. With every step Adam expected the sirens to explode into life and the spotlight to pin them down. He wasn't sure what he feared more – the humiliation of being caught dressed like this, or the punishment that was certain to follow.

The walkway seemed to take an age to come round to the library's wing, and when it did Adam was dismayed to see Scarecrow and Jonkers loitering on the island in the centre of the chasm.

"That's all we need," he said.

"Piece of cake," Doughnut murmured. "Just act natural."

Easier said than done, Adam thought to himself. He kept his head down as they crossed the walkway, praying that he wouldn't trip over on his heels. Thankfully Scarecrow and Jonkers were engaged in a sniping argument with each other and didn't give them a second glance.

"Told you," said Doughnut.

They had walked on several paces when there came

a high-pitched wolf-whistle from behind them. Luca pirouetted around and waved coquettishly at Scarecrow and Jonkers, who were now watching with smiles on their faces. The two boys nudged each other, laughing.

"What the hell are you doing?" Adam hissed.

"Got to give my fans what they want," Luca replied, his eyes twinkling. "You're just jealous."

Adam shook his head in disbelief. Luca had come out of hiding after all this time, risking everything – and he was treating it like a game in the playground!

They had timed their run to reach the dormitories just after dinner, when the inmates would be returning en masse from the mess hall. Following Luca's lead, Adam fell into the ranks, convinced that every giggle and laugh was aimed at him. He was glad that his long blonde wig covered his face, which he could feel burning with embarrassment.

As the boys splintered off along the lower two floors, Adam saw the hard-faced Miss Roderick standing guard at the staircase leading up to the girls' quarters. He shuffled forward in the queue, trying to avoid her gaze. Luca and Doughnut slipped past her – but as Adam put his foot on the first step, the guard cried out:

"What do we have here?"

Adam's heart missed a beat as Miss Roderick dived into the crowd towards him, only for her to haul the girl next to him to one side, grabbing a necklace from around her throat.

"Thought I wouldn't notice, did you?" she gloated.

"This isn't a school disco – you can't wear jewellery here. Give that to me."

The girl's protests followed Adam as he scurried up the stairs, unable to believe his luck. They were in. He caught up with Luca and Doughnut and followed them along the third floor corridor, slowly taking in the unfamiliar surroundings. Although the girls' dormitories had the same layout as the boys', they felt like a different world. No impromptu games of football cluttered up the hallways, and the mushroom clouds of sweat and farts that polluted the air in the boys' dormitories had been replaced by faint wafts of perfume. Through the open doors, Adam saw girls sitting on the beds, brushing each other's hair as they chatted.

"Turn right up ahead," Doughnut muttered.

Adam gave him a questioning glance. "How do you know your way around here, anyway?"

"This isn't the first time I've done this," Doughnut replied, his eyes warily scanning the hallway.

"No kidding!" Luca exclaimed, bounding around the corner. "You're a dark horse, and no—!"

There was a startled cry as he collided into another girl, nearly knocking her to the ground. It was Jessica.

"Sorry," Luca squeaked.

"What are you. . .?"

Jessica trailed off as she looked at Luca's face. Her eyes widened with alarm. Adam leapt forward and grabbed her arm.

"It's OK, Jessica!" he whispered. "It's me!"

"Adam!" she gasped. "What on earth are you doing?"

Adam put a finger over his lips. "No time to explain," he whispered. "Don't say anything, OK?'

"But—!"

Before she could say any more, a firm hand grabbed Adam by the arm and dragged him away. Over his shoulder, he saw that Jessica remained motionless in the corridor, frozen with surprise.

"Let's not hang around," Doughnut hissed. "You can talk to your girlfriend tomorrow."

"She's not my girlfriend!"

"But you'd like her to be, eh?" Luca asked slyly.

"I knew this was a bad idea," the fixer muttered to himself. "I might as well walk over to the punishment cells and hand myself in now."

Glumly, he led them onwards through the warren, up another flight of stairs and across the fourth floor. Towards the rear of the building, they came across a battered storeroom door built into the side of a staircase.

"This is the one," Doughnut said. "Keep watch while I open it."

Feigning casualness, Luca and Adam took up positions on either side of the fixer as he dropped to his knees and began jiggling a wire in the lock. It was deathly quiet – a sudden scream of laughter from the floor below made Adam's heart leap into his mouth.

There was a muted click, and Doughnut pushed the door open.

"Nicely done," Luca said admiringly.

"I may not be as pretty as you, but I've got my uses," Doughnut replied, tucking the wire back into his belt. "Let's get the canister and get out of here."

The dingy storeroom was piled high with all sort of bric-a-brac: planks of wood, rusty toolkits and lengths of copper wire. Rooting through the mess, the fixer came up with a metal cylinder, and gave his companions the thumbs up. They locked the storeroom behind them and hastened back down through the levels.

As they were nearing the third floor staircase that led back to the boys' quarters, a gaggle of girls appeared in the opposite direction, nodding supportively as a familiar voice complained loudly.

"If you ask me, Adam Wilson's got a little too big for his boots," Shelley griped. "All I've done for him, and he still ignores me! It's not like he's even that good-looking. I might get together with Corbett instead. He's a real man."

As her friends chimed in supportively, Doughnut quickly shifted the canister behind his back, and Adam silently cursed his luck. Their only escape route lay beyond the girls. He dropped back behind his friends, his eyes fixed on the floor. As Shelley approached, he turned his back slightly towards her – only to catch his heel in a knot in the floorboard and stumble over.

There was a loud rending sound, and the back of his skirt split open, revealing a pair of very grey – and very unfeminine – shorts.

236

Doughnut gulped. "That's torn it."

Shelley stopped; stared; then opened her mouth and screamed.

Immediately the corridor descended into chaos. Everyone turned at once, and saw Adam scramble to his feet and sprint down the corridor after Doughnut and Luca, his shoes forgotten and his wig slipping from his head. As other screams joined Shelley's, Miss Roderick came thundering after them, a second female guard hot on her heels.

"You there!" she screeched. "Halt!"

The boys raced away, pursued by several piercing blasts on a whistle.

"Forget the exit!" Luca shouted. "This way!"

The entire floor had come alive, prisoners dashing out of their rooms to gasp and giggle at the commotion. Luca ran pell-mell down the corridor, bouncing off girls like a pinball. He reached the end of the corridor and hauled open a window, then clambered on to a drainpipe running down the outside wall. Doughnut followed, handing him the gas canister before swinging down after him. As sirens began wailing across the Dial, Adam glanced over his shoulder and saw Miss Roderick struggling to get through the packed corridor. He suddenly realized that this wasn't by chance: the girls were helping them.

Gritting his teeth, Adam reached out of the window and clutched the drainpipe, clinging on to the cold metal as his feet dangled in the air. Beneath him, Luca had shinned down to the boys' floor and was pushing up a window.

Adam waited for Doughnut to disappear inside after him and then went hand-over-hand down the drainpipe, alert to the spotlights humming into life in the watchtowers. He nearly lost his footing a couple of times before he reached the safety of the window and tumbled into a dark and empty room. Luca slammed the window shut and dived to the ground, seconds before a searchlight swept across the back wall of the room.

Adam lay very still, his chest heaving with exertion.

"That was too close," he panted.

The dazed silence was broken by the sound of Luca bursting into laughter.

"It's not funny!" Adam protested. "We were *this* close to getting caught!"

"Not funny?" Luca wheezed. "That was the funniest thing I've seen in years! Your face!"

As Doughnut spluttered with amusement, Adam couldn't help joining in. The three boys rolled around the floor, weeping with laughter, celebrating with the gas canister as though it were a pricelsss gold trophy.

CHAPTER TWENTY-EIGHT

Following the raid on the girls' floor, the prisoners' quarters were placed in lockdown – the Wing II gate was bolted shut, and searches declared in all the dormitories. The boys hurriedly threw their girls' clothes into a sack and changed back into uniform, Luca looking faintly comical in Doughnut's oversize spares. With the sack under one arm and the gas canister under the other, Luca was hustled down to the cellar, where Doughnut hid him in the secret tunnel behind the chest. In under ten minutes, Adam and the fixer were back in their dormitory, trying to catch their breath as they laid out pieces on the chessboard.

It didn't take long for the guards to arrive, with Mr Harker a weary presence at their rear. As his men began rifling through cupboards and looking under beds, the affable guard plumped himself down next to Doughnut.

"Evening, lads," he said. "Take it you've heard about the ruckus in the girls' quarters?"

They nodded.

"And I also take it that it's got nothing to do with you?"

They nodded again.

"I thought as much," sighed Mr Harker. "So it's just another mess that Mr Pitt will blame me for. Sometimes I wonder why I bother, I really do."

Not for the first time, Adam felt a small pang of sympathy for Mr Harker as he and his men trudged empty-handed into the next dormitory.

Careful not to arouse suspicion, Adam and Doughnut carried on playing chess for another couple of hours, chatting lazily to their roommates. Eventually a siren signalled the end of lockdown, and the inmates were free to move around again. When Adam stole back to the cellar to let Luca out of the tunnel, he was surprised to find the boy had re-covered his face in bandages.

"I always keep a spare supply on me," he explained, stretching stiffly. "Never know when you might need to hide your face."

"You think of everything, don't you?" Adam said admiringly. "Lockdown's over, and most of the guards have gone back to their quarters, so you should be all right getting out of here. What about the canister?"

Luca grinned. "That's where Doughnut's clothes come in handy," he said, rolling up a voluminous trouser leg and strapping the canister to his calf with another length of bandages. "I could smuggle an elephant out of here in these things."

He firmly tied off the bandages and rolled down his trouser leg, which fell shapelessly around the canister, masking it from view. "Might have to walk with a bit of a limp, but that's the advantage of the bandages. No one questions an injury."

"You're the expert," said Adam. "Ready?"

He nodded. "Thanks for helping me, Adam. You and Doughnut. I couldn't have done this without you two."

"Don't worry about it," Adam replied. "It was nothing."

"No, it wasn't, and I appreciate it. Friends like you make me think twice. . ." He trailed off.

"About what? Escaping?" Adam laughed. "Don't stay here for us, mate."

Luca looked away. "Yes, of course," he said quickly. "I was just being silly."

They walked stealthily out of the cellar and up to the ground floor, which had regained an air of calm following the evening's excitement. Near the front exit, Adam asked softly:

"So now that you've got what you need, when are you going?"

"Soon," Luca replied. "You'll know, believe me."

He patted Adam on the arm, turned on his heel and marched purposefully past the guards and out of the prisoners' quarters.

Though he should have felt triumphant at the successful theft of the canister, something about his exchange with Luca had troubled Adam. He couldn't escape the suspicion that there was more going on than met the eye, and that the other boy was hiding something. The next day, Adam roamed restlessly around the Dial, trying not to think about balloons and explosives and escape plans, refusing to let his gaze wander to the top floor of the infirmary. But by evening time, Adam's patience had snapped, and he was crossing the walkway to Wing VIII. Thankfully it was Nurse Waters sitting behind the reception desk. Her face lit up as he approached.

"I need to visit a friend," Adam whispered. "Matron's not about, is she?"

The nurse shook her head conspiratorially. "Coast's clear – she's been summoned to the guards' quarters. Best hurry, though."

"Thanks," said Adam. "I owe you one."

He hurried up to the top of the staircase and pushed through the swing doors into the Infectious Diseases and Hysteria Ward. The room was cloaked in darkness; not a murmur or a stir greeted his entrance. Adam tiptoed through into the next room, shivering at the instant, eerie drop in temperature.

He was about to slip through the curtain around the far bed when there was a movement in the darkness, and suddenly he realized he wasn't alone.

"Luca?"

A hand snaked out from the gloom, grabbing his arm. Startled, Adam tried to pull away, only to find himself face to face with the sallow features of Echo.

"Get out of here!" the boy hissed.

Adam stared at him in amazement.

"Didn't you hear me? Go! You've been betrayed!"

Before Adam could reply, footsteps loomed on the staircase outside. Echo swore, then grabbed Adam with surprising strength and bundled him down to the floor, rolling the pair of them beneath the bed opposite Luca's hiding place. The door to the ward flew open, and a pair of feet marched in. They beat a tread that Adam had learned to fear above any other, whether it was devouring the gravel of the exercise yard, striding across the walkway, or hungrily pacing the mess hall. His heart sank.

"Keep up, Matron!" Mr Pitt said briskly, marching into the ward.

"I'm doing my best!" the woman panted.

From his hiding place beneath the bed, Adam saw a pair of gleaming leather boots stride past inches from his face, followed by a worn blue pair of women's shoes.

"Wait down here," Mr Pitt ordered. "This won't take long."

Adam heard the creak of bedsprings as the warder climbed on to the bed directly beneath Luca's attic. Part of him wondered whether he should rush out to try and stop the warder, but Echo caught the look in Adam's eye and shook his head silently.

"Not now," he mouthed.

There was a rattle as Mr Pitt opened the hatch up to Luca's attic and the rope ladder tumbled down. Adam heard

Luca cry out – there came a series of thumps and muffled shouts, and then a loud crash as a heavy weight hit the ward floor. It was followed by a more measured creak of the rope ladder as someone descended it.

"Get up, D'Annunzio," said Mr Pitt. "It's not that far a drop."

There was a faint groan in response.

"Do you have any idea," the guard continued conversationally, "how often I've dreamt of this moment? I genuinely thought you'd outwitted me – that you'd worked out my and Caiman's little trap and hotfooted it away on the *Quisling*. Escaping on my watch! Every night for an entire year, I went to sleep with a smile on my face imagining you back in my grasp. Every morning, I woke up, heavy-hearted, with the realization that your throat was out of reach of my fingers. Not any more, sonny. Not any more."

"Thought you were so smart, didn't you?" crowed Matron. "Hiding away in your little cubbyhole, wrapping up your face in bandages? Well, it turns out Mr Pitt's smarter."

There was a short pause as Luca considered his response.

"Shove it up your arse," he muttered.

As Matron screeched with indignation, Adam heard Mr Pitt haul Luca up and deliver a series of methodical slaps to his face.

"You. Will. Not. Speak. Like. That. To. A. Lady!" the guard barked.

"Hit me all you want!" Luca shouted back. "Stick me in solitary for a year – I don't care! Whatever cell you put me in, I'll get out eventually, and then I'll trap us all here in no-time! Just you wait and see!"

"Solitary?" Mr Pitt repeated, in a mock-quizzical voice. "Who said anything about that?"

"But you're not just going to let me go free."

"Oh, no," Mr Pitt laughed. "There's no telling who you might talk to. If Mr Cooper finds out that I encouraged Caiman to betray you, he's certain to fire me. And I like the Dial. I like taking you miserable traitors and reminding you what worthless wretches you are. I like it when you cry. So I thought that we might take a little trip down to the Re-education Wing. After all, if anyone needs re-educating, it's you, D'Annunzio. I'd imagine that, with such a tricky case as yours, we might have to turn the machinery all the way up – not just make you forget the Dial, but wipe your mind completely. Leave it as clean as one of Matron's bedsheets."

Luca gasped. "You can't do that!"

"Really? Who's going to stop me? The only people in this prison who know that you weren't on that wretched airship are in this room. Are you going to tell anyone, Matron?"

"Not a living soul," she replied.

"No!" Luca howled. "Help me! Someone help me!"

Mr Pitt cleared his throat. "Matron?"

Luca yelled with pain, and then there was a thud as he slumped to the floor once more.

"That shot should keep him quiet," Matron said, with husky satisfaction.

"Good girl," Mr Pitt replied. "Take him to the ground floor. I'll follow you down in a minute."

The burly woman grunted with effort, and there was a soft sliding sound as Luca was dragged across the floorboards. The sight of the boy's glazed eyes chilled Adam to the core.

Mr Pitt waited until Matron had left the ward, tapping a steel toecap impatiently on the floor. One minute passed, and then another. Adam frowned. What was he waiting for?

His answer came when the guard said: "You can come out now." Adam stiffened, convinced for one terrible second that Mr Pitt was talking to him. Then the swing doors at the end of the ward creaked open, and soft footfalls crept through the shadows. Mr Pitt emitted a rasping chuckle.

"Even in a prison full of traitors, you take the biscuit," he told the newcomer. "Is there anyone you wouldn't sell out? Still, I can't deny your efficiency. First you lead me straight to the Tally-Ho's tunnel, and now you've handed me Luca D'Annunzio on a plate. Never let it be said that Mr Pitt doesn't keep his word. You'll be out of here on the next flight, free to return to whatever miserable existence you lead on Earth. No one here will ever be the wiser. Does that sound good to you?"

Adam held his breath, waiting for the traitor to reply.

"Perfect," said Jessica.

CHAPTER TWENTY-NINE

At the sound of her voice, all the certainties in Adam's world shattered. Jessica was the traitor? The girl he had fallen for, the girl he had kissed, the girl who had saved him when a knife had been at his throat, had all this time been an informant, selling out inmates for her own freedom?

"I thought I'd seen it all," Mr Pitt marvelled. "But you, girl, are a Judas and no mistake."

"It wasn't that difficult," said Jessica calmly. "The Tally-Ho are just little boys playing at escaping. All I had to do was bat my eyelashes at Corbett and he was putty in my hands. He'd have told me Major X wears a bra if he thought it would impress me. He was also amazingly careless when it came to handling top-secret plans – especially those describing tunnels beneath theatres. It's a miracle the Tally-Ho managed to get as far as they did."

"But D'Annunzio," Mr Pitt said admiringly. "Now that was another matter entirely. How did you find out he was still on the Dial?"

There was a pause. When Jessica spoke again, her voice had lost some of its certainty. "That was by coincidence.

I ran into Luca in the girls' dormitories – I wouldn't have recognized him if I hadn't seen a picture one of Adam's friends had drawn of him. When I realized who he was, I stayed up by my window and waited until I saw him walking back to the infirmary. Luca's so cocky, he didn't expect anyone to follow him. He led me straight back to his hideout."

"You're a treasure, my girl!" Mr Pitt barked. "A dirty piece of gold. One of Wilson's friends, you say? Don't suppose he was involved too, was he?"

"I brought you Luca," replied Jessica, with a note of defiance. "You didn't say anything about Adam."

"Come, come," said Mr Pitt. "Let's not sour the evening. You don't want me changing my mind now, do you? There's always room for you alongside D'Annunzio in the Re-education Wing."

"Please, sir, no! I'm sorry if I sounded ungrateful."

"That's the spirit. The next time the *Quisling* is scheduled to fly, I'll make sure you're on it. We can arrange for you to make a daring escape of your own back on Earth. In the meantime, I trust I can rely on your discretion?"

"Of course, sir." Jessica hesitated. "There's just one more thing."

"Spit it out then, girl. I've got a mind to wipe."

"It's just . . . all these years we've spent copying out the *Betrayals* in class. All the guards are in there apart from you. Why is that, sir?"

Mr Pitt snorted with laughter. "Of course I'm not in there! No one would ever *dare* betray me!"

"But that's impossible!" said Jessica. "How did you find out about the Dial?"

"Back on Earth that idiot Harker used to be one of my teachers. Even at that age, he was scared of me. One time I stole his briefcase and found a letter from the Dial inside it. I cornered Harker and made him tell me all about it. Instantly I knew I had found my home: a proper prison, with good honest sentences for dishonest little rats. So I waited, every now and again writing to Harker to make sure we stayed in touch. I think the old coot thought I genuinely liked him. Then, when the time was right, I made up some cock-and-bull story that I'd also been betrayed, and had Harker vouch for me with Cooper. He didn't take much convincing. Finding guards to work here is ten times harder than finding prisoners. People have grown soft and weak. They whimper about 'cruelty' and 'human rights'; they don't understand the need for rigour and discipline. But I do. I understand it very well indeed."

There was a long pause, and then Jessica said quietly: "Oh. I see."

"Glad to hear it," snapped Mr Pitt. "Now scram."

Adam heard Jessica walk away, and the swing doors creak open.

"Hold on a minute," the guard rapped suddenly. "You say you ran into D'Annunzio in the girls' dormitories. Miss Roderick's reports said that he had two accomplices. Did you catch their faces too?"

There was a pause.

249

"No – just Luca's," Jessica replied levelly, and pushed her way through the doors.

With a hoarse chuckle of triumph, Mr Pitt followed her out of the ward. Echo waited until the guard's footsteps had died away before rolling out from beneath the bed. Adam followed suit, feeling sick to the pit of his stomach.

"I can't believe it," he said faintly. "I can't believe she did that."

"A traitor on the Dial?" mocked Echo. "Who'd have thought it?"

Adam gave the boy a sharp glance. "What are you doing here? Why did you save me?"

Echo shrugged, pushing his glasses up his nose. "I didn't come here to save you – but you blundering around was going to get us all caught. I came here to save Luca."

"Why?"

"Why do you think? He's my brother."

Adam's jaw dropped. "*You're* Nino D'Annunzio?"

"The one and only."

"You're lying!" Adam protested. "You're the guards' pet! Everyone hates you!"

"A necessary price to pay," Echo retorted. "For our plan to work, no one could know the truth about me."

"What plan? You and Luca don't even talk to each other!"

"We didn't – for a long time. But we are brothers, after all. And we found there was one thing we could agree on: this place. We made up the morning Luca was supposed to escape with Caiman. That's why he called it off – he didn't want to go without me. All those years, he waited for me to finish my sentence! Can you believe that? So when I was through, I repaid the favour. I stayed on the Dial and got a job with the guards so I could warn Luca if they came sniffing around while he was finishing the balloon – and so I could steal some proper food for him."

Adam thought back to the night in the guards' pantry, when he had become angry watching Echo stuffing his pockets with chocolate bars. They had been for Luca! And his first meeting with Luca in the chapel, when the Collaborator had left minutes before the guards had caught Corbett tunnelling. Adam had thought Echo's message had been aimed at him – as with so many other things on the Dial, he had been wrong.

"It worked like a charm," Echo said proudly. "No one suspected a thing. Our plan was set to come into operation tonight." His face fell. "And then Jessica ruined everything."

"You have to help me!" Adam urged. "We've got to stop Pitt before he wipes Luca's mind!"

"Easier said than done," Echo replied grimly. "He'll be halfway to the Re-education Wing already, and even I don't have a key for that gate."

Adam perched on the end of the nearest bed, his face etched with thought. He glanced up at Echo.

"What did Luca mean earlier – when he told Mr Pitt he was going to trap everyone in no-time?"

Echo looked uncomfortable. "Look, I know what Luca told you about our plan, but he wasn't being entirely truthful. He wasn't going to use the Volcano Chilli to blow up the granary. He was going to blow up the Commandant's Tower."

Adam gasped. "But if the warphole machine was destroyed we'd be trapped here for ever! Why would he do that?"

"To put an end to this. The way Luca sees it, we're all traitors one way or another: me, you, Mr Cooper. How come it's only us who get punished? Even if we *could* escape, tomorrow there'll be another shipload of kids arriving for more centuries of punishment." Echo's voice hardened. "Either all of us escape, or none of us do. One way or another, this has to stop. The Dial has to be closed down."

Adam couldn't believe his ears. All this time, he had been unwittingly helping Luca in his attempt to trap every-one in no-time! Had Luca gone mad? Wasn't a three-hundred-year sentence enough? Wasn't there enough misery and despair on the Dial as it was, without stripping the prisoners of their one and only hope – that someday they might be set free, and be allowed to return home? Though it hurt Adam to admit it, maybe it had been for the best that Luca had been caught, and kept away from the warphole machine. . .

"That's it!" Adam cried, scrambling to his feet. "If we can open the warphole, that'll shut off the Dial's power.

Mr Pitt won't be able to turn on the machines in the Re-education Wing then."

"And how are you planning on getting into the Commandant's Tower?" enquired Echo. "Knock politely on his door and see if he'll let you in?"

"I'll go the same way Luca was planning to. Come on!"

Adam raced over to the hatch above the bed and scrambled up the rope ladder into Luca's attic. The room bore the scars of recent battle – a desk had been overturned, and the floor was strewn with torn plans. But as Adam crept through the door and out on to the balcony, he saw that Luca's patchwork balloon had been inflated and was still moored to the side of the building, bobbing proudly in the air, sheltered from view by the slanting infirmary roof.

As Adam scrambled inside the crate beneath the balloon, Echo gave the home-made contraption a dubious appraisal.

"You really think you can fly that thing?"

"What choice have I got?" Adam called out over the roar of the burner. "There isn't time to try anything else."

"Watch out for the Volcano Chilli!" Echo warned. "Luca wouldn't have set off without it."

Looking down by his feet, Adam saw that a bulky sack had been stored in a corner of the crate. It had to be the explosive. In a typically mischievous move, Luca had drawn a large smiley face on the fabric.

"Thanks!" Adam called back. "What are you going to do now?"

"Get back to the radio station," Echo replied through cupped hands. "If you can't stop Mr Pitt, maybe Mr Cooper can. Good luck!"

The boy cast off the guide rope, and with a sickening lurch the balloon wobbled into the air. Caught by surprise, Adam had to grab on to the side of the crate to stop himself from toppling out of the basket. He tugged on the burner, and the balloon rose higher. For the first time, Adam became aware of the incredibly dangerous nature of his journey. For all the months that Luca had laboured building the balloon, he had never been able to test it properly. If the burner failed, if a rope snapped or a seam tore, if the crate cracked under Adam's weight, it was a long, long way down to the ground. Even if the balloon held, there was no guarantee that Adam could wrestle it in the right direction – he could be swept out over no-time, condemned to float above the wilderness until the gas canisters ran out and he crashed to the earth. As the wooden slats beneath his feet creaked painfully, Adam felt his mouth go dry with apprehension.

At least some parts of Luca's scheme were going to plan. No one noticed the small craft as it floated past the radio station and through the darkness on the other side of the prison, bursts of flame hiccupping from its burner. A strong gust caught hold of the balloon as it passed over the punishment cells, propelling it further north. The Commandant's quarters loomed increasingly large in the foreground. As he remembered the detailed plans of air currents littering Luca's attic, Adam felt a newfound surge of respect for Luca. He had predicted that the prevailing currents would take the balloon in the right direction, and he had been dead right. Adam's confidence was growing now: the whistling of the wind through his hair felt exhilarating, not threatening, and he had to stop himself from whooping with glee.

But as the balloon maintained its collision course with the tower, a new thought made him falter. Reaching the tower was all very well, but how was Adam supposed to get inside? At this rate, all he was going to do was crash straight into it. A crosswind caught the balloon, sending it floating past the left edge of the tower. With a jolt Adam realized that the nearest window had been flung wide open, and a shadowy figure was standing watching him.

The Commandant.

The silhouette held out a hand and gestured at Adam to throw the mooring rope to him. Adam hesitated, paralysed by indecision. There was no way of knowing whether he could trust the Commandant – but if he floated past the tower, Luca was a dead man. Taking a deep breath, Adam picked up the coiled mooring rope and hurled it over to the window. The Commandant caught it smoothly, and began powerfully pulling the rope towards the window. Adam had to cling on to a guide rope as the balloon veered sharply towards the tower, until the crate was nearly touching the stone window ledge. The Commandant disappeared into the darkened room, and the mooring rope went taut as he fixed it to something.

Gritting his teeth, Adam wrapped a hand around the guide rope and stuck a leg out of the crate and on to the ledge, slowly shifting his weight towards the safety of the window. As he tried to bridge the gap, another gust of wind caught the balloon, and for a horrifying second Adam felt the crate slipping away from him, but then a strong hand reached out from the tower and pulled him through the window.

Adam tumbled to the floor, thankful to feel solid ground beneath him. As he lay on his back, panting, there was a small whoosh of flame as a gas lamp was lit, casting a wavering light over the room.

"All right, mate?" a familiar voice asked.

Adam's eyes snapped open.

CHAPTER THIRTY

Through the suffocating layer of drugs pressing down on his mind, Luca D'Annunzio was dimly aware of being marched across the Dial's walkway. The prison was engulfed in noise, sirens pounding his skull, shouts raining down from the perimeter wall. There were people on either side of him, roughly pulling him along by his arms. They came to a halt by a heavily padlocked gate – there was a jingle of keys as it was unlocked. The gate swung open, revealing a squat windowless building beyond.

Though he was too dazed to comprehend what was happening, something about the structure sent a nameless shiver of dread down Luca's spine. As he passed underneath the gate sign marked "Wing XII – Re-education Wing", Luca's head began to swim, and he was grateful when the blackness enveloped him once more.

"*Danny?*" gasped Adam.

It seemed impossible, but somehow his best friend was standing in front of him, wearing his favourite jeans and baggy T-shirt, his dark hair cropped short as usual, and the same slight smile playing on his lips that appeared every time Danny knew something Adam didn't.

"Hello, Adam," he said.

"You're the Commandant?"

"Looks that way, doesn't it?"

"But that's impossible!" Adam stammered. "You can't be!"

Danny raised an eyebrow. "Sure about that?"

"But this doesn't make any sense," said Adam, slowly picking himself off the floor. "You set up all of this just to get back at me?"

"Partly."

"What about everyone else? Doughnut, Luca, the Tally-Ho? They didn't do anything to you. Why are they being punished?"

"If they were here, they wouldn't be seeing me. They'd be seeing the person they betrayed. Only you see me like this, Adam."

"But this is your prison. You're the reason why we're all here."

"You've got it the wrong way round," Danny replied, with a shake of the head. "Sure, it's my prison. I built it myself, so long ago that if I told you when it'd make your head spin just thinking about it. But only traitors get sent to the Dial, Adam. If you hadn't betrayed me, you'd still be on Earth now. I only opened the gates. You're the ones who walked inside."

"Yeah?" Adam retorted. "And who put you in charge?"

"Did anyone need to? There are traitors, so there's a

Dial. It's necessary. Or do you think people should just be allowed to get away with it?"

"But it's not fair!" Adam protested. "Lots of people do bad stuff – liars and robbers and murderers. Why don't you kidnap them too?"

"How do you know that I don't?" Danny said sharply. "No-time's a big place, Adam. You don't think there's not room for another Dial here? You don't think there's room for another *thousand*?"

As the boy's voice dropped to a hiss, the hairs on Adam's arms rose in warning. He reminded himself that it wasn't his friend standing there in front of him, but a powerful potential enemy. And Adam was here for a reason. As he scanned the room for the warphole controls, his gaze settled on a large machine by the far wall, its nozzle pointing directly towards a set of bay windows. The Commandant followed his gaze with interest.

"Maybe we should catch up another time," he said. "After all, you're running out of time to save Luca."

So the Commandant had known all along. Of course he had. He appeared to know everything. But did that mean that he was going to stand aside and let Adam turn on the warphole machine? In Danny's frame, the Commandant was several inches taller than he was, and much broader across the shoulders. And if he fought like Danny did, Adam didn't stand a chance.

"Are you going to try to stop me?" Adam asked, his heart pounding.

The Commandant studied Adam's face intently for a moment before seemingly reaching a decision. Then he stepped to one side and gestured invitingly towards the warphole machine.

"Be my guest," he said.

A hand was slapping Luca's cheek.

"Wakey, wakey, D'Annunzio!" Mr Pitt said pleasantly. "You won't want to sleep through this."

Luca stirred reluctantly, shying away from the powerful light burrowing into his eyes. He tried to sit up, but there were leather straps digging into his wrists and ankles, pinning him to a chair. Through half-closed eyelids, he saw that Matron was fixing wires to his forehead, pinching his skin with metal clips. Somewhere beyond the deadened senses in his mind, a voice was warning Luca that he was in desperate trouble and needed to fight his way free, but so faintly that he could barely hear it.

Mr Pitt walked over to the small machine wired up to Luca's head and began adjusting the dials on a control panel.

"How much power are you going to use?" asked Matron.

"Quarter power is usually enough to remove memories of the Dial." The guard's monocle gleamed. "So I thought I'd turn everything up to full."

"Quite right too, Mr Pitt," Matron agreed. "Can't be too careful with a troublemaker like this."

Mr Pitt flicked a row of switches on the machine, bringing forth a high-pitched noise that shivered around the Re-education Wing. Resting his hand on a lever, the guard smiled thinly at Luca.

"No. . ." Luca mumbled. "Please . . . no. . ."

"Sweet dreams," hissed Mr Pitt, and pulled down the lever.

Adam ran over to the bay window and threw open the shutters, sending a gust of night air into the room. There were no complicated controls on the warphole machine – just a steel wheel. But no matter how hard he tried to turn it, the wheel stuck fast. The Commandant looked on emotionlessly, his hands clasped behind his back. Adam knew better than to ask for help.

Throwing his jacket to the floor, Adam adopted a bracing stance and grabbed hold of the wheel again. Gritting his teeth, he pulled with all his might, every muscle in his arms straining with the effort. He cried out as the wheel gave – suddenly it was spinning freely, and the warphole control began to hum. Adam spun faster and faster, ignoring his aching arms, completely focused on the whirling wheel.

The hum grew louder and louder, until it felt like a swarm of bees had flooded into the room, and then a dazzling beam of light shot out from the nozzle of the warphole control, arrowing straight up into the night sky. The blast sent Adam sprawling to the ground; shielding his eyes, he watched as the air around the beam rippled and writhed, and then the warphole sparked into nebulous life above the prison, fiery tendrils creeping across the sky, and the Dial fell abruptly, gloriously, into darkness.

Mr Pitt howled with rage as the lights went out in the Re-education Wing and the machines around Luca died.

"What's happening?" wailed Matron.

"They must have switched the warphole on!" Mr Pitt replied. "Damn it to hell!"

There was a loud crash: something thrown against the wall. Luca was too woozy to feel any sort of triumph. Somewhere in the pitch-black, a loudspeaker crackled into life.

"Attention! Attention!" Echo's voice rang out around the room. "Emergency at the Re-education Wing! Illegal mind wipe in progress! All guards to Wing XII! Repeat: all guards to Wing XII!"

"Mr Pitt!" screeched Matron. "The little brat's set the guards on to us! How are we going to explain this?"

"For pity's sake, woman, keep it down!" snapped Mr Pitt. "I'm thinking!"

"Let's leave the boy and get out of here," Matron said, in an imploring tone. "If the warphole's open, we could go back to Earth!"

Mr Pitt laughed hoarsely. "Whoever said anything about 'we'?"

There was a thud, and a woman's weak moan of distress.

Luca felt a draught of stale cigarette smoke in his face. He flinched.

"Maybe you think you've won, D'Annunzio, but this isn't over," a voice hissed in his ear. "I'll be waiting for you when you get out."

Footsteps moved away through the darkness, and a door creaked open as Mr Pitt strode out of the Re-education Wing, leaving an acrid aftertaste of smoke lingering in his wake.

From his vantage point at the tower window, Adam watched as the Dial's guards responded to Echo's alarm, hurrying down from the perimeter wall and congregating by the nearest wing gate. But the walkway was already moving, the two giant stone hands sliding into place outside Wings XII and I. A figure hurriedly opened the gate outside the Re-education Wing and strode stiffly in the direction of the Docking Port.

"Looks like you did it," the Commandant remarked. "Judging by the hastiness of Mr Pitt's exit."

Adam was still straining at the wheel of the warphole machine, only now he was trying to turn it in the opposite direction and shut it off. But in his efforts to save Luca, he appeared to have jammed the mechanism completely. There was no shifting the wheel this time.

"I think it may be broken," the Commandant said evenly.

"You have to do something!" cried Adam. "You can't

just let Mr Pitt get away with this! He's not even a proper guard – he lied about being betrayed!"

"I know."

Adam stared at him in disbelief. "You *knew*? Then why did you let him come here?"

"Maybe I was waiting for a prisoner with the will and the heart to expose Mr Pitt. A prisoner who displayed sufficient bravery and loyalty to make me question whether the Dial needs to stay open at all." A faint smile played on the Commandant's lips. "After all, no-time is an eternity, even for me."

"Then help me stop him!" urged Adam.

The Commandant shook his head. "You asked me to stand aside earlier. The rest is up to you, I'm afraid." He paused. "Where are you going?"

"To get my balloon," Adam replied, moving back towards the window. "If you're not going to do anything, I will."

"You think you can steer it down to the Docking Port before Mr Pitt escapes?"

"I don't know. But I've got to do something."

"I suppose you could go that way," the Commandant said. "However, it might be easier if you took the corridor."

Adam stopped in his tracks. "What corridor?"

"The one that runs from here to the Re-education Wing. If you hurry, you can follow Mr Pitt across the walkway to the Docking Port." A reflective look crossed the Commandant's face. "Of course, there's always another option. The warphole's open. The guards are occupied with Mr Pitt. You could use your balloon to go back to Earth, if you wanted. You know I won't stop you."

Adam glanced up at the warphole, which was pulsating invitingly only metres from the tower. He couldn't deny the powerful tug of the thought of leaving the chaos and the confusion behind him, the sirens and the gunfire and Mr Pitt and the figure standing in front of him – who was his best friend and at the same time something completely alien and unimaginably powerful. Adam had spent months dreaming of returning home, to his family and his friends, to the blissful monotony of school lessons and television programmes and summer holiday lie-ins. And now that dream was within his reach.

"No." Adam's voice rang around the tower. "I'm not leaving my friends behind."

The Commandant nodded. "Fair enough. Take the lamp with you. I wouldn't want you tripping in the dark."

"Thanks." As he reached up and unhooked the lamp from the wall, Adam glanced back at the Commandant. "Listen, if there's any way you can speak to Danny somehow, tell him I'm sorry. I never said it at the time, but I am. Really sorry."

"I know you are," the Commandant replied. "And he does too. I promise you that."

"Good," Adam said uncertainly. "I hope so."

The other boy's face broke into a grin, and at that moment Adam was certain he was talking to his best friend.

"What are you waiting for – a hug?" Danny urged. "Go and stop Mr Pitt!"

Adam nodded fiercely, then ran out of the room. Halfway down the tower, a corridor branched off from the staircase, leading directly into the Re-education Wing. Taking a deep breath, Adam plunged down the passageway.

CHAPTER THIRTY-ONE

Adam came out on to a small semicircular platform high up on the wall of the Re-education Wing. From here the Commandant would have had a bird's-eye view of the departing prisoners as their minds were sieved for memories of his prison. Swinging the gas lamp in a wide arc around him, Adam saw that the room below was laid out like a dentist's surgery – a single chair in the middle of a white tiled floor, surrounded by squat machines. Luca D'Annunzio was strapped into the chair, his head lolling to one side.

A set of steps curved along the wall from the platform to the floor; on reaching the bottom, Adam nearly tripped over the slumped figure of Matron. She groaned pitifully as Adam ran past her and over to the chair.

"Luca!" he cried out, wrenching the straps from around the boy's wrists and ankles. "Are you OK?"

Luca stirred, groggily clutching his forehead. "Yeah, I think so," he mumbled. "Where's Pitt gone?"

"He's making a run for the *Quisling*."

"Then what are you waiting for? Go after him."

"What about you?"

"Don't worry about me," Luca said, hauling himself out of the chair. "Don't let Pitt get away!"

He pushed Adam towards the door. After a brief hesitation, Adam pressed the gas lamp into Luca's hands and slipped outside, where the warphole was still shining brightly in the sky like a second moon. Although the power was down around the prison, Adam could see candles flickering in the windows of the prisoners' quarters, the red glow picking out faces pressed up against the glass. There was no sign of Mr Pitt. Adam leapt up on to the walkway and hurried towards the Docking Port.

He had reached the island in the centre of the chasm when a sharp report, like the crack of a whip, made him falter. Glancing to his left, Adam saw a detachment of guards had lined up by the gates of the prisoners' quarters, and were aiming their rifles at him. They must have thought he was trying to escape!

"Stay where you are, inmate!" a loudhailer shouted. "Put your hands up!"

Adam looked over to Wing I, and back at the waiting guards. If he hesitated much longer, then Mr Pitt would be in the air and no one would be able to catch him. There wasn't time to explain. Whispering a quick prayer under his breath, Adam slowly raised his hands in the air – and then bolted towards the Docking Port.

There a shout of alarm, and then a bullet whizzed over his head. Adam ran on, his heart pounding violently in his chest. He was aware of the loudhailer shouting at him to stop, and then another bullet flying past his nose, and one biting into the frame of the Wing I gate. Then Adam was jumping down from the walkway – grateful that the power outage had dimmed the searchlights – and scrambling into the shelter of the Docking Port.

He slammed the door behind him and leaned against it for a second, catching his breath. The registration area was cloaked in darkness, and at first Adam thought it was empty. Then he made out the form of a guard sprawled in the shadows. Clearly Mr Pitt hadn't had time to explain either. Looking down at the unconscious man, Adam was reminded why he was pursuing the Assistant Chief Warder: the beatings and the persecution, the bullying and the cruelty, Luca sitting senseless in a chair, seconds away from having his mind wiped. . . There was no way Adam could let this man escape. Roused by a cold thirst for revenge, he rushed through the registration area and back out into the fresh air.

The *Quisling* cut an ominous outline on the landing strip. The zeppelin's engines were already throbbing, severed mooring ropes scattered across the tarmac. As Adam sprinted over to the airship, it began to lift slowly off the ground. Coming alongside the gondola, Adam saw that one of the lounge windows was open – he reached up and grabbed the sides of the window as the *Quisling* rose higher into the air. For a second his feet were off the ground and he was dangling dangerously in the air. Then, summoning the last vestiges of his strength, Adam hauled himself through the window.

The lounge of the *Quisling* had been restored to its former glory, the slanting windows boasting new panes of glass, the plush armchairs re-stuffed and re-covered, bottles of spirits glinting temptingly along the circular bar once more. This room had been the scene for Adam's first meeting with Mr Pitt. It felt like a lifetime ago. Mr Pitt wasn't in the room now, of course – there was only one place he could be.

Taking a deep breath, Adam strode over to the Control Room door and pulled it open.

Doughnut and his roommates watched, faces glued to the dormitory window, as the *Quisling* struggled into the air. Since the warphole had exploded into life, the Dial had been in a state of complete chaos, the mayhem only compounded by Echo's alarm and the sudden take-off of the Dial's only zeppelin.

"What the hell's going on out there?" Doughnut murmured.

"Search me," replied Mouthwash. "The *Quisling*'s not meant to be flying tonight. I reckon someone's making a break for it."

"The guards had better stop them, then," an unwelcome voice chimed in. The pandemonium had even managed to drag Caiman out of his bunk to join them by the window. He squinted through the glass. "If the *Quisling* goes, none of us will ever get out. Why don't they just shoot it down?"

270

"And risk blowing up our only airship?" Doughnut gave Caiman a scornful look. "How would we get out then? Give each other a leg-up to the warphole?"

"Well, someone had better think of something quickly," Mouthwash said nervously, watching the zeppelin as it stuttered towards the swirling vortex. "If the *Quisling* goes back to Earth we're stuck here too."

The boys jumped as one as the dormitory door crashed open and Corbett's head jutted into the room.

"Evening, lads," he growled.

"All right, Corbett," said Doughnut. "Any idea what's going on?"

"Bits and pieces," the Tally-Hoer replied. "The guards are taking potshots at anything that moves. Word is that Pitt has just stolen the *Quisling*. There's something else that Major X thought you boys should know. Some nutter of an inmate just went for a run over to the Docking Port after Pitt and nearly got turned into Swiss cheese by the guards."

"Really?" exclaimed Mouthwash. "Wonder who that was?"

"Who d'you think?" Doughnut replied grimly, looking pointedly in the direction of Adam's empty bed.

Whereas normally the *Quisling*'s cockpit would have been busy with navigators, now there was only Mr Pitt scurrying around the cabin, shuttling between instruments like a stiff-backed spider as he attempted to pilot the giant zeppelin on his own. Wisps of smoke were rising from a cigarette in an ashtray balanced on the dashboard. Through the window, the Dial was slipping from view as the zeppelin continued to rise.

At the sound of the Control Room door sliding open, Mr Pitt glanced up from an altimeter.

"Wilson!" he said, through clenched teeth. "What a pleasant surprise. Anything I can do for you?"

"Go back to the Dial," Adam replied. "Land this thing."

Mr Pitt shook his head. "This flight is going directly to Earth. No unscheduled stops."

"Not if I can help it," said Adam, swallowing nervously.

The guard stepped away from the altimeter, amusement etched across his face. "Are you trying to threaten me, Wilson? Haven't I taught you enough lessons in that department? If you've got a single ounce of sense in that skull of yours you'll shut up and let me pilot this ship out of here. Maybe when we get back to Earth I'll even let you live."

"We're not going back to Earth," Adam maintained. "We're going back to the Dial."

"So be it." Mr Pitt briskly unbuttoned his shirt cuffs and rolled up his sleeves. "If you want to return to the Dial so much, I'll help you," he snarled. "I'll throw you out of the flaming window!"

Mr Pitt lunged towards him, hands outstretched, fingers twitching in their desire to grasp Adam's throat. Adam ducked instinctively, driving his shoulder into Mr Pitt's midriff. The guard grunted as the air was knocked from his lungs, and the two of them staggered backwards into the dashboard. Adam heard a click, and then a pained creak from the aft of the airship as the *Quisling*'s rudders swung to one side. The zeppelin veered sharply back towards the Dial, sending both Adam and Mr Pitt stumbling to the floor.

With a snarl, the guard fastened his fingers around Adam's neck and began to squeeze. Adam tried to break free, but the grip around his throat was mercilessly strong. Mr Pitt's pressed his face up close to Adam's, his filmy left eye glinting with triumph behind its monocle.

"I always knew I'd be the last thing you ever saw," he spat.

Adam's lungs were pleading for air, dark spots exploding in front of his vision. As light-headedness threatened to overwhelm him, his left hand reached up to the dashboard and scrabbled frantically for some kind of weapon. His fingers closed upon a heavy circular object: Mr Pitt's ashtray. With a last, agonizing effort, Adam grasped the ashtray and brought it down hard on the guard's head.

Mr Pitt howled with pain, his hands springing free from Adam's throat. The guard clutched at his head, which was covered in ash, discarded cigarette butts and a streak of blood. Adam rolled away, wheezing for breath. Through tears of pain, he saw a large black handle built into the dashboard. He dived over to it and jerked the handle down as far as it would go, dipping the front of the *Quisling* and sending it nose-diving towards the prison below.

"What are you doing, you fool?" Mr Pitt screamed. "You'll kill us both!"

Adam wasn't listening. His gaze was fixed on the window. The Commandant's Tower was looming larger and larger before them, until it filled the view, and he could make out each individual tile on the roof and brick in the wall. Numbly, Adam realized that he was going to die. Thoughts of his family flashed through his mind, and Danny, and his friends on the Dial, and – unexpectedly – of Jessica.

Then the *Quisling* ploughed straight into the Commandant's Tower, and there was no time to think about anything any more.

CHAPTER THIRTY-TWO

The airship shuddered as it crumpled into the tower, and there was a deafening boom as one of the fuel tanks exploded. As the aft of the *Quisling* was swallowed up in flames, the cabin sloped sickeningly upwards until it was almost vertical. Adam clung on to the handle on the dashboard, watching Mr Pitt go rolling across the floor. They had only seconds before the airship crashed to the ground.

As he looked desperately around him, through the cabin window Adam caught a glimpse of something bobbing outside. It was Luca's balloon, still attached to the side of the Commandant's Tower. There was a chance – a slim one, but a chance all the same – that he could reach the balloon through the hatch in the Control Room floor.

Adam let go of the handle and slid down to the hatch. His trembling fingers struggled to undo the catch, and it took an age to spring the hatch open. The *Quisling* was sinking past the tower – if he was going to jump, he had to do it now.

A hand fastened around Adam's leg.

To his horror, he saw that Mr Pitt had clawed his

way back over to him, murderous intent in his eyes. Any thought of escape and survival seemed to have vanished from the guard's mind. Adam cried out and shook his leg free. Before Mr Pitt could come at him again, the airship rocked violently, sending the guard sprawling backwards.

Adam didn't think twice. Pulling himself through the hatch, he leapt out of the *Quisling*. The second he was in the air seemed to stretch out for hours, the wind whipping by him – and then his right hand latched on to a guide rope, and there was a tremendous tug on his arms as his plummet was brought to an abrupt halt. His legs flailing in the air, Adam grabbed hold of the basket with his other hand and pulled himself inside the balloon.

Breathless, he looked up to see the *Quisling* sliding past him in a fiery free fall. Over the roar of the burning airship, Adam heard a rage-filled scream – the final cry of Mr Pitt, as the zeppelin hurtled to the ground and buried him in flames.

With gunfire crackling across the Dial and the *Quisling* fleeing in the direction of the warphole, Mr Cooper swung into action, quickly declaring an emergency roll call. The inmates surged across the walkway towards the exercise yard, urged on by the guards' loudhailers. The elder children took care of the younger ones, who were pale and shaking at the chaos.

Once the prisoners' quarters had been emptied, the

walkway swung round from wing to wing, collecting everyone else from the prison: guards recalled from their watchtowers; nurses helping the patients out of the infirmary; even a grumbling Bookworm, torn from his beloved library. Before long there were several hundred people milling about in the exercise yard, guard and inmate alike staring pensively at the warphole, united in their unspoken fears.

Doughnut was trying to find Adam amongst the crowd when a commotion in the corner of the yard caught his eye. A circle of inmates had gathered around Corbett, who was standing menacingly over another boy lying on the ground, with Major X an interested spectator on the edge of the circle. As Doughnut pushed his way forward he saw that the boy on the ground was Echo. In the confusion, no one had noticed the announcer slink nervously into the yard – and now the guards were too distracted by the *Quisling* to step in and save him. Doughnut groaned. A fight was the last thing anyone needed.

Echo cowered as Corbett kicked a shower of gravel over him. "Not so high and mighty now, you little suck-up," growled the Tally-Hoer. He looked over to Major X. "This runt needs a lesson, boss. Permission to teach him?"

A weary voice answered before the Major could open his mouth.

"Leave my brother alone," said Luca D'Annunzio, pushing into the centre of the circle. "He's not what you think."

"*Luca?*" gasped Major X.

"Your brother?" gasped Doughnut.

Corbett merely stared, his jaw dangling open. He was too stunned to stop Luca hauling Nino to his feet. Side by side, it was just possible to see the family resemblance, even if it was little more than a shared gleam in their eyes.

"Someone had better tell me what's going on here, and fast," rapped Major X.

"Pitt finally lost it," Luca replied. "He tried to wipe my mind in the Re-education Wing. Adam stopped him by turning on the warphole, and then he went after him."

Major X looked over towards the fixer. "Did you know about this – that Luca was still here?"

Doughnut nodded. "Only found out recently. It took me a while to get my head round it too. But Luca's on the level, so I'm guessing Echo is too."

"One thing's for sure," said Luca, "we won't get anywhere fighting amongst ourselves. We need to—"

He was interrupted by the throbbing of zeppelin engines. The *Quisling* had abruptly changed course, and was cutting through the sky like a shark back towards the prison. Straight towards the Commandant's Tower.

"It needs to pull up!" Mr Cooper shouted. "Pull up!"

The *Quisling* ploughed into the tower, causing shrieks of panic amongst the children. As the airship went up in flames, the inmates turned to one another, fearful questions trembling on their lips.

Doughnut's face went pale. "Adam!" he whispered.

*

Adam hauled himself out of Luca's home-made balloon and through the window of the Commandant's Tower, still not quite able to believe that he was alive. By rights, he should have consigned with Mr Pitt to the pyre of the *Quisling*, which was burning furiously at the base of the perimeter wall.

He wasn't safe yet, though. Already the temperature was rising inside the tower, and Adam could hear flames crackling across the roof. The Commandant was looking out through the bay windows up at the warphole, his form flickering like a television screen as it shifted from one victim to another – one moment a young girl, the next an old man, the next a teenager with a wounded expression. He stood motionless, hands clasped calmly behind his back, apparently unmoved by either his constant transformations or the fire now clawing at the edges of the window frame.

"Come on!" Adam cried, grabbing the Commandant's arm. "The Volcano Chilli is still in my balloon! If that catches fire the whole tower's going to explode!"

The Commandant nodded. "So be it," he said calmly. "I cannot leave."

"Are you crazy? If you stay you'll die!"

The Commandant changed shape once more, reverting to Danny and this time holding the form. Carefully but firmly, Danny removed Adam's hand from his arm.

"You need to get out of here, mate," he said. "It won't be long before Luca's explosives go up."

279

"And then he'll get his wish, won't he?" Adam said bitterly. "The warphole machine will be destroyed and we'll all be trapped in no-time."

"Maybe," replied Danny. "Don't be too hard on Luca, though. He could have got out of here years ago, remember? But he didn't. He stayed behind for his brother, and wanted to blow up the warphole machine because he cared more about the freedom of future prisoners than his own. Not bad going for a collaborator, if you ask me."

Things slowly began to fall into place inside Adam's head. "That's why you let him hide away all these years, wasn't it?" he asked. "You wanted him to do something right!"

Danny shrugged. "Everyone deserves a second chance, I reckon. Look at you. You could have left Luca and been back on Earth by now, but you're still here. That's loyalty. That should be worth something."

"It won't be worth anything when the warphole closes," Adam said quietly.

"Don't be so sure. Luca may have been wrong about a few things, but he was right about one. Maybe I can help bring a dream of his true."

Before Adam could ask him what he meant, Danny gave the vortex a critical glance. "Enough talking," he said. "Time for you to go."

"Go? Go where?"

"So many bloody questions!" exclaimed Danny, exasperated. "Just get downstairs and leave the rest to me, eh?"

"OK," Adam said dubiously, "but are you sure you won't—?"

"GO!" Danny roared. "And don't leave anyone behind!"

Adam raced out of the room and down the stairs, with a final glance back at the Commandant, who quietly closed the door behind him as the first sparks of flame spat on to the carpet by his feet.

When the *Quisling* ploughed into the Commandant's Tower, there were cries of dismay in the exercise yard. Several of the younger children burst into tears; even the guards looked shocked.

Doughnut saw that a couple of the guards were remonstrating with Mr Cooper, jabbing fingers in the direction of the Commandant's Tower.

"We have to put the fire out now!" one shouted.

Mr Cooper shook his head. "Too dangerous," he said. "It's already an inferno up there. Anyone trying to put out the fire will only get themselves burnt to a cinder."

"But if the warphole control goes up we're all stuck here!" the other guard yelled, hysteria creeping into his voice.

The Chief Warder folded his arms. "I said no – and I'm the only person in this prison with the key to that wing, remember? We're in the hands of the Commandant now. Trust in him. I do."

One of the older prisoners elbowed his way forward and jabbed a finger at Mr Cooper.

"It's all Pitt's fault!" he yelled. "And you goons call *us* traitors!"

As the crowd descended into squabbles and recriminations, fingers levelling against one another, Luca and Nino D'Annunzio trudged away and slumped down on one of the benches. After a minute or so a figure appeared out of the darkness and took a seat beside the brothers.

"You two OK?" asked Doughnut.

"We should be," Luca murmured. "This is what we wanted. It's just. . ." He gestured at the bickering, bewildered throng in the yard. "All these years we've been telling each other that we were ready to be stuck here in no-time – we didn't really think about them."

"Be careful what you wish for," Nino added gloomily.

Luca stared at the Commandant's Tower, which was blazing like a beacon. "I never wanted Adam to get caught up in this. Do you really think he was on the *Quisling*?"

Doughnut shrugged. "Hope not," he said. "For his sake."

The boys lapsed into an uneasy silence, listening to the soundtrack of crackling flames wafting across the prison.

"Come on," Doughnut said eventually. "We're not doing any good feeling sorry for ourselves. Let's go look round the Dial, see if we can find Adam."

Luca was about to reply when he felt the bench shiver beneath him.

"Did you feel that?" he asked.

Nino frowned. "Feel what?"

The bench shivered again, more insistently this time, and a deep rumble emanated from the belly of the Dial.

Doughnut scrambled to his feet. "What the—?"

The rest of the inmates and the guards were backing away from the centre of the yard, which was now churning and rolling like a storm-tossed ocean. Suddenly a giant stone outcrop erupted from the ground in a shower of gravel, shooting up into the sky, knocking everyone in the yard off their feet. It was a hollow, drain-like cylinder formed entirely from rock, which thundered upwards over the prison at a sharp angle, rising over the chasm and the Docking Port and continuing onwards all the way up to the warphole. By the time it had come to a shuddering rest, it had formed a slanting covered passageway that led from the yard to the heart of the vortex.

Doughnut's jaw dropped open. "What *is* that?"

"A sky tunnel!" Luca yelled, grabbing the fixer's arm. "It's my sky tunnel!"

CHAPTER THIRTY-THREE

The inmates crowded around the mouth of the tunnel, their faces bathed in wonder as they peered inside. The passageway was smooth, the incline gentle enough to be climbed without steps.

"Incredible," Luca whispered, reaching up to touch the rocky surface. "He's given us a way home."

Nino scratched his head. "Who has?"

"The Commandant, dozy!" laughed Luca. "You think anyone else could do this?"

As the unexpected possibility of leaving the Dial sank in, the prisoners turned and eyed the guards uneasily. It was all very well a tunnel appearing in front of their eyes, but would they be allowed to use it? When a bold inmate placed a foot inside the tunnel, one of the guards hesitantly raised his rifle in warning. The tension in the yard rose, fingers tightening upon triggers.

Then a loud clap of the hands interrupted the stand-off, and Mr Cooper stepped forward.

"What are you waiting for?" he boomed. "Everyone line up in ranks of four! No pushing! Children before adults!"

Doughnut blinked. "You're going to let us out?"

"Of course I'm letting you out!" Mr Cooper replied. "You were brought here to be a taught a lesson – not killed, or trapped for ever."

The fixer nodded towards the tunnel. "Are you sure it's safe?"

"Only one way to find out." It was Major X who replied, pushing forward to the front of the throng. "If anyone knows about tunnels, it's me. Tally-Ho?"

His men snapped to attention behind him, saluting sharply.

"Give us two minutes to see if we can get to the top safely and then follow us up," the Major said to Mr Cooper, straightening his cap. "See you on the other side."

Taking a firm step forward, the leader of the Tally-Ho led his men up the tunnel towards the warphole, the tread of their marching feet falling smartly in time with the rhythm of his echoing cries of "Left, right, left, right!", until the Major's voice faded and then disappeared completely.

Back in the yard, Mouthwash gave Doughnut a bewildered look. "Am I dreaming? Are we getting out?"

"Looks that way," said Doughnut. "But I won't believe it till we're back on Earth."

With the Tally-Ho seemingly safely through the warphole, the guards helped organize the remaining children into ranks, all the while keeping watch on the beam of light still defiantly emitting from the fiery summit of the Commandant's Tower. At a signal from Mr Cooper, the

Dial's inhabitants began their ascent to freedom, old feuds forgotten and past tensions ignored. Bookworm walked beside Caiman, Scarecrow beside Mouthwash, Paintpot beside Jonkers; and then came the guards, Mr Harker and Miss Roderick dragging Matron's prone form behind them, a smiling Nurse Waters accompanied by Mr Cooper. The prison was rapidly drained of its occupants, until there were only three people left standing in the exercise yard, a pair of brothers and a fixer, all aware that two other prisoners had yet to appear.

"How long do you think we've got until the warphole closes?" asked Luca D'Annunzio.

"No idea," Doughnut replied. "Not long, I guess."

"Maybe we should head up the tunnel, then," said Nino D'Annunzio.

"Maybe," said Doughnut, scanning the prison for movement.

"You really think there's a chance Adam's alive?" asked Luca.

"I do," Doughnut murmured. "And I'm not leaving until he does."

Adam stumbled down the stairs of the Commandant's Tower, choking in the smoke, his eye stinging with tears. Behind him the fire roared joyfully as it consumed the upper reaches of the building, tongues of flame licking the lip of the top stair in anticipation of a larger feast. Adam burst outside, coughs racking his lungs, to be confronted by the sight of the stone tunnel bursting out from the heart of the exercise yard, leading straight into the maw of the warphole. A disbelieving smile crossed Adam's face. The Commandant had been true to his word.

Thankfully, the fire hadn't spread far enough to affect the walkway – Adam called it over to Wing XI and scrambled on to the broad path. At once he saw a girl ahead of him, sitting in a disconsolate heap on the circular island in the centre of the chasm. Jessica blanched at the sight of Adam, looking down at her hands as he approached.

"I know all about you," Adam said coldly. "I know you're the Traitor."

Jessica nodded. "I thought you might."

"That's it? No excuses? No lies? Not even a sorry?"

"Sorry?" She laughed bitterly. "I spend every waking moment wishing that I could turn back the clock, go back to Earth and put everything right. I'm not evil, Adam. I made a mistake! But they locked me up in this place . . . this hideous prison . . . and I felt like I was losing my mind. I had to get out, no matter what it took. It doesn't mean that I was proud of what I did. If I ever did return to Earth, I'd never betray anyone again. So yes, of course I'm sorry. But what does it matter? Does 'sorry' make up for what I did?"

"It's a start," Adam replied sharply. "I made a pretty big fool of myself, didn't I? Chasing around after you, telling you I liked you, kissing you. And all the time you were just trying to get information from me so you could sell us all out. You must have thought it was so funny."

Jessica shook her head. "I know you won't believe me," she said sadly, "but it was different with you. From the moment you landed here I tried to keep you away from me, but you wouldn't listen."

"I was in the infirmary when Luca got caught," Adam said. "You lied to Mr Pitt. You said Luca was on his own in the girls' dormitory. You didn't tell him about me."

"I didn't want him to hurt you again."

Adam folded his arms. "But you were happy for him to hurt Luca, and to try to wipe his mind."

"I didn't know Mr Pitt was going to take him to the Re-education Wing! I thought he'd just put him in solitary!" Jessica turned her back to him. "Oh, what's the use?" she sighed. "I know what I did. It doesn't matter what I say now."

There was a crash as a piece of burning masonry fell from the roof of the Commandant's Tower. The warphole beam wavered uncertainly, its brilliance diminishing as the power began to fail.

"We can talk about this back on Earth," said Adam. "The warphole won't stay open for ever."

"Good," Jessica replied defiantly. "I'm not going anywhere."

"What? You have to!"

She shook her head again. "After everything that's happened? After everything I've done? I'm a traitor, Adam. This is where I belong."

"On your own? For ever?"

"If need be. Please, Adam," Jessica whispered. "If you care about me, please let me stay here."

She reached up and kissed him softly on the lips, then pushed herself away and ran back towards the Commandant's Tower. Before Adam could chase after her, he heard a voice crying his name.

"You're alive!" Doughnut shouted, his face pressed up against the exercise yard gate. "I knew it! Get over here!"

Adam took a final agonized look at the fleeing figure of Jessica. He didn't want to leave her here, but what could he do? She wanted to stay here. Was he supposed to risk everything for a double-crossing traitor? His heart hardening, Adam sprinted in the other direction.

As he stepped down into the exercise yard, he was enveloped in a fierce bear hug by Doughnut, while Luca and Nino D'Annunzio looked on with undisguised happiness.

"I thought you were never going to show up!" Doughnut exclaimed. "Everyone else has gone – Mouthwash, Paintpot, Mr Cooper, Major X, the whole lot! We're the only ones left."

Not quite the only ones, Adam thought to himself, as they jogged across the gravel towards the sky tunnel. There was still someone else on the Dial. As he entered the mouth of the tunnel, he thought about his family and friends back home, and the joy of seeing them again, and how he would try and make it up to Danny; and then he thought about Jessica, destined to haunt the prison for eternity. Adam looked to his left, at Doughnut beaming with joy as he tackled the incline, and to his right, where Nino and Luca were staring dazed at the shimmering warphole at the top end of the tunnel. He remembered the Commandant's last words – *Don't leave anyone behind. . .*

Adam stopped in his tracks.

Luca gave him a sideways look. "Everything all right?"

"Fine," Adam replied. "Only I've got to go back."

"You've got to *what*?" yelled Doughnut. "Are you crazy?"

"Maybe. I'm still going, though."

Doughnut stared at him in amazement. "Why?"

"It's Jessica," said Adam. "I can't leave her alone here."

"But she's a traitor!"

Adam shrugged. "Isn't everyone?"

"Are you sure about this?" asked Nino. "There's no going back on this, you know. You could be stuck here for ever."

"I know," Adam said simply. "But I have to."

Doughnut reached out to grab him, but Luca caught the fixer's hand.

"Come on," he said softly to Doughnut. "We'd better go." Luca smiled at Adam. "Always knew you were trouble."

"I learned from the best," Adam replied. "Look after yourselves – all of you."

As Adam turned around and hastened back down the slope towards the ground, the D'Annunzio brothers stepped either side of Doughnut and guided the flabbergasted fixer away up the tunnel. Glancing back over his shoulder, Adam saw the three distant figures pause by the warphole entrance, turning to wave farewell before stepping into the vortex, and back to freedom.

Adam's feet had barely touched the ground when the fire on the Commandant's Tower reached Luca's balloon – and the sack of Volcano Chilli stashed in its crate. There was an apocalyptic bang as the tower exploded, and the warphole beam abruptly disappeared. Deprived of its life source, the warphole writhed in agony, churning and twisting before folding in on itself as it closed for the final time. Adam sprinted across the yard and dived on to the ground, throwing his hands over his head as the sky tunnel began to shake above him, before suddenly disintegrating into a shower of dust and tiny pebbles that rained silently down like a soft grey curtain.

Adam lay still for several minutes, convinced at any moment a giant slab of masonry was going to drop down upon him and crush him. Finally he sat up, brushing the debris from his hair. The night sky was smooth once more – the turmoil of the warphole already a distant memory. Fire continued to rage around the Commandant's quarters: in the top tower window, he thought he could make out a blurred movement – someone else saying goodbye? Perhaps Adam should have been overwhelmed by the enormousness of his decision, but he felt strangely calm. For the first time in his life, he was absolutely certain that he was doing the right thing. The thought comforted him as he headed back towards the exercise yard gate, his feet crunching on the gravel.

It appeared that the walkway had shifted position whilst he had been inside the sky tunnel. Adam called one hand around to him, taking comfort from the deep rumble as it slotted into place. He hopped up on to the path and crossed the chasm, whose inky depths no longer seemed quite so threatening. The second hand of the walkway would lead him to Jessica, Adam knew. But he didn't need its help – there was only one place she was ever going to be.

Even with parts of the Dial crumbling and aflame, the theatre still retained a hushed grandeur. Jessica was sitting at the grand piano, her head bowed, her hands clasped in her lap. At the sound of Adam's emergence from the staircase, her eyes widened.

"What are you still doing here?" she gasped. "You have to go!"

"Easier said than done," Adam replied, crossing the hall. "The warphole's shut."

Jessica's hand flew to her mouth. "Why didn't you go through it?"

"I nearly did," said Adam, sliding beside her on to the piano stool. "But then I thought about Luca. I think he was right about one thing – we're all traitors, one way or another. I know you've done some bad things, but it shouldn't mean you have to spend for ever on your own here."

"But what about your home? Your family, friends?"

Adam shrugged. "As far as they know, I haven't been gone a second. If I return today, or in a thousand years, it isn't going to make any difference to them."

"But the warphole machine is broken!" Jessica protested. "Don't you see – we can *never* go back!"

"You never know – I might be able to fix the machine. Maybe the Commandant survived the explosion, and he can get us out. Maybe this is all just a bad dream."

"You're crazy," Jessica said softly. "I can't believe you've done this."

Adam squeezed her arm and smiled. "Hey – what are friends for?"

There came a thunderous explosion from outside, as the Commandant's Tower gave up its futile fight for life and came toppling down to the ground. Jessica shivered.

"So what do we do now?" she said.

Adam looked thoughtfully around the theatre.

"I don't know," he admitted. "Anything we want, I guess. Go look around the guards' quarters. Have a food fight in the mess hall. Play a rumble of Bucketball." He lightly pressed a key on the piano. "You could teach me how to play."

"You want to learn the piano?" Jessica gave him a dubious look. "I'm not sure you're the musical type. It could take a while, you know."

The hall resonated with the sound of Adam's laughter.

"How long have you got?" he asked.

EPILOGUE

Dawn broke out over the Dial like birdsong. In the empty corridors and dormitories of the prison, centuries-old echoes had finally been set free: the countless protests of innocence, destined to fall on deaf ears; the clinking of coffee mugs and the slap of spit-palmed handshakes, as new escape plans were agreed upon; the whispers of remorse in the chapel pews, acknowledging old wrongs. No sirens would ring out again; no sputtering radio announcements would intrude upon the quiet. Smoke was still curling into the air from the smouldering remains of the Commandant's Tower, leaving a dark trail across the bright blue sky. Amid the wheezing husk of the *Quisling*, something glinted in the balmy sunlight. It was a sovereign ring, its golden surface scratched and tarnished.

On the other side of the prison, two figures could be seen sitting on the perimeter wall, their feet dangling over the edge. Their hands were locked tightly together. As the last of the flames crackled out, a soft giggle could be heard as the two traitors inched closer to each other, settling down to share an eternity of forgiveness.

ACKNOWLEDGEMENTS

Although *The Traitors* is a work of fantasy, it owes an enormous debt of inspiration to these real-life prisoner-of-war stories from the Second World War: *Boldness Be My Friend*, by Richard Pape; *Colditz*, by Pat Reid; *Dare To Be Free*, by W.B. Thomas; *Wingless Victory*, by Anthony Richardson; *Farewell Campo 12*, by James Hargest; *Reach For The Sky*, by Paul Brickhill; *The Wooden Horse*, by Eric Williams; and *Colditz: The German Story*, by Reinhold Eggers. I heartily recommend these fantastic reads to anyone searching for further heroic escapes and general derring-do.

Getting a book published is always a team effort, and I'd like to thank everyone at Scholastic, my agent Sam Copeland, and Matt Drew, who helped bring the Dial to life in the early days of its construction. Finally, my love and heartfelt gratitude to Lindsay, for painting my world anew in such glorious colour.